SECRET SHOPPER

BY

Tanya Taimanglo

∞ ∞ ∞ ∞ ∞ ∞ ∞ ∞ ∞ ∞ ∞ ∞ ∞

D1739090

Other Titles By Tanya Taimanglo

Sirena: A Mermaid Legend From Guam
(Children's Book-Authorhouse 2010)

Attitude 13: A Daughter of Guam's Collection of Short Stories
(Fiction-Authorhouse 2010)

www.GuamBooksAndBeads.Com

SECRET SHOPPER
By Tanya Taimanglo

Cover photo by: Tanya Taimanglo
Design by: Tanya Taimanglo & Sonny Chargualaf

Author Photo by: Mark J. Pacheco

ISBN-13: 978-1482313772

ISBN-10: 1482313774

ACKNOWLEDGEMENTS

Special thanks to my husband, *Henry*
and my children, *Elijah* and *Samantha*
for putting up with me for three and a half years
as I molded this novel.
I love you three lots and lots.

To my omma, *Un Cha Chargualaf*
for hearing the story first as it was freshly born in 2009/2010.

To my kid brother, *Sonny Chargualaf* for inspiring me.
And, for helping with the evolution of the book cover.

To my late father, *Tedy Gamboa Chargualaf*
for always being the voice in my head
and the man I want to impress.

DEDICATION
I dedicate Phoenix's story to the ladies who hold me up:
Kimberly Untalan Taisipic (my real life Rachel),
Alison Taimanglo Cuasay,
Desiree Taimanglo Ventura,
Dr. Patricia Taimanglo,
Nari Taimanglo,
Angie Barker,
Raquel Santos
and
Denise Avitia.

Special thanks to authors,
Carlene Rae Dater and Lani Wendt Young
for your advice and guidance.

TABLE OF CONTENTS

Chapter 1

Stand by Your Chieftain

No one on a talk show ever tells you that divorce makes it hard to breathe. When Dr. "Feel" tells the pretty, plump lady in a pant suit that she can move on and heal from heartbreak, she nods obediently and smiles with hope. I see the cracks in her brave mask threatening to reveal her true face. The line of tears blazing through her foundation tells me that she'll go home, beg her husband to take her back, eat a ton of chocolate and curl up in the fetal position under her favorite blanket, for weeks. *At least that's what I did.*

I never wanted to move to California from Guam. I didn't like shifts in my universe. I didn't want to change my Facebook status from married to single. I had convinced myself that I could take Bradley back even after he cheated on me. Jem, short for Jemima, was an agent in his real estate office who doubled as Bradley's part-time lover. Nix, short for Phoenix, was the gullible wife who thought that dropping thirty pounds was the way to save the marriage. *Phoenix is my name.*

"Bradley! I got the job!" I yelled from our second floor office. The Lure Company was San Diego's largest secret shopping firm and they hired me after a trial evaluation. It was the dream job for me. I was going to be paid to buy iced coffees, deli sandwiches and if I was lucky, clothes. All they wanted was a customer evaluation and my spy skills. Writing a customer service evaluation was mundane, but easier than a master's thesis. And, I always have an opinion. I'm not always heard, but now I had an outlet.

"I'm in the bathroom!" I heard Bradley from the third floor of our towering condo. I never liked the idea of stairs in our home, back on Guam life was simple in a single level, solid concrete abode. Here, there were too many places to hide from each other, although the "acoustics are great," *Bradley's words*, not mine.

I felt my belly jiggle as I bounded up our carpeted stairs. Catching my breath at the top step, I thought that at twenty-five-years old, I should be fit without having to work at it yet. My usual choice of exercise was a leisurely walk hunting for lucky pennies.

The sound of rushing water and the wispy steam emerging from our master bathroom told me that Bradley was preening himself in front of the mirror, again. Something he did a lot more of since Easter, when business slowed in the real estate market.

"Dear husband, I am a certified secret shopper!" I yodeled. He should be proud of me since it was his suggestion that I get a part-time job. Bradley hadn't sold a house in two months. We weren't starving yet, but we were about six months away from calling mom and dad on the island for some floatation money. We only had to do that once, just before we refinanced our home at a better rate. I was darn proud of weaning ourselves off our parents, even though the occasional twenty dollar bill in a birthday card was always thrilling. *Mom, you can't send cash in the mail. It's not safe.* I once told her half-heartedly.

The smell of shaving cream reminded me of my dad and as the fluffy white clouds settled, I saw Bradley's muscular bronze back first. His leaner hips minus its love handles were wrapped tight in a white towel. He was the sexiest man burrito I had ever seen.

In the past month, Bradley had been on a fitness quest— exercising six days a week and cutting out everything bad from his diet, including me. As I enjoyed the yummy contours of his body, my sights elevated to Bradley's newly bald head. My eyes darted to the sink which cradled clumps of brown hair. I felt like I was karate chopped in the throat and no speech could escape. I loved his floppy hair and now I had Mr. Clean. The softness of his once longer locks preserved the boyish face I was so fond of. Now, he looked hard, older and determined.

Bradley's eyes were intent on his reflection. I watched as he seemed appreciative of his new look. He didn't hear me or ignored me as usual. I cleared my throat and his eyes flickered to me. They were dark and intense, daring me to object. For a second, I did not recognize the man I married, the man I had my first kiss with, the man who had been my classmate since the first grade. I felt like the cute puppy I fell in love with had grown into a large unmanageable dog I couldn't wrangle.

"So, you got a job. Good for you, Phoenix." Bradley was indeed listening. "When do you start this little job of yours?"

Little, that stung, but I didn't tell him that. "I start on Monday. You do realize that you look like a Chamorro Mr. Clean." I became better at ignoring the arrogant tone he whipped at me.

"And you do realize that I'm a new man. I have a new mission and a," Bradley broke his glare with me and pulled his towel off roughly. He retreated to the shower. I wondered if his new mission was to actually sell a house this month. We needed the commission. I surveyed Bradley's scattered locks and fought the urge to keep some for my scrapbook. I cleaned the sink, humming a sad melody to myself like a funeral song for Bradley's hair. It seemed like Bradley had molted and was now washing away his old life.

"Are you joining a Buddhist nudist colony? Or, is there a Chamorro Chief Club out here?" I said more for my amusement.

I got on my knees and wiped up the stray hairs on the floor with a wet tissue. Bradley pulled open the shower curtain dotted with tiny coconut trees. Finding the curtain at the dollar store had been the highlight of my week. My sight gravitated to his man parts and a pint of blood raced to my eyeballs. The realization that Bradley hadn't touched me in weeks weighed heavy on my mind, among other parts.

I heard Bradley sigh. He grabbed his robe and as the soft flannel enveloped him, it took the edge off his tone. "Nix, get up. I can clean up after myself."

"I was wondering when you were going to call me *Nix* again." I staggered to my feet, cursing the bad knees I inherited from my dad's side of the family. Around the same time Bradley started his extreme hottie makeover, he stopped calling me Nix, only referring to me by my full name. I didn't ask him why. I didn't want to know.

"We need to talk." He pointed to our bedroom and I washed my hands twice and let the last of the hot water scald my hands. I looked at my reflection in the hazy mirror. My almond eyes were plain and set too far apart for my liking. My brown hair was long and wild. My high cheekbones were the only saving grace of my face, that and maybe the creamy skin I snagged from my mom. I flattened my unruly hair with my damp hands. I bit my lips to make them pink, then pushed up my breasts. Maybe I would get lucky today.

Bradley waited, arms folded by the head of our Ikea bed. His new look had stirred something in me. I realized my eyes were batting more than usual, well ever and my chest heaved. He was the embodiment of a strong Chamorro man, the type of man from Guam who could rip a coconut tree out of the ground and hunt a wild boar barefoot. Before I could stop myself, my inner seductress—*didn't even know I had one*, emerged. Bradley stood in protest with a scowl in place as I stripped. I tripped over my jeans tangled around my ankles and disappeared from view at the foot of the bed. I heard a giggle escape from the Chieftain's mouth, a good sign. I peered over the bed and Bradley sat now. His light

9

brown eyes were softer and his robe lay open. I continued my strip tease, secretly hoping I wouldn't have a concussion before climbing into bed. Well aware of my best features, I sucked in my belly, held my hand over my now unfastened bra, keeping the cups over my breasts. Then, I scaled the side of our bed. I kept my plump back side away from his line of vision. Bradley's jaw tensed and he lay back in invitation, but his face had the same look he made when he was in the dentist's chair. This confused me. Did he or did he not want this?

Although making love to my husband after a month was exactly what I wanted, I cursed being a woman whose mind could juggle several thoughts at once. First, I remembered that I didn't lock the front door. The part of San Diego we lived in was safe, but not *Little House on the Prairie* safe. Two flights of stairs down and back up half-naked I went. Secondly, I realized that the blinds were wide open and it was the middle of the day. If Mrs. Salter was on her elliptical machine, she'd have my boobs in plain view. Like a soldier doing secret ops, I gestured to Bradley with my face and hands. I pointed to the blinds. I held onto my white bra and tiptoed to the window. I didn't want any sudden movements drawing Mrs. Salter's attention our way as she was indeed doing her daily cardio, pumping her fists to music.

Bradley sighed in frustration and after I twisted the wand to the blinds, I turned my head slowly to give Bradley my sexiest gaze. As I peered through my curtain of chestnut hair, I saw a flash of disgust on his face. He did not make eye contact with me, but was instead eyes wide and mouth gaping, looking at my marshmallow back. My rolls of flesh and fat, like that of a camel. The kind of fatness that is only cute on a baby. I whirled around and wrapped my arms around my waist. Insecurity bubbled in my gut and tears threatened to flood the room. I hated that I cared so much about someone's body language and facial expressions, especially my husband's.

"What?" Bradley sat up, snapping his mouth closed.

"Why did you make that face?" I asked softly.

Bradley hurled himself off the bed, looking ready to brawl. "What look?"

"I saw you look at my back and make a vomit face!"

Bradley grabbed my camel humps and said, "This stuff? This is mine. You're on a diet anyway, right?" The meat handling and the mention of the "D" word didn't help put me back into the mood.

"Did you or did you not make a gross out face?" I asked as I maneuvered out of his clutches. I walked backwards to the bed. In one swift move, I hooked my bra and put on my shirt. Bradley grunted or maybe his penis protested.

"Hey, why are you getting dressed? I did not make a face because of your back, Nix."

I knew what I saw, but I didn't want to ruin the rest of the night with my self-image issues. I wasn't always this heavy and I knew that the miscarriage I endured just a month after our wedding sent me on a downward hormonal and mental spiral. My parents didn't even know. By our first anniversary, after eating the secret of being pregnant and then not, I was thirty pounds burdened.

Bradley sat next to me and stroked my thighs. He kissed me hard, which marked the end of my protest. Typical. Once the engine was started, he had places to go. His destination was in my pants and I wasn't going to set up any more road blocks.

I tucked my resentment away and enjoyed our pre-dinner escapade as best as I could. I tried not to think of his face at the split second of disapproval. I lay back and let him have at it. I opened my eyes to get a glimpse of him when his face should have expressed pleasure, but regretted it immediately. Bradley's eyes were squeezed shut, his face contorted. I didn't realize how large his nostrils were from this vantage point and his lips curled in a way that was reminiscent of Elvis Presley, my first true crush. But, this was not Elvis gyrating on top of me and I had to bite my lip to keep a giggle from escaping.

We didn't typically do it in daylight, so this must have been the face he made in the dark. I learned something new everyday. The orchestra of grunts and groans that Bradley created was hard to ignore. He seemed different, like a new lover. Angrier even. I was on auto-pilot at this point and willed myself not to look at Bradley again, but my eyes popped open anyway. *Yep, Elvis was still in the building.* His eyebrows wiggled rhythmically and that's when a flurry of giggles broke forth.

Bradley's face resumed normalcy and he looked down, eyes wide in disbelief as I covered my mouth. Although I convulsed from laughter, not pleasure, Bradley still pumped along. His confused look made things worse and I burst into a fresh round of laughter. Bradley's face grew sinister. And yet, he still wanted to finish his mission. I pulled a pillow over my face and did my best to stop my hysterics.

Ten seconds later, after a lot of bouncing, Bradley was done. He hopped off the bed and retreated to the bathroom. I gave him points for actually completing the task, but why? Why didn't he just get pissed and roll over or ask what was wrong? Why was I so mean? Feeling my sweaty fat back, I remembered. I hated feeling ugly, and he made me feel like an ogre.

I knocked on the bathroom door. Bradley didn't answer, so I let myself in. He was in the shower again, his usual after sex, and I pulled the curtain aside and stepped into the warmth. I hugged his back as we wasted water together. We didn't speak, although I knew I needed to apologize and explain myself. I soaped his back and enjoyed the contours. My husband was a beautiful specimen. It dawned on me that while Bradley offered me this I needed to do the same. I was immature and selfish, yet another lesson learned that day.

"Honey. I'm sorry." I sang into his back.

Bradley turned around, held my wrists at my side and then kissed me on the cheek, lightly enough that thought I might have imagined it. He surveyed my face and took a long look at my naked body. I squeezed my eyes shut. I didn't want to see his disapproving face again. As the warm water changed to cold,

Bradley stepped out of the shower. He looked over his shoulder and said, "Phoenix, I'm leaving. I'm joining the Army reserves."

Chapter 2
Meet my Friend, Gym

I was a woman in limbo. Bradley stranded me in San Diego for boot camp. After several days of eating my loneliness, I dusted off my gym clothes and activated the membership Bradley gave me for my last birthday. I thought it was so romantic at the time with the contract wrapped in a red satin ribbon. I know now it was his way of telling me I was a fat ass.

My sadness turned into anger as the summer heat arrived. I fought the urge to buy a one way ticket to Guam, where I could find refuge in my old lavender room. My parents maintained hope that we would move back home. I love my parents, but they were smothering and always in my business, even down to the type of shoes I should be wearing. The burden of being their only daughter. I liked my liberation from them, but I knew that I could land softly back home if I really needed to.

In the meantime, I wanted to keep up appearances. Most days I harnessed enough energy to workout and learn the ropes of my secret shopping job. With the help of my Thomas Guide maps and GPS, I hit every Flex Gym within my evaluation target parameters. I turned my new job into a game. I was on the hunt for targets, people I needed to evaluate. I tried every machine at each gym branch, and scheduled secret shopping around exercise classes like Zumba and Hyper Hula. I used my credit card to buy the latest and greatest shoes, sweats and Ipod gear.

Bradley endured boot camp, while I navigated San Diego solo. Customer evaluation was challenging enough to keep me in motion throughout the day. My best friend for more than half my life, Rachel Untalan was the only person who knew of my loneliness. She owned her own clothing line boutique and was busier every day, but it was early morning on Guam, so I ventured a call.

"Hello?" Rachel's voice dripped with sleep.

"So, guess what Bruce, my boss asked me to do this weekend?"

"Don't tell me you're sleeping with your sixty-five-year old boss!" Rachel yelled, now totally awake.

"No, dork. Angelica, remember I told you about her? The extra friendly secretary and scheduler at Lure? Well, she and I have a hit on a strip club next weekend."

I requested more work, which perhaps translated to Angelica—Lure Company's only secretary and task master that I would do just about anything. The Tiger Gentlemen's Lounge needed evaluation. My boss wanted to send females, since evaluations conducted by male secret shoppers were always suspiciously stellar. Angelica was tapped to drag me along, because I was the newbie and would be less likely to say no.

Angelica had always been overly friendly. I never accepted her invitations for lunch or coffee, that gal pal realm was reserved

16

for Rachel. I never minded having a very tight circle of friends, in my case only room for one, but it was becoming harder to deflect her genuine niceness and concern for me.

Angelica's gay cousin, Gerard would get his macho on for the evening and we would escort him. I had to admit I was curious to see what the big deal was with strip clubs. Maybe I could learn pole dancing moves before Bradley came back because that always boosts relationships, at least that's what Cosmo experts claimed. *That's why I killed my subscription.*

"No, shit? I tried to drag you into one of those here, but you were so frigid! You probably still are." Rachel said.

"Yeah, I remember. And, no I'm not! I'm married. Did you really have a research paper on the topic?" I had always been suspicious.

"No. I heard my second cousin was dancing under the name, Virgin Chi Chi and I wanted to see for myself." Guam goes totally nude, which is a great tourist attraction I guess. Many strippers are recruited from the mainland, Asia or Europe based on the giant ads in the newspapers I'd see when I was back home. By the time I left Guam, local girls were beginning to make their way into that seedy world, which irked the hell out of the elders. A good Chamorro girl just didn't do that. "She has two kids now, so I know she's retired. Shit, who knows."

"So, what would be your stripper song, if you were Rachel Raunchy Rockets?" I asked. Her twinkling laughter made me miss her all over again.

17

"Good name! Not so prudish then. Well, hmm. How about, *Milkshake*? And you? Sounds like you've already thought of one." Rachel teased.

"If I was a stripper in an alternate universe, my stripper name would be 'Fancy Faith' and the song would be *Personal Jesus* by Depeche Mode." I loved the cowboy sounding guitar licks in the beginning of the song, proper gyration music. The first line of the song made me imagine the moment a dirty old man would touch me and I would Kung Fu kick his arm off. I guess I did put a lot of thought into this. Rachel had a psychology minor; if I chose to share this fantasy with her someday, she could analyze it and tell me what was wrong with me.

"Ooh, naughty! Well, make sure you wipe the chair you sit on." Rachel spoke like I was going on my first field trip.

"My, my. You sound like you've had experience in this matter." Rachel laughed. "A *Febreze* spritzer before I sit, aye!" I replied.

Rachel encouraged me to befriend Angelica outside of the office, since she could provide in-person buddy services that Rachel couldn't offer. Maybe I would because I had my best friend's blessing. If anything, I was loyal always.

After our little phone therapy session, I checked my laptop. I wanted to read the evaluation guidelines for the strip club and check out their website. I surfed my usual sites in the usual order, Facebook, e-mail, bank account, and then searched for my stripper song on Youtube. As the melody swirled around me, I did a chicken like dance routine with my computer chair. Naturally, I made sure my blinds were completely shut first. After stubbing my toe on my desk, I retired from in home stripping and settled in to check out the club's website. The Tiger Gentlemen's Lounge looked like a classy spot with many hot guys in the audience, instead of the pervy dudes who really frequented such spots. They must have been models, I deduced. I called Angelica that evening and she was ecstatic to meet me for lunch with Gerard to discuss our plan of attack.

We met at *Denny's* since Gerard insisted on using his employee discount. As long as they had good salad choices and I could save a buck, I was happy. Gerard was a beautiful man, Hollywood beautiful. His licorice black hair and hazel eyes were vibrant. His olive skin, flawless. I wished I could be tanner. I was the one who hailed from an island after all. My father being Chamorro was not enough to eclipse the milky skin I inherited from my Korean mother.

"So, Phoenix, will this be your first time at a strip club?" Gerard asked me excitedly.

"Never mind me, is this yours?" I asked back.

"Why, yes it is! I'm excited, but grossed out by it too!" Gerard gave me a friendly slap on my thigh. Angelica smiled and rolled her eyes. "I've only really seen a few women naked, my mom, my grandma and beautiful Angelica here!" He declared.

"I can't believe you said that, G!" Angelica feigned shock.

"I don't even want to know the story." I added and we all laughed. No, *really*. I didn't want to know and was glad when our food arrived.

Gerard said that next weekend's strip club visit was his last big hoorah before leaving San Diego. He had recently broken up with his long-time boyfriend and wanted to head to Las Vegas for greener pastures. I didn't ask him if he knew that Las Vegas was really a desert, but I got his point.

Angelica was like a warm glove. She was comfortable and easy-going. We didn't often meet face-to-face, but she showed her heart easily when she added a happy face to sign off her e-mails to me. Angelica was an ethnic sampler like me. She had a Mexican mom—who passed away a year earlier from breast cancer and an Irish-American father—whom she hadn't seen in the last ten years. She had a bright, pretty face. She was about a size 16, but her curves were in all the right places and she wore her weight well. She always had beautiful blond highlights in her auburn hair and her manicures were perfection. I foresaw a mani-pedi adventure in our future.

It was the end of July and we set up our sting for ten o'clock on a Saturday night. The warm balmy evening reminded me of home. I was giddy that I fit in my clothes from a year prior. I shimmied into my size 10 jeans and added a cute graphic tee with little pandas. I completed the look with two inch black heels. I didn't want to be too dressy and Gerard and Angelica coordinated their outfits with mine minus the pandas.

We parked at the neighboring lot. The orange neon lights of the strip club were retro 80s. The exterior of the club was adorned in gaudy black stripes on orange. If the interior had mounted tiger heads I might lose it. I was half right, with the tiger skin theme displayed on the chairs and booth benches. There were three runway aisles and mini-stages, and one large center stage. A beautiful Asian woman with peroxide blond hair was gyrating in a neon green thong and pasties. Her crystal clear stiletto heels looked hazardous and I hoped she had great health coverage. The almost four foot fall to the floor could prove deadly. I could see the headlines already: *Asian Stripper Stabbed in the Head and Torso by her own Stripper Shoes.*

Angelica and I were charged with separate reports. I was to evaluate the wait staff specifically and Angelica needed to attack the bar staff. We found a clean corner booth and I quickly scanned my seat for weird stains. Management was smart to have the tiger stripes on the seat for camouflage. I didn't want to run my hands over the synthetic fur and shivered, imagining the deposits. I could only hope that gum was the only gross thing under the table tops too. I would just burn my clothes when I got home.

I was smart enough not to mention this assignment to my parents. The less they knew about my job, the less grief I would receive. I had to tell my kid brother, Pharaoh though. He flipped out and bragged to his brawler buddies that their fantasy job did exist and his sister had it.

Heavy hip hop music pounded in the background. Ms. Asia Beauty Queen finished her set and the ten or so men present applauded and barked like seals. I was right, these guys looked nothing like the hot men on the website. Bills floated like fall leaves onto the stage and Ms. Asia crouched on the floor to collect her pay out, looking graceful as she did so. I wondered what would compel a woman to do this job, but gathered from media's fixation on this world that anyone from sexually abused women to girls trying to pay for college to moms with bills did this erotic entertainment. By the looks of the bundles of cash she cradled like a baby, Ms. Asia could definitely pay the bills, and the night was still young.

Finally, a rock song started and Gerard bopped his head back and forth in an effort to look interested, eager and straight. He put each of his arms on the booth seats to show anyone who cared that he was with Angelica and me. He nearly knocked the top of my head off as he did so. Angelica and I erupted in laughter. Keeping up airs, Angelica would kiss her cousin on the cheek and I would rub his chest. Gerard smelled wonderful, my acting probably looked genuine as I kept my face close to his chest.

The next dancer strutted on the runway as a Hoobastank song blared. Tigress—as she was introduced by the D.J., was a fine specimen. The way her legs formed pretzels around the pole was intriguing. Our mouths half-open, I wondered out loud if she needed Vaseline to slide so effortlessly on the length of the golden pole. My partners just laughed at me. I later discovered that Tigress was the owner of the club and I was strangely proud of her for that.

After another hour and five dancers all named after jungle animals, Angelica and I had enough data to do our reports. Before leaving, we asked a group of young fellows to snap a picture of us in front of the neon sign. I immediately sent it to Bradley. I wanted him to know I was having fun without him. I hadn't heard from him in three days, not even a goodnight text.

We left the club feeling fat thanks to the gorgeous dancing felines and decided to make matters worse by heading to the Asian smoothie shop for Tapioca pearl drinks. We sat among the crowd of college kids, fitting in, barely. We sucked on our fruity blended boba drinks as we hashed out our new experience. Several times in the tiger booth, Gerard had looked like he was going to be sick from all the *boobage* he saw. He did declare that the perky butts kept him sane.

"You'll like my husband then. He has an awesome bubble butt!" I checked my Blackberry as I thought of Bradley and saw that he had called twice in the last half hour. My picture must have worked. The loud conversations from the wired college group extended to the parking lot, so I sought refuge in my car. Bradley's message said to call him back as soon as possible, no matter how late. I missed his voice and I called him back right away.

"Hey, Bradley. It's Nix. Are you okay?" I was afraid he would tell me he was injured or failed some test and would have to be sent home.

"Hey, Phoenix. No, I'm fine. I just wanted to talk to you about something. Boot Camp Graduation, actually." He sounded hoarse. I felt bad for the physical strain he endured. I could hear a few people in the background.

"Are you out?" I pried. "Did you receive the picture?"

"What picture? Oh, I got a notification, just didn't open it. Just a few of us sharing a smoke." Smoke? All that fitness just to start smoking?

"You're smoking? What smoking a pig?" I really hoped that he was.

"Get serious, Phoenix." I waited to hear that he missed me, but heard him say, "I don't want you to come to the ceremony."

"Why? Am I not allowed? I swear, I'm not on the terrorist list." I joked. I began to hyperventilate.

"Phoenix. Just focus and hear me out." I hadn't heard from Bradley in the last three days and now he had something serious to talk about. I got used to his absence and I felt like he was enjoying his vacation from me too much. Three weeks earlier, I noticed that he didn't say two crucial things to me anymore: "I love you" or "I miss you." I chalked it up to stress.

"What is it Bradley? Believe it or not I'm working now."

"You are? Isn't it late? Are you by yourself? Where?" He sounded like my dad. Before I could share my night, he plowed through. "Nevermind. I called because I think we're done."

"Finished with boot camp?"

"No. Phoenix. You and me. I want out." His words didn't sink in. They came out all jumbled like he was talking in a Peanuts cartoon. All I heard was *wah-wah-wah.* "Phoenix. Are you listening?"

"So, you're done with boot camp early, right?" I had a communication glitch and my hearing malfunctioned. I watched a young couple making out.

"Phoenix. I'm sorry. Let me put this plainly." I heard a woman's voice in the background asking for the phone. Bradley muffled the cell phone and yelled back at this familiar voice. "Phoenix. I've been meaning to tell you this since before I left for boot camp. I mean, I wasn't even really sure what I was feeling until just recently, but," I felt my limbs go numb and panic bubbled in the pit of my stomach. The declaration from Bradley was like a bullet moving in slow motion straight for the space between my eyes.

"Bradley. Please." The words floated painfully out of my throat.

"Phoenix. I've been doing a lot of changing in the last few months. And I want us to separate."

"Separate? Why? Bradley please tell me. Is it my weight? Because I've already lost twenty pounds!" I heard him exhale and I swore I could smell the cigarette smoke.

"Phoenix, that has nothing to do with it. I'm actually with, well, I'm with someone else now." The kissing couple realized I was gawking at them and I dropped my eyes.

"Doesn't she know you're married? Who is it?" In the back of my mind I already knew the answer. I wanted him to say it was someone else, anyone else but the person I had suspected long before this conversation happened. Jemima, known as Jem, the most beautiful real estate agent in the east county was always a threat. Real Estate Barbie, I called her once, which made Bradley angrier than warranted. Now, I knew why. The wicked woman who mentored Bradley. The one who suggested that the entire office go out clubbing once a month to "build rapport" when she actually just wanted permission to bump and grind on Bradley. The final stake was when she coerced Bradley into joining the Army reserves with her. I hated women who went after claimed men. They should all be rounded up and have their uteruses removed. Government sanctioned hysterectomies sounds harsh, but my anger sky rocketed.

"Phoenix. I think you know." Bastard was going to make me utter the words!

"No. I don't. You tell me!" I was on fire. I was suffocating. I needed oxygen and I immediately wanted comfort from Rachel.

"Phoenix, I've been with Jem for the past two months now. I mean it started out with just friendly flirting and stuff, and then I thought it was just physical, but now," Bradley was really trying to explain the evolution of this sordid affair?

"Shut up! I don't need a play by play! Do you love her or me?" I was yelling into the phone now.

"I'll always love you, Phoenix." Bradley whispered. "We've been together for ten years. Of course, I'll always love you."

"Bull. If you loved me, you wouldn't have an affair! So, what? You want a divorce?"

"No, not necessarily." What was I hearing? Bradley didn't want me, but he didn't want a divorce?

"Please, Bradley. Don't play games with me. You've already had the affair. Next logical step is a divorce. I don't want to be anyone's ex-wife. That's not what I imagined when we married." Tears welled in my eyes.

"Phoenix, I can't ask you to wait for me while I figure this shit out. All I know is I'm going through some stress and I care about you, but I am having these feelings for Jem." There was a finality to his words and I felt defeated, so I came out swinging.

"Well, crap, don't let me stand in your motherhumping way." I was cursing like a sailor now, sort of.

"Phoenix. I *knew* you wouldn't understand." Did Hillary understand when it got out that someone else sucked her husband's presidential lollipop? Outside of the glare of the media, I'm sure she went ballistic too.

"I don't understand you! Love is absolute. You can't have your *thingee* swinging from here to there. It needs to land somewhere and when you decide, I might not be there to accept it. You're filth to me right now." My words exploded like fireworks. I had to concentrate so I wouldn't beg him to come back to me. I wanted him back already and I hated myself for that.

"Well, all I know is that I don't want us to call it quits on our marriage. I would feel better if you tried dating someone else." Was he serious?

"Two wrongs don't make a right, Bradley." I countered trying to sound even keeled.

"I know, but who is the guy in the picture? He seems nice." He finally saw the picture of me and Angelica hanging on Gerard outside of the club.

"No. You don't know, or else you wouldn't be trying to pimp your wife out to someone else. Gerard would be more into you than me anyway! We were doing reports at a strip club! Did you even read the message with the picture! You need to think about what you say before you put it out there. And as for Jem, you better get checked, she might have fleas and if you think I would let you touch me after the stunt you just pulled. Thank Buddha, I forced you to wear a condom before you left!"

"Fleas? God, Phoenix. You're so dramatic!" He yelled, then I heard the flea bag's voice in the background. "If you need to call Rachel, do so. If you want to go to Guam just charge the credit card and I'll take care of it." I saw red.

"Don't worry about me. I won't be able to keep a straight face anyway if I went home. Put Jem on the line now." Bradley hesitated, but I heard a shuffling.

"Phoenix." Jem started.

"Listen here. Don't even speak to me. You will just listen. Please, keep Bradley. I won't argue with you. You took a married man and he was weak enough to go for you, so great! You are one *powerful* lady. Best wishes, now put *your* man on the line."

"No, you listen here, bi…" Jem started and I heard scuffling as Bradley grabbed the phone away from her. I felt like I was on that stupid cheaters show except the truth came to me. I just had to sit back and the guilty parties came knocking.

"What did you say to her?" By the hero voice Bradley took on, there was no denying he was into this girl. Bradley defended Jem like I wished or hoped he would support and defend me since the tenth grade.

"She can explain, but she might get it twisted. I basically told her in a professional manner—no name calling mind you, that I wished her luck with her budding romance with you. I even said she was a powerful lady. Nothing but compliments." I stated sarcastically. Kill them with kindness I thought, but I was dying on the inside. I didn't want Bradley to hear me cry, so I clutched the steering wheel with my left hand, digging my nails into it so hard that it left marks in the leather. I glanced at his grandmother's ring, my wedding ring and it felt heavy. I wanted to cut my finger off. I had grown fond of my wedding ring, happy to accept a family heirloom. Now, I would have to return it.

"Phoenix, I, I," Bradley kept talking and I felt like he was slashing me over and over like some psycho killer in a horror movie, with no expression on his dead face.

"I don't want to hear it." I cleared the sadness out of my throat. "Should I tell our parents or should you?"

"Just give me until I return to decide, please."

"Whatever, Bradley. Enjoy the rest of boot camp. Oh, and you screwed up a lot in our checking account ledger, but I've got it all correct now. Your end balance was off by almost three hundred bucks. I used the extra money for workout gear." I hung up on the new couple and finally came unhinged.

After realizing that I wasn't in a nightmare, I called Rachel. Blow by blow, quote by quote I told her my sob story.

"Nix, that, uh, that's so unfair. I'm sorry, babe." Rachel lost her voice for a few minutes and listened as a fresh round of tears burst forth. She waited, as my crying fogged up the windows of my car. She made me promise that I wouldn't do anything crazy like plow into a tree or get drunk and sleep with a homeless guy. I promised. And, I made her promise not to tell anyone, especially my family about this impending status change.

Angelica and Gerard appeared at my window. I opened the car door and swung my heavy legs out, but I couldn't find the strength to stand. My puffy eyes told a story. Gerard's kind face and Angelica's warm hand on my shoulder provoked a fresh round of tears. They were probably wondering if someone died in my family. It felt like someone did. I felt like I was in mourning mode. I looked up at Gerard and asked, "Can I go to Vegas to look for greener pastures with you?"

Chapter 3

Bag It and Blonde It

I ran my hands over the leaner and smoother lines of my body. It was a relief to have wiggle room in my clothes. And five pounds ago my thighs stopped rubbing in an effort to make fire. I would have called Rachel to celebrate this achievement, but the internal rearranging of my being and soul killed any good news. Bradley smashed me and Jem took the shattered pieces and flung it up in the air. I watched and waited to see where all these parts would land. Would certain pieces disintegrate on impact, others be warped, still others go missing? And more importantly, what would remain unchanged?

That summer fluctuated hot and cold, much like my marriage. Within three months, I transformed from a happy plump wife of a semi-successful real estate agent to the unjiggly possible divorcée of an Army man. The volatility of it all made my head spin. I craved constants and neat boxes. How was the divorce going to change me? What was going to happen to all that I've known? I wavered on the edge of a very high cliff, uncertain of how to proceed. Bradley wasn't there to hold my hand anymore. Where would I be this time next summer? Who would I be? Throughout this chaos, I suppressed my anxiety with the mundane of the day. A day, like the previous seventy eight days, I got through alone.

Bradley was at Fort Benning, Georgia for officer training. My only consolation—he was in a different state than Jem. She was training at Fort Polk, Louisiana—she didn't have a college degree, which caused a rift in their training paths. Thanks to Facebook, I was able to track their happy existence in the military world. Torturing myself with the details, I know.

Bradley wanted a trial separation. I felt like training wheels, but I wasn't a piece of machinery that he could detach. The month leading up to his leaving for boot camp had been glorious. We did everything right and prepared meticulously. In retrospect, whether he was aware of it or not, it was like Bradley groomed me for my involuntary independence. He made sure I had a job, he paid our mortgage forward three months, he had me lose weight and eat healthier. He dangled gifts we couldn't afford in front of me like I was a jackass after a carrot, when all I wanted was him. Did he want me to be a better me for life without him? Did he want to minimize his guilt and say, look I helped Nix elevate herself? Within the first three weeks of his boot camp training, he grew distant—fewer calls, e-mails and texts. A shift in my husband's heart and mind occurred and I had no power to redirect the tide. The depression I went through made it tougher to keep food down. My favorite position lately was the fetal position.

With the change of my probationary status to full fledged Field Agent with The Lure Company, I had just enough going on in my miserable life to keep me motivated. The energy it took to sound normal on the phone with my parents was exhausting as well.

Rachel was the only one I called on doomsday, a hot night in July. All I heard was, *I'm with Jem now. I'll always love you, but . . . Give Rachel a call. If you want to go home to Guam, charge it to my card and I'll take care of it.* It was a thirty minute call, but that's all I recalled. I was so pissed off and I knew I spewed a lot of venom that night. I should have been embarrassed that Angelica knew all my marriage drama, but I was not. She had been a great comfort since then.

What made things worse was my family's loss on Guam. Dad was under a lot of stress, with his older brother dying. I couldn't make it back to Guam in time for the funeral for Uncle Joaquin. Traditionally, there would be nine days of rosaries, then the viewing, then a burial. Uncle Joaquin died of a heart attack. He was 60 years old. That number frightened dad, since he was only a year younger than Uncle. My grandpa died at 60 too when I was in the 5th grade.

Uncle Joaquin specifically had in his will to bury him within three days. I couldn't negotiate the ticket to get home. I would be lucky if I landed in time to make it to the cemetery. That compacted by the fact that it takes a minimum of eighteen hours of travel time to get to Guam from California. Times like that, I wished I could teleport home. But then again, it wasn't a good time to be under the lens of my family and friends. I could hear it, *Hey girl, why are you so skinny? Is your husband cheating on you?* Why, yes. Yes, he is.

The Lure Company placed a special assignment in my workbox. I had some experience with hits, as we called them, but it was still a new facet of my job.

"Phoenix Rose, agent 1021, you are called into duty. Target, Thomas P. Roberts. Destroy this message immediately. It will self-destruct in 5-4-3-2-1." *Kablooey*, so the scene goes. My boss, Bruce Lure wasn't as dramatic in reality.

With a bowl of baby carrots and vitamin water, I sat at my computer to review my week's hit list from Angelica. Happily, I didn't have any more strip clubs. Coffee, sandwiches and banks. *My usual.*

Thomas P. Roberts worked at Bag It, a sandwich shop, which despite its vulgar name was popular. It was situated at a strip mall near the naval base. I had seen it a few times, since I passed it often on my way to the base commissary.

I planned my secret shopping missions with my own military precision. My target, Thomas, was described as Caucasian male, medium length wavy brown hair, gray or blue eyes, early 20s, 6', slim build, gold necklace with pendant. A very general picture, but with gray eyes, he could either be captivating or scary.

I slated my pre-visit for a Sunday. I had Thomas's schedule and knew he would work during the lunch shift.

I had decided to start going to church on the base, since the hours offered were more suited to my sleeping in on Sundays. With no one to wake up to, I had been doing a lot of sleeping in. And, it wasn't odd to see a single woman alone at mass, since many spouses had to deal with deployments.

I wore my dark blue pant suit with a pinstriped silk blouse. A small part of me still languished in the fact that I was a size 8 again, and I enjoyed the professional look of the outfit. It made me feel older than my 25 years. My patent black chunky heels were broken in nicely. I wore my hair in a tight ponytail and was mindful of keeping my large knockoff Coach sunglasses on. My pearl choker and matching stud earrings polished off my look. It was the dawn of October, and the late summer heat still lingered in San Diego, but being from a tropical humid island, the San Diego mornings were still chilly for me.

My battle plan was to attend mass, then visit Bag It. I would be dressed up for church, so I made a mental note to be casual on the Tuesday visit for the actual evaluation to avoid recognition.

Bag It was the last shop on the left side of a strip mall. The *mall*, which was probably erected in the 1960s, housed only five businesses. Three were closed on Sundays, and Bag It and the smoothie shop only had lunch hours on the weekends. It made sense since most of their traffic was on the weekdays with the Navy contingent providing the bulk of their business. According to my notes, the target was not very personable. His boss was his older sister, Tamara Roberts-Barrett, and according to Angelica, she wanted something in writing to motivate Thomas to adhere to her customer service standards.

Bag It was surprisingly busy for a Sunday. There was a mix of church folk and the Navy enlisted who had weekend duty. The shop smelled of baked bread and bacon. If I wasn't so damned depressed I would have salivated. The five hundred square foot shop had ten circular dining tables with vinyl red chairs. There was nothing unique or distinct. No pictures on the plain beige walls, aside from a large sign for the fire extinguisher. The gray vinyl tiles looked like the same ones at the George Washington high school cafeteria back home. Bag It had been in business for as long as I was with The Lure Company, three months. Its popularity was growing in the area, and Tamara's staff went from just her and her husband to including her brother and two others. Perhaps, more personality would be added to the overall look of the place once she got a handle on things. If I was Thomas, I would be pissed that my sister would hire our company to evaluate him.

I stood behind seven customers and reviewed the menu. There was a large dry erase board with neat handwritten descriptions. Each of the eight sandwich options seemed very unique. My taste buds warmed up as I read the contents of each sandwich type. Words always got me aroused. There were some cute names like the *Navy Launcher Sub* or the *Loose Lady Sub*. I could just imagine the sailors going back to the office saying, "I had a *Loose Lady* for lunch." *Ba-dum-pah.*

As I scanned the items to the last sub, I was shocked to see Guam on there. There was a *Guam Sub*! I smiled, a wave of pride washed over me. There were others who knew of my home island.

37

I had to remind myself that I couldn't give away who I was. It would be too obvious for me to even order the Guam Sub. I imagined the flavor as I read the contents of this homage in sandwich form to my home: BBQ chicken *kelaguen*, red onions, lemon mayonnaise, lettuce and jalapenos on a corn roll/corn tortilla, optional. Darn, that sounded extra yummy. They even spelled *kelaguen* correctly. The original dish included a heavenly concoction of smoky chicken with onions, lemon and peppers. I immediately peered behind the counter to catch a glimpse of Tamara. She must have been there to have this knowledge of Guam.

A petite Asian female was posted at the register. She was busy taking sandwich orders. My physical assessment skills kicked in. Her name tag read, Alma, and she had a jet black blanket of hair, which reached her waist. I coveted that hair. My hair could never decide whether to be curly or straight, hovering somewhere in between. It was very thick thanks to my Asian lineage, but something in the mix with my dad's Chamorro DNA made my *blah*-brown hair very temperamental. Alma obviously didn't make the subs, at least for today, since she wasn't donning the required hair net. She was all of barely five feet tall. She wore gold hoop earrings and what looked like a Swatch. *Did they still make those things?* Her pink t-shirt was form fitting with Bag It in bold letters across her petite chest. Then I looked behind her and ascertained my target.

As described, Thomas was a tall, lanky Caucasian twenty something male. I saw tufts of honey colored hair underneath his red baseball cap. He wore it backwards, his substitute for a hair net I presumed. He was hunched over severely, hands busy with food. I guess the counter was too low for his height. He worked diligently at making sandwiches. A statuesque woman emerged from the back. She must be Tamara I thought to myself. Side by side, Tamara and Thomas were indeed siblings. She too hunched a bit, like she didn't want to be noticed. She had a lovely square face, with fine features and light colored eyes. It was hard to see them behind her black rectangle framed spectacles. I could tell that she was one who downplayed her natural beauty. I loved women who did that, like my Rachel.

Rachel could roll out of bed in her boyfriend's shirt— whoever the flavor of the month was—and look stunning. Her ebony hair was always layered just right. She wore it just past her shoulders. Rachel was known to experiment on occasion with her hair and her make-up, but she was one who could look gorgeous even with no hair. The image of a bald person dragged me back to the night Bradley shaved his head and got his first tattoo, a tribal tattoo to match his hunk make over. His face filled my mind, threatening the tears to burst. I did a mental mind swipe and got back to work.

Tamara kept her hands on her waist and looked like Wonder Woman as she surveyed her restaurant. She smiled, perhaps more to herself and seemed pleased that the shop was busy even on a Sunday. She whispered something to Thomas and they both giggled. It was cute to see them interact, and I missed my kid brother then.

I still had five people in front of me so I finalized my decision settling on the *Rock Lobster Sub*. I made a mental note to return as a regular patron if the sandwich was scrumptious. I watched Thomas intently. He seemed unconcerned by his surroundings, working on the task at hand, maybe wanting to be somewhere else. He wore a plain gray t-shirt and blue jeans. I couldn't see his footwear, which would give me a gage to the type of person he was. Sneakers, *laid back*. Running shoes, *sporty*. Loafers, *old man at heart*. Barefoot, *disgusting*. Guam *zoris* aka flip flops, *cheating, lying bastard*. Wait, that was Bradley.

About the time that Bradley busted my heart, I started caring about the people I evaluated and wanted to understand what motivated them to offer good service or not. I always wondered who they were, what they did when they left their place of work, what car they drove, what astrological sign they were…a ton of questions. There had to be an explanation as to why one person was a jerk and another a saint. I wondered too if I really knew my husband. What would motivate him to cheat and end our marriage after over a decade together? Did our relationship get stale? Did I lose my allure? Did our time together run its course?

I wasn't sure if I would get to see Thomas in action, since Alma was manning the counter at that moment. When the line decreased by three, Thomas approached the counter, but kept his eyes downcast. He placed what looked to be a turkey avocado bacon sub, on a tray for an awaiting customer. That must have been the *Caddy Classic*, number 2 on the menu. He didn't even make eye contact with the young woman, who was obviously attractive in a Megan Fox kind of way. Thomas just slid the tray to her and brusquely asked what kind of chips she wanted for her meal. Three of the men in the line glanced over at this woman often. She must have been barely legal and obviously unaware of the effect she was having in the room, or at least pretending not to notice. I, on the other hand, was keenly aware that I was not causing any ripples with any of the male specimens here.

I was still a married woman, one who wore her wedding ring like it would ward of any evil spirits trying to tear apart the last shred of her marriage. Even with the knowledge that I was at my high school weight of 130, I was a woman in limbo. I couldn't move on, not that I wanted to, because the man I loved had put me on a time out. Bradley said I should try dating since he was doing that with Jem, but I couldn't bring myself to even start. I had no dating experience beyond what I knew with Bradley. I felt so old-fashioned, so out of it. I was clueless as to the dating realm in this day and age aside from what I saw on the tube. And what I saw was that everyone was dating everyone else after a mere hello.

I agonized over the prospect of being a divorcée, but I also wanted my marriage to be fixed or broken, not in between. If Bradley was certain about Jem being his soul mate, then I wished he would just declare that instead of keeping me on the side in case he changed his mind. I was thankful that I was wearing my large sunglasses. My eyes welled up. I looked into my purse for a tissue when someone tapped my shoulder.

"He's ready for you." A Navy chief dressed in his crisp khaki uniform pointed to Thomas. Culver—I read his nametag with my special ninja move. Bruce Lure taught us to see without seeing. The Chief was perhaps ten years older than me. He had warm chocolate brown eyes and he smiled a bright white smile. I made many assessments of his physical features, which I was getting very good at since taking on this secret shopping business. It happened whether I liked it or not. I could tell you the outfits and hairstyles of my librarian for the past month if you really wanted to know.

I offered *el Jefe* a half smile as thanks. If the kind Chief was flirting with me at all, I couldn't tell. Bradley plucked me from the grapevine so early that I never developed a sense of my feminine powers. I didn't know how to *work it* so to speak.

About a year before I was engaged, I went out to a karaoke club with Rachel. We were both eighteen, which used to be the legal drinking age on Guam. I think it should have been twenty one, but maybe that's because my cousin died after he got drunk and plowed into a concrete power pole on his eighteenth birthday. A couple of military guys flirted with us, at least that's what Rachel said. She kept nudging me to mingle with them, even though I was only on a break with Bradley for the weekend. We had one of our first major blowouts, but Rachel took that as a pass for me to meet other men.

One of the men, Isaac, was decent looking. His blue eyes I remembered the most. He jokingly asked me to show some teeth, give him a smile. So, I did. I looked like a lioness baring my chompers and the look on his face was that of shock. I realized that

42

Chief Culver was still eyeballing me as he cleared his throat and tilted his head at me towards Thomas.

"Oh, sorry, sir." I stepped forward two paces and was suddenly looking at my Tuesday target. Maybe my dark sunglasses allowed Thomas to look directly at me, but I was sure he couldn't see my eyes. I was speechless for a second as I looked at Thomas's face. Seeing it whole for the first time was like seeing an entirely different person. His eyes were definitely gray and the opposite of creepy. He gave me a half smile, which made his eyes crinkle a bit. His height was intimidating when he corrected his posture. I shook my head to come out of my trance as Thomas cleared his throat. He waited for me to make a move. That move was to pick a sandwich.

"Sorry, can I get the Gua, I mean the, uh, Rock Lobster Sub?" I posed it as a question like he would tell me no.

"Sure. The works?" He asked, his face returning to a stoic mask. I nodded to affirm this and then he asked, "What size?"

"Oh, there are sizes?" I was really distracted today.

Thomas tapped his pen impatiently on his yellow notepad. I looked up at the board again and saw at the very top of the menu the three sizes: *Just need a snack, Fill me up* and *Give it to me good*. As tempted as I was to tell Thomas, *Give it to me good*, I couldn't do it. I gave him a crooked smile instead. I wanted to maintain my weight loss with the hopes that Bradley might take me back, so I asked for the snack size. Thomas requested my name, his voice strumming my chest so unexpectedly. I said, "Sirena."

Bruce recommended that we had a set list of fake monikers ready. I decided on Sarah for everything because of my love of Sarah McLachlan, but my brain froze. I must have been missing Guam, as I offered the name of my favorite Chamorro legend instead.

"S-I-R-E-N-A." Thomas spelled the name of the legendary mermaid correctly, without hesitation. I watched the long creamy fingers of his left hand jot down my fake name in capital letters. He looked at me more closely and it seemed like he wanted to ask me something, but closed his plump lips instead. Maybe I wasn't worth the question.

Thomas nodded his head and proceeded to the sandwich creating station. Alma waited for me to pay, her childlike smile greeting me. She rang up the order correctly and provided my receipt. I stood along the wall with the other customers, eagerly and hungrily awaiting our delights from Thomas the sandwich monger. I wondered why he was the only person actually making sandwiches. Maybe that was Tamara's intent, keep us waiting, so in our starved state we would rave about how delectable the subs were. Everything tasted better if you let yourself get hungry enough, right?

Almost ten minutes later, while I checked for a text from Bradley, Thomas sang out, "Si, Si –Rey-na." He sang the distinct tune for the *Sirena* song by Johnny Sablan, a Guam singer. Was it Thomas who had been to Guam? If I wasn't on assignment, I would ask him about it, my curiosity piqued. My Guam pride strengthened now that I lived away from my home. Tamara looked amused that her brother was singing out my name, well my fake name. She hit him playfully on his arm and his faced transformed to a thing of beauty. Earlier, with his small smile I was only witnessing a flower bud, but now his face was natural and in full bloom. I surprised myself when an electric shock ran through my body, tickling the dormant places of my body. This was not a reaction I ever had for a man since being with Bradley.

Once Bradley chose me and we were together, I switched all those feelings off. I never lusted for another, never felt I needed to. Any tingles and feelings of desire were solely for Bradley. Even though Thomas stirred something in me, I wasn't one to flirt or make my attraction known. I still held on to the hope that Bradley would come back to me.

Thomas didn't look at me as I walked to the counter. Maybe he assumed I had no connection to Guam, since I wasn't bronze or have ebony hair. His laughing eyes and flushed cheeks were reminiscent of someone. I couldn't place the face, but I lingered a few seconds longer to watch him. I heard Tamara ask about the song and Thomas just shrugged and glanced quickly at me before he returned to the sandwich making counter. Alma smiled at me and raised her eyebrows, perhaps wondering if I wanted something more.

"He's single by the way. At least for this week." Alma commented, tilting her head back in Thomas's direction. I noticed that Chief Culver turned his attention to us when Alma declared this. I didn't know if she was serious about my chances with a man like that or just teasing. I opted for the latter possibility and got flustered. I hoped that Thomas didn't hear Alma.

"Huh?" I was shocked back into reality. "No, I, um, I'm married." I waved my left hand at her and grabbed my bagged sandwich. I bolted and wished my heels didn't clack loudly as I exited. How could she even think I was interested? Was I really staring at him for that long? And, I was still married, technically.

I retreated to the safety of my Rav4, which I parked behind the strip mall. I didn't want to be identified and on the field agent tips, parking away was highly suggested. I removed my jacket and unbuttoned the top two buttons of my silk blouse. I sat in my car, breathing heavily from the idea of even dating anyone again, Chief Culver—whom I noted did not have a wedding band on or Mr. I've Been to Guam Thomas.

I pulled out my Blackberry for the umpteenth time to check for a text or message from Bradley. I didn't notice the approaching footsteps as I was about to check my voicemail. A light tapping on my window made me jump like a skittish colt. I immediately threw my jacket over my Lure documents and looked up slowly. I saw a gray t-shirt marked with the Bag It name. It was Thomas. My shirt was unbuttoned to my bra and it must have looked like I was having a hot flash. It was warm now that noon loomed. I didn't hit the button to roll my window down, but yelled through the glass instead.

"Yes!?" My mind raced as I thought of reasons why he would knock on my window. He tapped each of his fingers on my window again. This time he lowered his face to look in. I saw the gold necklace and pendant that was described by a previous field agent. The pendant was intricate and beautiful. It looked like a Celtic symbol I once saw on a CD. Yes, I went through an Irish music phase in college. Thomas had an amused look on his face. I felt like a caged gorilla being gawked at by zoo visitors. Maybe he had a banana for me? *Wow! My mind had not been in the gutter in a long time, even my dirty jokes were limp.*

I wiped the hair that came loose from my ponytail out of my face and quickly put on my sunglasses. I rolled down the lightly tinted window a few inches and brought my lips to the opening space between us.

"What?" I asked, trying not to sound too mean, but failing.

"You forgot your chips and drink, ma'am." Thomas was now eye to eye with me. I didn't remember ordering a meal. Thomas's eyes darted around the interior of my vehicle and his glance grazed lightly over my cleavage. Caught. Men will be men. Rachel once caught a deacon staring at her boobs. I wasn't flattered at all by such behavior.

In the tenth grade, I kicked Jose's *jewels* in P.E. class because he sneered and made a vulgar comment as I crouched opposite him during volleyball. This was before I knew what a sports bra was, satisfied with my undersized, ill-fitting K-mart two for ten dollar cotton bra. It was the first time I was sent to the principal's office. Luckily Mrs. Flores, the discipline principal was a big-breasted woman herself. She heard me out and let me off with a warning and advice on proper boulder holders.

Modesty overwhelmed me and as I pulled my jacket to my chin, Thomas's prying eyes landed on the Guam flag dangling from my rearview mirror. He smiled widely and his eyes did that thing that tickled my tummy. His iridescent eyes looked like horizontal crescent moons and his face took on an anime effect. When he smiled so brightly his eyes almost closed completely, which made him look younger in a flash. His long lashes made me jealous. His lips were a bit pink and glossy from when he licked them. *Yes, I watched.* They were pretty plump for a man, I thought. His teeth were immaculate, perfectly straight and white. My insides flip flopped again when his warm minty breath invaded my car. Maybe I was just light-headed from being really hungry.

"Are you from Guam, Sirena?" Thomas asked excitedly, pointing to the evidence.

"No. My husband is." I stated rather bluntly. I felt trapped and I didn't want to blow my cover. Although I was dying to know how he had any knowledge of Guam, I had to leave for more reasons than one.

"Oh." He sounded disappointed. Thomas looked over my face again, probably wondering what was lying beneath my huge sunglasses. "Well, you can come back to get your drink and chips, or I can bring it out to you if you tell me what you want."

Tamara rounded the corner now and headed in our direction.

"Tom-Tom! People are waiting. Come on." I was thankful that she went back to the shop. I smiled at the sound of a big sister calling her little brother by his pet name. I dropped my smile as soon as Tom-Tom returned his gaze to me.

"Well, ma'am?" I wished he would stop calling me "ma'am"—did I look that old? I shifted into drive. I would make things worse if I requested the additional food.

"I'm fine. I'm on a diet. Thanks." And, then I drove off. Thomas stood there and watched my retreating car. I finally released my breath when I saw him turn around and walk back to the shop. I was able to make out that he wore a pair of plaid Chuck Taylors and I smiled liking his style.

Once I was a safe distance away from the shop I headed back onto the base. I made a quick decision to go to the military exchange. There was something I had been meaning to do since the hatchet came down on my marriage.

I picked out a box of blond hair dye. I flashed my military dependent card and paid with cash. My Blackberry chimed indicating that I had a text. It was Bradley.

be back in town by nxt wknd. Can you pick me up?

A dull pain started in my chest and then I realized I was gulping for air. If I texted back right away, would he think I was desperate? I decided to wait to respond and drove home on auto pilot. This was my husband, but because of the predicament he put me in, I didn't know how to act. I hated not being in control of my feelings. I gripped my steering wheel tighter and drove a little faster. My Weezer CD blared in the background like the soundtrack of my day. I sang along with all my might, my voice wrought with all the dramatic flair I could conjure.

Once I hit the 54 West, I thought about our condo. It was still filled with Bradley's things. He made no immediate plans to move. Before boot camp, we talked about moving up north together closer to Sacramento, to be near the Army base.

He gave me a list of things to do while he was at AI training. For the first time, as I thought about this, I was angry. I thought, *how dare he put me on notice and still expect me to take care of his crap.* Was I going to start his car up every other day anymore? Did I have to continue paying the bills? That was Bradley's duty up until he decided to leave me. The condo was too large for me. I toyed with the idea of moving out. I really only needed a small one bedroom unit. This was the first time I allowed myself to really think about being solo.

The last time I was a single woman, I was a sophomore just getting to love music by Dave Matthews and Sarah McLachlan. I was interested in reading the classics. I stocked my closets with the rebellious fashions of the day. One constant was my obsession with Hello Kitty. Basically, I was still a kid finding her way in life; I wasn't a woman at all.

Thinking about being single was both scary and a relief. My anger fueled this thought process. I had a right to be angry right? Was I in the wrong? No. I finally saw my situation in a new light. The sadness in me was turning into rage. The blues were turning red. Maybe Rachel was rubbing off on me. Maybe Chief Culver and Bag It Thomas rattled my feminine wiles. Whatever they did, something was definitely awakened in me.

Chapter 4

My Fairy Spa Mother

I pulled up to my condo and there was a bright orange taxi blocking the path to my door. Mysterious spy music played in my head, as usual. I parked and peered into my rearview mirror. I couldn't see the passenger and my heart fluttered, putting me on guard. I opened my car door slowly. For a moment, I imagined that Thomas might have followed me home with my bag of chips and drink. That seemed so illogical the thought fizzled in my cup before I could take a sip.

A woman. She had wild pixie hair and large dark sunglasses. I walked behind the car, keeping my most intense stare on the passenger. I reached my door and fumbled with my keys. My nerves were pretty rattled for a laidback Sunday, first from Thomas almost making me as an evaluator and next by Bradley's text. The old me pleaded that I text him back, but this new fiery me screamed, *Screw that, let him wait!*

I opened my door finally, when a familiar voice called to me from the taxi.

"*Hafa adai*, sexy biatch!" I recognized my best friend's voice at once, greeting me in our language. Was I dreaming? I looked into the taxi. It would be like Rachel to hold the taxi guy there until I showed.

"Rachel? What the hell? What are you doing here?! And, what happened to your long hair?" I raced to the other side of the taxi as she made a dramatic exit. I half expected to see flames shoot out or doves racing for the sky from behind her. The driver made a sour face and started his car. She threw the poor man a hundred dollar bill and told him to keep the change. The airport was only ten minutes north, so I knew her tip was rather indulgent. It must have been Rachel's way of apologizing for the fact that this poor guy had to witness estrogen-drama at all.

Rachel wrapped me tight in her arms, "I missed you. My hair is just hair, it'll grow back. I was bored." With sweetness in her eyes, Rachel held me at arms length. She cranked back her little fist, then punched me swiftly on my arm. *Ouch.* "What the hell, Nix!? I thought you electrocuted yourself in your tub or jumped off Coronado Bridge. I almost came two weeks ago if it wasn't for updates from your dad! When you didn't answer your phone or respond to my e-mails the other day, that's when I freaked out and hopped on a plane, make that three planes, to get here." I gave Rachel strict instructions to keep my separation private.

"Sorry." I rubbed my arm and smiled at my best friend.

Rachel looked ragged from the long flight over, but still beautiful. Her new pixie hair was stunning. How could she possibly get more gorgeous? She gave me a once over and did it again for good measure, holding my hands the whole time. Rachel walked around me. She smacked my butt playfully.

"Are you *that* depressed? You look hotter than your wedding day! And your ass, it's so, so firm!"

"We haven't been in each other's presence for three minutes and you're already touching my *dagan*." I teased.

"I missed you! How long has Bradley been gone? I bet he hasn't seen you *this* hot. He's going to bust a nut!" I'm sure she meant to compliment me, but bringing up Bradley let alone my wedding day, was not the right thing to do. I started crying, wailing actually. *Okay, banshee shrieking if you must know.* Rachel walked me to the door like I was a lost puppy. She plopped me on my couch and ran outside to get our stuff.

I composed myself quickly, I didn't need to drag my bestie into my pit of sadness. Rachel held the box of dye with a questioning look. When I told her of the dual purpose of the drastic change—one to make going back to Bag It easier and two because Bradley liked blondes apparently, Rachel agreed to help. She did not agree with the reasons, but came up with a new one, a better one. She wanted me to have a fresh start.

In college, Rachel went blonde and wanted me to try it too. She wanted to run a social experiment for her psychology paper, "Guam Blondes and the Effect on Chamorro Men." I had avoided her for a week. I hoped she just didn't want payback for forcing her to choose another research paper topic.

Rachel searched local spas that were by chance open on a Sunday and by a miracle accepting appointments. I cooked up a hot batch of *kimchee* fried rice, knowing Rachel loved my mom's recipes. I had the *Rock Lobster* sandwich sitting on the counter. It called to me. My mind wandered deeper into my morning encounter with Thomas. I marveled at the thought that what sat in that very bag was created by his lovely hands. Once I completed Rachel's lunch, my curiosity and my awakening appetite got the better of me.

As Rachel sat in front of the steaming bowl of spicy carbs, she inhaled the vapor like it was an elixir for jetlag. I told her to save the spa day for when she was feeling normal, but Rachel is an *I'll sleep when I die* person. This was why my best friend was so successful.

We had an hour before the Diva Spa could take us. She included time for me to get my hair dyed professionally. I guess it was a good thing that there was a pre-season Chargers event today. Everyone was either at the stadium or glued to their flat screens.

Rachel ate her bowl of rice slowly, savoring each morsel. I wondered if my rendition of *kimchee* fried rice was as good as my mom's; probably not, but Rachel's vulgar moaning each time she shoveled a mouthful suggested otherwise.

I ceremoniously pulled the wrapped sub from the plain brown paper bag. I removed the blue plastic tipped toothpick that pierced the wax paper. As I opened each corner of the crisp wrapper, the smell of lobster and celery and creamy mayonnaise invaded my nose. I hadn't had mayo for months now and my mouth watered. Angels may as well be singing in the background as the lobster sub was finally revealed. My eyes flickered to

Rachel, making sure she was actually with me and not just a figment of my imagination. Her mouth was opened and her spoon suspended over her jade green bowl. I guess she watched my sandwich strip tease. She smiled widely, rice still in her mouth and laughed. I realized how silly I must have looked, and laughed too. The delirious raucous we created permeated through my condo and for a moment I felt normal. Rachel's presence was like extra strength Tylenol.

I explained the details of my new job and my target, Thomas. My stomach rumbled and Thomas's sandwich was begging to be eaten. Rachel's eyes glazed over a few times. I told her to nap on the recliner in the office. She needed to be upright with her belly full of food. I didn't want her to have indigestion, a residual lesson from my Korean mother.

"No way am I going to nap. I only have five days with you and I'm going to make the most of it. We'll eat, go to the spa early and take a walk before the appointment. I'll get a sextuple shot at Starbucks. Can you believe we still don't have a Starbucks on Guam?" Rachel declared. "I want to get up to speed on *Brad-lame*."

Rachel was right. With how tired she was, if she even blinked too long, I wouldn't see her until lunch the next day. On the way to the spa, Rachel heard my gripes about Bradley and Jem. When my conversation strayed to Thomas, she waved her hand like she was shooing a fly. "You're just having rebound feelings." Rachel, my life coach was right as usual. In between conversation time, Rachel and I sang along to Pink songs, growing more aggressive with each mile.

Poor Rachel slapped herself between songs to stay alert. Luckily, Pacific Beach was only twenty minutes north, or four songs by my measurement. After coffee and a quick walk, Rachel had the boost she needed to get through a *stressful* spa treatment.

Rachel and I held up the miniature robes given to us and guffawed in unison. Even when I was a size 14, the robes were smaller, barely covering my bottom. I would figure after losing thirty, I would fit into one of these. They must have someone in charge of assessing patron sizes and switching robes that are three sizes smaller. "This is a conspiracy!" Rachel and I said at the same time as we barely got the ties around our waists. Rachel hugged me before she was escorted away by a pretty girl who looked like a mannequin.

This sugar exfoliation treatment was a first for me. I thought of all the cookies one could make with the sugar that was about to be rubbed on me. The incense-filled room was dim and cozy with scented candles peppered all around the small sanctuary. The only odd piece of equipment was the stainless steel bed. I felt like I walked onto the set of *CSI* where autopsies are performed. I shivered. Having to take a shower horizontally seemed wrong to me, but Rachel swears by this treatment. Twenty minutes later, after being rubbed down and glazed like a doughnut, Mandy—the sugar fairy rinsed my entire body with warm water. I felt invigorated, but happy it was over because only two small towels over my boobs and crotch area saved me from complete nudity with a stranger.

Step two of our spa day included a full body massage. I did this for the first time with Bradley for our honeymoon in Hawaii. I was hooked since then, often getting weekly massages. That ended six months ago because of our shrinking budget. I was glad to be in the same room as Rachel so we could catch up. Aside from my drama, I wanted to hear about her clothing line's launch in Japan. ShinyPurpleThread was doing great on Guam. Rachel's profits this year alone were almost at half a million bucks. That's huge in a failing economy.

Rachel had requested, unbeknownst to me, male masseurs. She got Bret and I was paired up with Chazzer. Rachel had no shame in taking in every defined muscle of our masseurs. She must have absorbed the sugar right into her bloodstream, since she was very alert.

"What's going on with S.P.T. in Japan?" I asked.

"The show went well. I have about ten potential clients who want to carry my line. We're in negotiations right now." Rachel stated between moans of pleasure and grunts of pain. "I brought some samples for you, but I have them in size 12s and you're obviously not that size anymore. You look to be an 8, if not 6."

This wasn't exactly a topic I wanted to discuss in front of Tweedle Buff and Tweedle Guns. Rachel never filtered her conversations and I wasn't expecting her to start now, lying half naked with two men.

"I would still love to see them and try them on."

"Of course! You're going to wear one tonight when we go out to party! I can make some quick alterations."

"Party on a Sunday night?" I asked doubtful.

"Yeah, first dinner, then karaoke, then maybe dancing." Bret and Chazzer looked at each other and smiled. Maybe they thought we were lovers.

"My *husband* is coming back Sunday from training," I emphasized the word husband to clarify my unavailability. Also, I didn't want the masseurs getting too frisky with visions of girl on girl action in their minds. All I needed was to have Chaz junior poking my leg.

Rachel shot her head straight up, the sanitary white paper stuck to her right cheek, perky boobs gyrating unashamedly.

"What the hell are you bringing Bradlame's name up?" She growled. "You're divorcing that bastard and that's that!" Rachel put her head back down and Bret continued kneading her hips and legs. "Let him take a taxi home, and before Sunday, change the locks! Damn, he's lucky my flight leaves the day before. Maybe I'll extend my stay."

It would be nice to have Rachel with me when I saw Bradley, but I couldn't ask her to stay. I didn't respond to Bradley's text yet, and the me of last week would be fretting by now. But I was surprisingly calm about it. I would let him sweat it out until tomorrow.

Rachel and I settled into silence. I let Chazzer work out the knots in my back and squish and jiggle my aching limbs. I felt my body melt into the table and I was on the verge of sleep.

Human touch made me feel alive again and the new energy gave me the courage to change my hair. Rachel gave specific instructions to the colorist and hair stylists. She went into business woman beast mode. Rachel always had an air of authority. When she spoke, people listened. When I speak, people usually swat at their ears because a mosquito is buzzing.

After almost an hour and a half of tugging and pulling and sniffing harsh chemicals, I was more than ready to see the new blonder me. The make up artist, who smelled of delicious strawberries, did her magic. I was so close to her perfectly painted face that I could count every fake lash. Rachel acted like the host of a make-over show and turned the salon chair slowly. I kept my eyes closed ceremoniously.

"Okay, Nix, look!" Rachel demanded.

I opened my eyes to see a Diva like pop star, a Hollywood vixen. It was fascinating that I could even look this different. I wasn't a blond Barbie like Jem, but my hair color was like beautiful caramel. My locks were as straight as ever. It danced along my shoulders and chest so magnificently. I looked up at Rachel and had to keep myself from crying. The make up was more than I was accustomed to. The mascara wasn't Tammy Faye Baker, but it enhanced my almond eyes very nicely.

While I was getting my hair and faced pimped out, Rachel had brought along her sewing kit and a stunner design of her own. She got the management to loan her a room to work on the outfit to surprise me. I wondered if she told them I was a charity case from the Divorcée of the Month Club. Rachel didn't even need to measure me to alter the gorgeous hunter green wrap dress for my body. She whisked me into a room and dressed me like a doll. She had brought along my only used once, strappy black heels. Rachel fitted me with silver tassel earrings and a matching tassel necklace. Happy with the way I looked, she escorted me to the full body mirrors in the salon. Bret and Chazzer were punching out for the day when they both stopped to look at me. *Me?*

Chazzer looked at Rachel as if to ask, *Is this the same woman I was just touching?*

"Phoenix?" Chazzer asked in a deep voice, dripping with honey. "Wow, you look awesome!" He cleared his throat nervously. The salon divas were high-fiving each other and giggling.

"Doesn't she?" Rachel added excitedly. "We're celebrating tonight and you *boys* aren't invited." She added with a wink.

Bret, who was obviously the more professional one, pulled on Chazzer's huge bicep to drag him out the front door. I blushed as he held his position for a few seconds longer, his ocean blue eyes sparkling because of me.

"Damn, I'm good." Rachel declared. "Let's head out. I made dinner arrangements at a teppanyaki place in Kearny Mesa." I had to admit Rachel was indeed good. I felt like my fairy godmother flew in from Guam. I protested, but Rachel paid for the services and handed anyone who touched us a twenty dollar bill. After stuffing a few more bills in an envelope, Rachel signed it "Love, Phoenix," with instructions to give the masseurs their tip in the morning. "Best to keep the men waiting for their treat."

The sun was still setting and the gorgeous light added to the beauty of my day. As I slid into the driver's seat of my car, I heard my name.

"Phoenix? Ma'am." There someone went with the ma'am again. Chazzer strutted towards my car and Rachel chuckled, teasing me quietly.

"Hi, Chazzer." I said nervously. "What is up?" I was trying to sound like a *bro* to him, but he was a man who was probably used to girls batting their eyelashes at him.

"I, uh, well. I was wondering if you might want to visit the spa again. I'd like to make arrangements to, um, be your masseur." *Why?* I thought. Rachel hit my arm as I furrowed my brow. She whispered, "Damn."

"Why, is there a special next month or something?" I must have sounded like a diva myself, but I was serious. Chazzer smiled and blushed, his hot cheeks almost matched the deep red of his hair. He didn't look old enough to drink, and as red-headed men go, he was attractive in a Queens of the Stoneage lead singer kind of way. I realized he was nervous, and I cut him a break.

"Do you have a business card perhaps? I'll be sure to ask for you if I come back here again. It's kind of out of the way though." Even before I finished my sentence, Chazzer magically had his card in front of my newly painted face. I smiled at his enthusiasm, but I wasn't ready to be declared a cougar. "Chazzer, you realize I'm like five years older than you, right? You're just a kid." *And Phoenix and Chazzer didn't sound right together, too comical,* I thought.

Chazzer dug his hands into his snug-fitting khaki shorts and stepped back to look me over again. He seemed even younger then and he smiled wide, "I'm 20 and you can't be over 21! Even if you're thirty! That." He gazed at my face, his words coming out like gravy, "*That* is the way I like it."

I hate gravy.

Satisfied with himself, he turned and trotted away. I allowed myself to take this flattery in, to own it. This was a new phenomenon, and I wasn't sure I could handle it. He was indeed attractive in a caveman way. I tilted my head at his retreating hard body. A twinge of guilt made me think of Bradley, and I cranked my head back into position. Rachel was especially mum during this whole escapade. She pretended to text, but her body convulsed from holding in her laughter.

"I'm so proud of . . . me for making you the hottest you've ever been." Rachel said.

"Yeah, yeah. And, thanks for footing the bill, I owe you." I said as I pulled out my Blackberry. Three missed calls from Bradley. Wow. Rachel peered at my phone and snatched it away.

"Let the fool simmer in it!" She dropped my Blackberry in her Louis Vutton bag with finality. I agreed and we were on our way to dinner. The new me, the blonde me was starving.

When we walked into the waiting area, it felt like the restaurant bustle froze. I was used to this with Rachel, but for me—it was like having a new super power. I didn't know what to do with it.

I was relieved to be seated in a dark area, but we sat with eight strangers around the hot teppanyaki grill. I was never good at eye contact in general and the amount of face time dudes were expecting from me was awkward. Rachel sat back and observed this new phenomenon. Snickering or pushing my arm every so often. She wasn't being subtle.

I barely made it through dinner. I kept thinking I had stuff in my teeth. Even Yuki, our grill master was distracted by the pair of us, flinging shrimp that was meant for his hat at the table behind him. I was burning from this invisible spotlight cast on me. I could have sworn a guy at the other teppanyaki station took a picture of me with his cell phone. I was comforted when we headed out.

I paid for dinner. It was the least I could do for this reinvention of Phoenix that Rachel facilitated. I analyzed a massive collage of customer pictures while Rachel drained her oyster in the ladies room, *her phrase*, not mine.

"Excuse me, ma'am?" *The next bastard to call me ma'am was going to get a beat down,* I thought. I turned to look at the source of my disdain. It was a teenager, must have been barely fifteen years old. He looked at me with wide eyes. I held onto my purse a bit tighter and used it as a shield over my boobs, which were heavily accentuated by Rachel's dress.

"Yes?" I asked confused. "I don't work here."

"Oh, no. Weren't you in that movie, with the dogs and the snow and that actor from the street racing movie? You have a really cool name, I, uh, can't remember it."

"Heck no, kid. I'm not an actress." He looked me over in disbelief. His mom who was standing nearby looked disheartened when she heard me. Were these folks crazy?

"Oh, sorry. You just really look like her." I made a mental note to Google whatever movie this kid was ranting about, even with his vague summation. His mother took him by the shoulders and dragged him away just as Rachel exited the restroom, witness to the tail end of the scene.

"Damn, Nix, I can't leave you for a second tonight without you breaking someone's heart. That kid looked twelve!" She laughed after I explained the misunderstanding.

It was an hour away from midnight and I checked Rachel's vitals to see if she was still able to continue with her grand plans for her first day in San Diego. She really was the energizer Playboy bunny.

Rachel directed me turn by turn, freeway to exit to the karaoke bar she researched. It was down the street from a Guam restaurant I visited once with Bradley when we first arrived. The food was a nice substitute for Chamorro cuisine, but it paled in comparison to the dishes I had to master quick since our transplant. When we drove down the familiar street, I saw the restaurant was closed, its windows boarded up. A small wave of remorse crashed in my heart at the sight.

Pass The Mic was a trendy karaoke lounge. There were more women than men in the joint. It was a good mix of ethnicities, which is why I love San Diego. There was a comfort here. A Shania Twain song was being belted out by a woman who looked like a younger Betty White. She had some pretty good pipes and a sweet twang in her voice. Rachel honed in on a booth in the corner. She let me lead. I kept my purse up again like a shield and pushed through like a linebacker.

I finally exhaled when we made it through the curious crowd and plopped into the booth. Within seconds, a waiter magically appeared at our table. He handed us a song binder and went into a very animated speech about how the process of selecting a song went. He pointed to the cup of pens, each tipped with colorful origami birds and photocopied song request chits. He kept his eye contact between my face and my boobs as he spoke, stuttering on occasion. Rachel nodded her head in an exaggerated manner and pretended to be following along. She was really testing to see if he would even glance at her. "That guy was all about you!" She declared after ordering drinks and choosing her song.

"Whatever." I smiled, but draped my hair over my chest.

Rachel was due to sing in three songs according to the flashing marquee over the stage. If I did actually get buzzed enough to sing out loud, I wondered if management would allow me to do it from the booth. Wireless mics, I spied. Good.

I perused the binder and was impressed by the list of contemporary songs. As much as I loved oldies, which was commonplace in karaoke lounges on Guam, I wanted to also sing what was on the radio today. My karaoke experience was limited to our home entertainment center and my family as an audience.

My dad had purchased a karaoke system for me one Christmas. It was nice to hear my mom sing in Korean and my dad with his vintage croons. He loved himself some Everly Brothers. Maybe I would choose one of their songs, since I knew them by heart and I missed my parents.

Impatient Rachel wanted our drinks yesterday, so she went to the bar and was gone for too long. Knowing her, she was chatting up some handsome fellow, but I was happy to be sitting in the corner. It was my thing.

Rachel maneuvered gracefully through the crowd with two martini glasses. Her smile was mischievous. Talking over a Bon Jovi song, Rachel told me she met some guy at the bar who lived in Guam for a month. That seemed more like an extended vacation to me. She said they didn't speak for too long because he was about to go on stage with his sister. He told Rachel that he and his co-workers had their company meetings here once a week.

"What's his name?" I asked excitedly, happy to meet anyone who had visited Guam.

"I don't know. I didn't get that far. He was just so damned cute I started chatting with him. He is a dead ringer for Edward!" That got me excited, and I'm sure Rachel meant *Robert Pattinson*. I don't think any man in his right mind would be glittered up in a pea coat at this bar. It was Rachel who sent me the Twilight series many Christmases ago. I plowed through the books in a week and Rachel and I chatted, texted and debated about the stories for about a month. Once the movies hit the stores, Rachel sent me the five-disc set. She really was my fairy godmother. We debated the movie and the books as well, often to the dismay of her sales staff. Rachel was more a Team Jacob girl, so I was curious to see this guy since I was more attracted to Robert.

I craned my neck to see the commotion on stage and my question was answered. First, I saw a tall beautiful woman step onto the stage. She wore a pink t-shirt. Two little words popped out at me. Bag It! I looked closer and lost my breath for a moment. It was Tamara, owner of the sandwich shop, minus the glasses. Her long flowing amber hair was undone. I shook my head and thought, *sister, brother.* Crap! It was Thomas whom Rachel spoke to. The connection was clear. Nice way to advertise the shop I thought. Sure enough, Alma and three other people in Bag It shirts were seated at a table by the stage.

Thomas still wore his gray t-shirt. He did not have the baseball cap and I could see that he did look like a Cullen, except not as pale. His light brown hair was neater than the actor, but still reminiscent of the original. I fervently told Rachel about the precarious position I was in and who the Bag It crowd was to me. Her wide eyes told me she finally connected the dots too, "That's the rock lobster guy?"

The gorgeous siblings sat together on a couple of barstools. The crowd became electric when they saw the pair on stage. Their own fan club? Tamara thanked everyone and stated that this was their last song for the evening.

"We've got a kid to get home to! I do, my kid brother is single though, ladies. Slinging tasty sandwiches at our shop. We'll be back next week." Tamara calmed the crowd of about fifty people.

A familiar tune started. It was Smokey Robinson's *Cruisin*, the movie, Duets' version with Huey Lewis and Gwyneth Paltrow. Thomas sounded so much better, so much smoother than Huey, but Tamara was just as beautiful and melodic as Gwyneth, *wait*, she was better too.

As much as I wanted to stay for the whole song, I didn't want Thomas making me. I told Rachel that I was going to hide in the restroom until the Bag It group got in their Partridge Family van and left. She thought I was ridiculous, but indulged me.

"Hey, Nix, if this dude was flirting with you, maybe you could date after the evaluation. He won't know it's you right?"

"I'll be sure to pencil him in after my date with Chazzer." I responded sarcastically. "And, what happened to no rebounds?" Rachel was so impulsive. I hustled to the restroom at the tail end of the duet.

When I walked into the ladies restroom, I scared myself, not recognizing my image in the gold framed mirror. I sat on a red velvet stool. Rachel had specific instructions to call me after Thomas left. I read Bradley's new texts.

Where r u? U ok? About Sunday, get back to me, kinda worried. Brad

Kind of worried about not hearing from his wife, soon-to-be ex-wife? I fumed but my rage was short-lived. A gang of Bag It girls invaded the restroom. They were making their final pit stop before heading home. I heard Tamara's voice in the doorway, and I pretended to be on the phone. I averted my eyes and was happy that my new blond hair shielded my face.

"Tom-Tom! Tell James we'll meet at the car."

Tamara bounded into the restroom and as a cacophony of pissing sounds erupted in the three stalls behind me, she stood uncomfortably close to me. I glanced at her jeans and shoes. She too was wearing a pair of Chuck Taylors in red. I wondered if that was part of their uniform. I found out moments later as Alma and another Bag It girl made their way to the sinks. They wore Nikes, so maybe it was just a sibling thing.

"Awesome dress!" Alma said as she walked by me. I gave her a thumbs up and kept my face hidden. *Crap! Get out already!*

When all was quiet, I dialed Rachel's cell number. As a Kiss song blared in the background, Rachel got on the phone.

"Hey, mom! Yeah, I'll call you later! Love you!" She hung up.

She must be talking to Edward, I mean, Robert, I mean Thomas.

I decided to text Bradley.

I'm fine. Will pick you up Sunday, text me your flight details. Phoenix

I hit send for the short and simple, non-emotional text. It would be my first since our break-up. Was this progress? Was this me moving on?

I jumped when my Blackberry vibrated in my hand. It was Rachel, the mug of her licking an orange popsicle suggestively appeared on my screen, her caller ID.

"Mom here." I answered.

"Hey, Thomas just left. He sat at our booth for a few minutes while the harem of coworkers was in there with you. It's safe to come out. I'll tell you more then."

I checked my reflection in the mirror and heard the start of Rachel's song. That meant mine was next. I decided on *When Will*

I Be Loved by the Everly Brothers. A little bit dramatic, but I was feeling a bit sorry for myself today despite my new exterior.

I headed for the bar and bought a shot to calm my nerves. I would ask Rachel to drive us back to the condo since I had more to drink than usual, aside from loyal, I'm responsible. I'd only seen this done on T.V., so I licked my salty hand and downed the shot. The hot liquid coated my throat and I felt it descend to my belly. Repulsed, I sucked on the lime wedge. When I looked up, my face contorted from the taste of sour, three college boys watched me. I smiled meekly and licked the side of my lips of the dripping lime juice. That must have sent the wrong signal and their matching sneers proved it, so I pirouetted and bolted back to my booth. I felt their eyes on my back and quivered from disgust.

Rachel did her best job at *Don't Cha* by the Pussycat Dolls. She beckoned me to the stage, but I refused and shook my head like a petulant baby. Rachel had a line of men in front of her waving their beer bottles and a group of college girls smirked, threatened by her confidence and beauty. This was the scene I was used to, Rachel breaking hearts and pissing off girlfriends. The pixie look was doing her well. Her lean body was well earned by all the hours at the gym and this audience appreciated it. She was definitely unique from the batch of pale women here. Her chocolate brown skin was inviting.

Someone yelled a marriage proposal, which Rachel took in stride.

"Sorry boys, I'm with her!" And she pointed to our booth. Rachel brought the cordless mic to me. I was definitely not drunk enough for this. She sat down and sipped her drink. She pushed me towards the stage, but I knew the song by heart and I didn't need to see the lyrics. I held my position at the comfy seat of our booth. This was short and sweet, like all oldies. Taking direction from Betty White's doppelganger, I sang with feeling and twang.

By the end of the song, the entire bar was singing along. Then I saw Thomas. He stood by the jukebox, far enough away, but too close for comfort. He stared in my direction with a sexy half smile on his face. His eyes did that thing to me again and I panicked. How long had he been standing there? I sank deep into my seat. I slunk to the floor and landed with a thud. Rachel shook her head at me. As the audience's cheering died down, I began my G.I. Jane crawl to the restroom. When I was safely shielded in the hallway, I stood and made my escape to the ladies restroom for the second time in fifteen minutes. Rachel laughed so hard, I heard her snort. She called out to me. "Don't ruin that dress!"

Miraculously, Rachel concocted a story of me being sick from major stage fright. Thomas said he was *compelled* to return to the bar when he heard the first few notes of one of his favorite songs. Rachel entertained him for a few minutes even telling Thomas how reminiscent he was of the beloved Twilight character. Rachel explained this as she drove us back to the condo. He had asked for my name and Rachel told him "Monica". Hopefully, Thomas was not into *Friends*. He had to leave because the Bag It

73

gang called him. Rachel told Thomas that I left in a taxi to our hotel room because she had more partying to do and he bought it.

"He said you sounded like Lisa Ronstadt." Rachel said excitedly.

"You mean, Linda?" Linda Ronstadt was an awesome singer from my dad's era. I appreciated her, but I didn't know if she sang a version of that song. Rachel didn't really care about oldies, her earliest music history being New Kids on the Block and, well The Doors, since she thought Jim Morrison was hot because Val Kilmer played him in an old biopic.

"Linda, Lisa, whatever, Thomas thought you sounded hot. He apparently has an appreciation for the dinosaur music like you." Rachel took direction well as she safely got us home.

"Sounded hot doesn't really mean I'm hot. Did he say anything else?" I was curious.

"He had a lot of questions about Guam, since I told him you and I were vacationing from there." There was no way Thomas would connect the brunette me from almost twelve hours ago to the blonde me of now, so I wasn't too worried. "He spent a month there in the summer, loving the culture, he said."

"Really? Wow, I wonder what brought him there."

"He's definitely hot and intriguing. I see you two making beautiful half-vampire babies." Rachel joked.

Chapter 5

Becoming a Golden Girl

Walking into the condo with Rachel, I imagined for a moment that I owned it, all alone. I was just a single working girl having her best friend over for a slumber party. I suggested a classic movie and after some cold showers, separate—not together, despite the fantasies many of the men from the karaoke bar might be having, Rachel grabbed one of my oversized Bruce Lee t-shirts, comfortable in her nakedness.

"You still have this! May I?" She pulled the enormous black t-shirt over her damp hair before I could answer. I wrapped my new caramel hair in a wet knot and pulled on my white Bruce Lee one-inch punch t-shirt, then removed my towel. We raced downstairs and popped in a movie. It was like old times, but back then we rented VHS movies from the local mom and pop store, sat with a tub of cool whip and Oreos and a liter of pop and burned the rest of our afternoon in sugary giddiness. Oh, how I wish my metabolism now was that of my fourteen year old self. Now, we sated ourselves with stale ranch rice cakes and diet pop.

Ten minutes into *Bridget Jones's Diary*, Rachel snored. I gently removed her head from my shoulder and lay her flat on the sofa. I had her company for four more days and I was grateful. Rachel was definitely in dreamland, mouth gaping open, legs sprawled over the back of the couch, very ladylike. She looked like she was in a pixie death match with Tinkerbell and lost. I wrapped her tight in my Hello Kitty blanket and kissed her forehead. Leaving the movie on in the background, I headed to my room.

I walked past the office, my laptop actually beckoned me. *Psst. Get your butt in here and tap this*, it said. I headed in and started it up promising myself that I would only be on for fifteen minutes. I unwound my damp hair. My finger hesitated on the Facebook button. It had been two weeks. I hit my e-mail button instead. I saw numerous messages from Rachel, a few from Pharaoh and three from Bradley. *Hmm.* Rachel was here already, so I skipped those. I didn't want to be cursed out via her e-mails. I clicked on Pharaoh's latest e-mail. He wasn't a man of many words and his correspondence wasn't any different.

Hey sis, training again, dumped Caroline, parentals are cool, but call. Funeral was typical, can't believe Uncle J is gone. Roar!

I wanted to give mom and dad space during this time. Didn't want to call them frequently, reminding them that I wasn't coming home. It was almost three in the morning, which meant it was about eight at night on Guam. They may still be at Uncle's post-funeral rosary, but I took a chance and called the house. They picked up.

I finally dragged myself to bed after an hour of tiptoeing around the topic of Bradley. I thought about my parents. Dad was so proud of this new direction Bradley took by joining the Army, being an Army retiree himself. I wondered what dad would think about the new direction of my marriage. When they asked about Bradley it took all my strength not to yell out, *He's screwing Barbie now and they're looking into adopting a bunch of kids from Korea and whatever third world country was in vogue at the moment!*

I looked at Bradley's cold side of the bed, the place I slept when I missed him. I went to my spot instead and stared out into the starless sky, wondering for the first time not about Bradley, but about Thomas.

After losing half of Monday to sleep, Rachel and I spent the second half of the day sightseeing. I was glad she didn't care to go to the zoo or Seaworld or any other touristy spot. We dined in the city and strolled around. Monday night was filled with Chinese delivery and just more great conversation and wine.

With Tuesday's evaluation looming, I spent the evening in my office preparing and reviewing my paperwork for Thomas. Rachel slept again, not completely recovered from her jet lag. I felt bad when I thought about her adjusting to our time zone, only to leave back to Guam to be a zombie again for a few days. She was the sister I never had and I hated for her to suffer because of me.

Rachel negotiated her way into going to Bag It with me. She even helped herself to a long raven wig in my closet, something I bought to spice up the bedroom which never came out of its original packaging. She wore some of my old clothes, which were baggy on her. Her mocha brown skin and the black hair made her look like her old island girl self from high school. Long hair and hot weather wasn't a good mix, and I wondered why more Guam girls didn't have pixie haircuts.

I indulged Rachel's dress up session because she enjoyed the whole secret agent element. I wore my faded jeans with a fitted black t-shirt. I slipped into my pink Converse All Stars with Hello Kitty laces, maybe because part of me wanted to connect with Thomas. I needed to get through this evaluation without being made, but I was making it hard for myself. Thomas was an oddity to me because he actually liked Guam. My experience thus far was of statesiders having something stupid to say about my home. *Is it true there are brown tree snakes everywhere? Isn't Guam just a military base? Don't teenagers have to lose their virginity at fourteen. Wow, you don't have an accent and you speak English good.* Speak English well, ignoramus, I thought. But, maybe the tides could change with a man like Thomas.

I wore my hair straight. Really didn't have a choice since Rachel ordered the stylist to straighten it. I grew fond of the lighter hue. I never thought I could ever embrace my mixed heritage. Growing up on Guam I wanted not so much to fit in, but not stick out in a crowd. I coveted the beautiful copper skin, dark eyes and ebony hair of my cousins. I was the direct opposite—fair skin, confused wavy brown hair, almond shaped hazel eyes. People didn't look at me and say, *hey, that's a Chamorrita.*

Rachel was exotic, her beautiful brown eyes were wide and eager to soak up life. Her eyelashes for miles were unworldly. Her physique was goddess-like and she didn't possess freakish height like me, but she walked tall and proud as a Chamorro woman. Now, yes, there was no such thing as a full-blooded Chamorro anymore, with war ravaging through the island after the first descendants discovered Guam in something B.C., every Chamorro was mingled with either Spanish or Japanese or *Haole—inclusive of all Caucasian* blood, amongst others. Some with all of that and then some.

Bradley and I joined the local Guam Club when we first got to San Diego in an effort to enjoy island life away from home. The food was a big draw, but the looks I received from Chamorros who either left the island decades ago or never set foot there were disheartening. One man who had been in the states for over twenty years eyed me curiously as I stood in the buffet line. I was already an emotional wreck having miscarried a few weeks earlier.

Fiestas were supposed to be a celebration of a village saint, open to everyone. After several more stare downs, he finally asked if I was from Guam. The interrogation began with him wanting to know my family name and village. Did I have to prove my connection to the Chamorros to eat? Bradley had a thicker skin about those matters, but then again, his bravado and physical traits marked him as a Chamorro.

I checked my attire in the mirror. A size 6 looked good on me admittedly. Rachel volunteered to do my make up and I begged her to keep it subtle. Three layers of mascara and a swipe of blood red lipstick later, I shook my head in defeat and we were set to go. Rachel did a Charlie's Angel pose at my car.

"Hey, miss! I told you not to come here again!" It was Frances, our condo's maintenance phenom. I turned around half-expecting her to be aiming her hammer at me.

"What? Frances, it's me, Nix." I said surprised, hands in the air. Frances was stunned and nearly dropped her rake. I realized that she must have not recognized me. I last saw her when I was fifteen pounds heavier and I was now a fair haired svelte rock star, *Rachel's words*, not mine.

"Sorry, Mrs. Farmer, I thought. . ." Frances dropped her eyes. "I thought you were someone else."

"Who? Was there someone here at my condo before?" Frances blushed a bright red. She was built like an ox, much like my late grandmother. Her knowledge of fixing things was vast and I always wondered why she was in this field. She looked like she should be baking cookies for her grandkids and not working so hard near her retiring age. Did she know something? No one in our neighborhood knew that my marriage was on the rocks. Not yet, at least.

"Frances? You can tell me." I reassured her.

"Awhile ago, I saw a woman enter your condo when no one was home. She was tall and blond. I saw her near your car the day before that. Then I saw her go to your door." Frances raced through the details. Rachel observed the exchange while sitting on the hood of Bradley's car. She probably didn't care that her studded jeans scratched the hood.

"She had a key, but I confronted her. She said she was Bradley's cousin and she was getting some paperwork for him."

Jem. It must have been Jem. I felt like racing into my house and setting fire to the king sized bed that I once shared with Bradley, barely shared at that. I mused that she met Bradley while I was out. I didn't want to visualize their dirty bedroom antics.

Frances didn't need to hear the gritty truth. I lied that we had a "cousin" visiting that week. Frances looked doubtful, but let it go. I didn't want to become a source of gossip here. Rachel rolled her eyes and I explained my suspicions about the mysterious scratch on my car door. She was ready to go psycho chick and track down Jem's BMW. I knew she wasn't serious, but Rachel's rage should never be underestimated.

"I'm loving Bradlame and Jem more and more." Rachel's voice dripped with sarcasm.

I stared at the little river rocks near my shoes. So smooth, so ordinary. "Let's go. Remember to stay under the radar."

"Are you talking about me or you here?" Rachel hopped off the car.

Within ten minutes, we were parked near Bag It. I used Bradley's leased Lexus GS, which was void of any Guam paraphernalia. Unprofessional, he once said. Rachel and I reviewed our game plan and she headed inside. She was going to text me details like the number of customers and whether Thomas was there or not. I wondered if I should give her a cut of my pay for this hit. This report was earning me twenty bucks, chump change in Rachel's world. I had to time my encounter just right so I was sure to be serviced by him.

I smiled as my mind envisioned Thomas moving in slow motion, smiling that big screen smile. Then an image of me naked on the counter with him placing tomatoes in just the right places and pickles elsewhere danced in my mind. An off camera fan would blow my hair back, slow motion, with the *boom chicka bow wow* porno music in the background. My phone buzzed waking me from my fantasy.

Rachel texted,

An Asian chick @ register. 10 people dining. 3 in line. Sexy vamp making subs.

Rachel agreed to engage Alma, the "Asian girl" in a conversation so I could order directly from Thomas. I grabbed my Hello Kitty book bag and checked my reflection before going in for the kill. The red lipstick was really too much. I French kissed a tissue until most of the color transferred off.

Rachel sat near Alma. My best friend overacted as I expected like the extras you see in a restaurant scene in a movie. I staked my spot in line behind two Navy men in blue uniforms. The shorter one of the two, the one without the wedding ring, turned to eye me. He said hello, a goofy smile greeting me. Just as he was about to speak I put my hand up, in a talk to the hand gesture, then pointed to Alma who was ready to take their orders. I didn't mean to be rude, *well, yes I did*, I was working after all. I pulled out my Blackberry and pretended to be texting. I glanced around the shop and didn't see any other employees. It was about eleven in the morning, just early enough that I wouldn't run into a lunch crowd. I glanced over my swap meet faux designer shades and saw Thomas working away. He wasn't wearing a baseball cap this time and his brown sugar hair flopped to the right. It was a perfect blend of proper grooming and wild child disarray. I blinked a few times to clear my head of his visage and reviewed the standards I needed to evaluate, which I thankfully uploaded to my Blackberry.

Like clockwork, Alma was about to call me and Thomas delivered several bags. He glanced up at me and held my shielded gaze for a few moments. He did a once over on me and his eyes locked on my shoes. A tiny smile danced on his lips and my heart fluttered. I wondered if he liked what he saw. I wasn't the dressed up fashionable karaoke diva from the other night. He went back to work at his station and I frowned. Why did I want him to look at me again?

I let the next customer cut, mumbling an excuse that I was still deciding. Thomas glanced at me a few times. I panicked for a second thinking he made me. But, unless his sister told him he was going to be evaluated, I had nothing to worry about.

Rachel watched the exchange, a silly grin on her face. Just as Alma was about to invite me, being the only customer in line for the moment, Rachel remembered her cue, jumped up and asked Alma for her recommendation of subs. She had other questions about catering and calories and just about anything else that would keep Alma busy. *God, she was so obvious, but it did the trick.* I took that as my chance to get Thomas's assistance. I stood by the counter and looked up at the menu, reading it like it was my first time. I had to get Thomas to engage in a conversation about one of the subs and my curiosity really wanted his take on the Guam Sub. Just as Thomas called out the two Navy guys' orders—"Chuck!" He turned his attention to me, after tossing the bags to the sailors. *Tsk, tsk,* that's why his sister hired me.

"What can I get you?" Thomas asked, his face very serious. I continued to look at the menu, distracted by Rachel's booming conversation with Alma and Thomas's nearness. I cleared my throat nervously then pushed my shades to my head, using it like a head band to get the hair off my face. Thomas's gray eyes rested on my face and I felt my cheeks burn. The microscopic movements of his haunting eyes told me he was examining my face. I wondered what he thought. I tried desperately not to smile, and his lips didn't betray his thoughts, staying in a straight line.

"I've never been here and I was wondering about number eight. What is Chicken Ke-La-Goon?" I slaughtered the pronunciation on purpose. Thomas tilted his head like he knew I was lying. I returned my gaze to the menu board and tapped my foot nervously.

"It's pronounced, *ke-la-gwen* and it's basically barbecue chicken with lemon, peppers and onions, minus shredded coconut. It's a specialty from Guam. I highly recommend it." Check that off the evaluation. He needed to use that phrasing—*I highly recommend* when discussing a specific sub. I hope I wasn't working too hard to get him to pass the evaluation. I did need to include that he wasn't wearing a hair net and that he practically flung the bags at the previous customers in my report.

"Okay, I'll get that."

"What size?" I played dumb again and took a moment before I requested *Give it to me good*, with a straight face. I ordered the Loose Lady Sub as well in the same embarrassing size. Thomas needed to upsell my order to a meal and also recommend a dessert. There was a selection of fruit filled pastries. I secretly wanted him to pass this evaluation, but he failed on both ends. Thomas passed another standard by repeating my order, which ended up sounding like a really strange list of porno movies that take place on Guam. I blushed, but Thomas was accustomed to this shop lingo. "What's your name?" I was set to be Kimberly—but my funny bone was back in commission and I blurted the first thing that appeared in my mind.

"Mufasa." I declared. *Damn, Lion King!* My favorite Disney movie.

Thomas guffawed loudly and whispered back as he wrote on the receipt slip, "Mu-Fa-Sa it is." He looked at me and beamed, his eyes transforming to a glorious set of mesmerizing forces of nature. He shook his head and laughed again. He turned on his heel and on the way to the sandwich station he hummed Elton John's *Circle of Life.*

Alma looked at me and smiled and also began humming and harmonizing with Thomas. These people with their weekly karaoke meetings.

I stood along the beige wall, beating myself up inside for letting my funny bone dictate my fake name. I hid my face and looked at the new décor. One 8 x 10 picture was of a beach and coconut trees. Something you could get at Bed Bath and Beyond, but it was strangely familiar. I have been there I thought and I moved closer. I recognized the beloved Camel Rock in *Asan*, Guam.

The second picture was a black and white print of a mermaid painting. I knew this one intimately too! It looked like the painting of the Sirena legend that used to hang at the old Guam Airport. I used to fantasize about that painting when I was a kid. This specific painting was my definition of beauty, maybe because she was fair like me. If this Chamorro mermaid could look like she did, pale, brown hair, fair eyes, then maybe I wasn't too shabby.

She sat atop a large rock in the middle of a churning sea, with men in a ship in the distance. I sighed loudly.

The third black and white photo was a beach shot of *Tumon* beach and hotels. I almost didn't hear Alma call out, "MUFASA!" Breaking free from my trance, I walked away from the pictures that made me suddenly homesick for Guam. "Do you want meals or just the sandwich, Mufasa?"

"Huh, no. I mean, yes." I stuttered.

I wrapped up with Alma, and saw that Rachel stood enraptured by the photos of the home we knew. How many people came to this very shop and knew or even been to these places from Guam? I gave Rachel a knowing look and turned my mind back to my assignment. We were really going to blow it if we continued to stare at the collection of photos like homesick island girls.

I had a great vantage point of Thomas's back. He worked quickly on my order and I kept my eye on my watch. For two large subs, he had to complete it within four minutes. There was a tiered scale for the time limits. Tamara was pretty detailed, since the evaluation was often created by the shop owners.

Moments later, Thomas turned around and had two bags with my orders. He smiled at me and bowed.

"Mufasa, your subs await." He laughed, then turned his attention to a couple of uniformed Navy women. I observed their reactions to him. They had been watching him since they entered the store. Maybe they too were Thomas fans.

I made several mental notes about the cleanliness of the store and the supplied stock of chips and cups and other paraphernalia.

Rachel walked out with a take out menu before me. When I plopped into the car, I was breathless with excitement.

"Did you see those pictures?" Rachel read my mind.

"Yeah, I haven't seen that Sirena painting since I was a kid!"

"I know, before the old Guam Airport shut down. I wonder how he got that?"

I wondered too. We drove to the beach, discussing the evaluation. My mind kept returning to Thomas's gorgeous eyes. My fascination with him swelled. Rachel and I followed the best friend code, even if I wasn't divorced, my claim on Thomas was understood.

"Hey, Nix?"

Rachel woke me from my reverie, the salt water air was warm and cleansing. "Hmm?"

"You have a pretty great job."

"I do, don't I, for now."

Rachel planned out the next few nights to a tee. It should have been my duty since she was in my new hometown, but Rachel was here to help me heal, help me move on. In my mind, I knew that that was supposed to happen. It was my stupid loyal heart that dragged itself along, branded with Bradley's initials.

Was there an official scale to healing from a broken heart? This was honestly my very first one. Back in high school, Rachel's first major heartbreak took her about three months to get over. Everything must be accelerated in our teen years though.

The three evenings I had with Rachel were going to fly by. When Rachel was with me, life didn't feel so dismal, so stuck in a slump. She picked up my weight and helped me glide through each second, each minute, each otherwise lonely hour of my day. I dreaded the day I would have to take her to the airport, and not just because I had to have her there so damn early in the morning. I was going to truly miss my sister.

Tuesday evening, Rachel found an advanced salsa class at the nearby YMCA. She convinced the handsome dance instructor to let us in for the hour and paid him double his fees. How could he say no? I mean, this *was* Rachel we were talking about. She could probably get Trump to shave his trademark head of hair with a wink of her business eye.

It was a crazy night of swinging and tripping over my shoes, but Rachel and I had a blast. We held our own and the teenagers seemed to enjoy the fresh blood and goofiness we brought. I asked Rachel jokingly if we were off to get matching tattoos next. She took too long to answer and was on her phone suddenly using Yelp to find a reputable parlor.

"No way, Rachel! I was only kidding. I chickened out with Bradley thank God, and I'm not ready to get something so permanent." Apparently, Rachel was. She already had Japanese blossoms on the small of her back, which she did as a college graduation gift to herself. I hid in the corner of the waiting room when it was my turn. Rachel suggested I get a huge red phoenix on my back and I thought of Bradley the night he got his tattoo and he suggested the same thing. Before I knew it, we were walking into InksRWe. Rachel chose a cute sprinkle of stars for her ankle.

"Just two for now." She instructed. She decided that for every store thereafter that carried the ShinyPurpleThread line, she would add another star. I think the Dixie Chicks gals did the same thing for each record they made or something, a cute pair of chick footprints on their ankles. Did that mean your success was limited to the space on your feet? I told Rachel to get a vintage sewing machine on her back and her face lit up at the idea.

"Next time I visit you." She declared.

Wednesday was a day of shopping therapy and a much needed nail salon visit. The pedicurist worked gingerly around Rachel's new tattoo and received a generous tip for doing so. After lunch, Rachel shoved me into Victoria Secret and had the resident bra expert measure me. I had been forcing my puppies into a 38 C for most of my post pubescent life, only to discover I was really a D cup, a 34 D to be exact. I had to admit, my posture improved instantly. I couldn't stop Rachel from spoiling me as she purchased over five hundred dollars of undergarments in every color possible. She steered me away from the blacks or whites—my standard.

"Just in case Bradley walks in on you as he's packing his crap or better yet, Thomas spends the night." The thought of being with another man intimately, even someone as divine as Thomas made my insides churn. I couldn't visualize it, maybe I wasn't ready to.

That evening, Rachel drove us to another dance studio. A surprise, she called it. She had set up a one time visit with a belly dancing class. I boomeranged back to the car as soon as I entered the studio and saw the many posters with seductive women and their glorious navels. Yeah, I lost a few pounds but I wasn't ready for my own jelly. Rachel dragged me back in just before I started the engine. I couldn't say no to her puppy dog eyes and whimpering.

"These are a bunch of strangers! You need to get in touch with your inner Shakira!" Rachel proclaimed.

"I can't wiggle it for strangers!" I cringed.

"Did you see the different sizes of women, Nix? Everyone is beautiful here! Let's do this, please, please, please?" I gave in. God, I dreaded the sight of my belly.

We met the instructor, the beautiful Bella Donna. She whisked us away to the costume room for some frilly chiffon and jingly belts. If we wanted to dress up further, we were welcome to. I stuck to the value meal outfit, while Rachel dressed up in the works. She was stunning in a fuchsia get up, prancing around like she was the lovechild of the I Dream of Jeannie icon and Prince Aladdin.

I wondered how much she paid for this class. I would have been happier in my sweats at home watching a DVD with a tub of popcorn with Tabasco. Rachel's enthusiasm was contagious and I thought about the sacrifice she had to make in her own life to come to California to get my ass in gear. I did a few jumping jacks and decided to just go with it tonight, to lose my inhibitions and *waka waka* like Shakira.

On Guam, there were many dance groups who incorporated Polynesian dancing, like hula andTahitian. It was a fantasy of mine to be one of *those* girls, but I felt like I was never worthy enough, beautiful enough or exotic enough. Perhaps belly dancing would be a good alternative.

Bella Donna played quick paced, entrancing music. The heavy percussion engaged us and I swayed with the group. She demonstrated a short routine. It was mindboggling how her hips seemed to take on a life of their own. Her chest was possessed by another brain altogether. She did this all with a Mona Lisa smile. Bella Donna did not have abs of steel and the femininity and softness of her belly were seductive. I wondered if my new smaller belly could compare. Would I be able to move like this gyrating, alluring siren? I had childbearing hips, I guess I could be proud of. The rotations and bumps Bella Donna demonstrated were like an advertisement of what she could do to a man in bed. I blushed. Was that was this was about? It's one thing to look the part, quite another to know how to use *what yo' mama gave you.* In my case, my Korean mama. The one who never gyrates.

I never teased Bradley with dance, ever. He asked a few times. "Dance for me," he would beg. I would usually do something dorky like the Running Man or the Dougie. Bradley liked pushing me past my comfort zone, which often times made me feel not good enough.

As I watched the dancing, my hips tried to mimic what I saw. I had to keep my tongue from sticking out because I was concentrating so much. After a few basic descriptions and demonstrations of several moves, Bella Donna started a new song. She told us to be a wave, to vibrate, to flow. From the Egyptian Shimmy to the horizontal hip twist shimmy, my hips were only beginning to feel unhinged when class was declared over. Rachel and I were panting and glistening with sweat.

"Thank you." I breathed into Rachel's ear as I hugged her.

"For what, silly?"

"For being my *Miyagi*." Rachel searched my face and smiled.

"You are welcome, Phoenix-san." She bowed and then hugged me again, "I love you."

Thursday started with breakfast at the Egg Shack where we shared a twelve-egg omelet. We walked around Pacific Beach to work off the cholesterol overload. Rachel did my hair that morning in lovely waves. And she finally granted me my wish, natural make up. It was nice to see her dress down for the day and we looked like two girls who didn't need to impress any man. I wanted the time to trickle by slowly.

"So, what are you going to do about Bradley?" Rachel wanted assurance before she left to Guam.

"I'm feeling like my legs are stronger figuratively and literally. I can stand on my own for once. Oh, and I can shimmy now." I demonstrated my best belly dancing moves and she joined in. A volleyball game stopped because of our impromptu show and a few guys whistled at us. We moved our shimmies further down the beach.

"So," Rachel pressed, "about Bradley?"

"I don't know. I've only known Bradley. I'm frightened of divorce. Thank God we don't have kids. How can I move on to another man when Bradley knows me through and through?" It didn't seem right. After Bradley and I made love for the first time, the summer after we graduated from high school, I made him promise to never leave me. If he did I threatened to join a convent to become a nun.

"And, I've only known every Tom, Juan and Harry on Guam—yes, I only dated the hottest Toms, Juans and Harrys—but with every man, I had a genuine connection. You can't live your life worrying about Bradley being your first everything. It's no longer special. He cheated for God's sake! And you're a hottie! Other men need to be blessed with your beauty."

"Yeah, sure, hottie. I blamed my weight at first, but what if on Sunday, with the new me and everything he asks me to try again? What then?" I was afraid, maybe more so of not knowing what I really wanted. I didn't want to continue with Bradley, yet I wanted validation from him, some kind of stamp of approval that I wasn't a waste of space.

"Do you hear yourself?" Rachel blew out her breath sounding like a deflating balloon. She paced like a crazy tiger in front of me, then kicked up some sand in anger and the wind blasted it into my eyes and mouth. After a thousand apologies, a trip to the public restroom to clean my face, de-sand my eyes and reapply some make-up Rachel treated me to some lemonade. We continued our conversation on the way to the car. The grit in my eye bugged me to no end. Perhaps, like her words, Rachel wanted her advice to stick with me long after she went home.

"Nix, I hope to God Bradlame tries to nail you this Sunday and I hope to Jesus Christ Superstar that you shut him down! Who knows what real estate Barbie gave him."

She was right. It would be kind of nice to see his reaction this Sunday.

"Nix, promise me that you won't still be undecided when he gets out of training. Promise me that you'll let this jerk go—out of your heart, mind and soul. Please." Rachel grabbed my face and squished my cheeks together. "He will just break your heart again. I don't want you hurt. Promise?"

"I proh-misshh." She released my cheeks so I could speak. "I promise I'll be a divorced woman next time we see each other."

And I finally felt like this was the right path to travel. Just needed that extra nudge from my best girl to make it official.

Divorce. D-I-V-O-R-C-E. It was so final. It was a sign of failure. I worried about what our parents would think, but pushed it to the back of my frazzled brain for now.

Several margaritas and ten shopping bags later, Rachel and I made it home. She commandeered my luggage for all the glorious items she purchased. As much as Rachel was a fashion designer, she loved buying high end designer clothes and shoes. Ever notice how food prepared by other people can be so much tastier? Same goes for clothes I guess.

Rachel and I spent the evening in. We watched old home videos marveling at our dated hair and clothes. My dad loved to video tape school functions, games, award ceremonies, chores, everything. At the time I was utterly embarrassed, but being older I was happy to have these memories burned onto tapes. So many of the images included Bradley and I was actually okay watching them. He was and forever will be a part of my life. He will always be known as my first love, my first husband and finally as the man who cheated on me and became the jerk I divorced. Rachel made me realize that I needed to push through my fears and face reality. I didn't do anything wrong. *I didn't do anything wrong.* And, I tried to do everything right to repair his damage.

"You're better off without him. Look how hot he was in high school."

"That's not helping." I pulled my knees to my face.

"Nix! He was hot, now he's not. He's not that smart too. And his hair is receding which is why he shaved his head, I'm betting."

"Okay, Rach, that helps a whole bunch." We laughed, stuffed our faces with dessert kabobs and crashed out on the couch together.

I woke up in a cold sweat. I dreamt that my legs were fused. I was a mermaid on land and I was being chased, but couldn't move. I must have made a hullaballoo in my sleep because I awoke to Rachel cradling me and whispering into my hair like I was a baby. "Hey, hey. It's okay."

I sat upright and flattened my bed hair. "What, what happened? Was I dreaming?"

"I'd say you were nightmaring more like. Are you okay?"

"Just a bad dream. Nothing. I'm fine. I guess all that sugar and the fact that my sister is leaving me again."

"Aw. I love you too. I just had a lovely snogging dream you rudely interrupted." Rachel frowned.

"You did?" I relaxed.

"Don't laugh though. I was with that red head, Chazzer."

"Oh! Nice! He's all yours. Want his business card?" I jokingly checked my pockets.

"No way!" Our laughter echoed and I hugged Rachel hard. Her visit helped me heaps and I really didn't want her to leave.

We kept our final goodbyes neat and simple usually, but I was an emotional mess. I felt like I was just rescued from a sinking ship this past week. Rachel helped me settle myself in the typhoon that was my life. She brought the eye of the storm and now things could begin to land and settle and be. All I needed to do was pick up the pieces I finally acknowledged as true and rebuild. I gave my best friend, my sister, a long tight hug. She was a good four inches shorter than me, but in many ways she was taller. Rachel lived her life for herself. Whoever, whatever man wanted to hop on her bus was welcomed if they followed her rules. I needed to charter my own bus and figure out my own life. I needed to figure out what moved me. Find my passion and do it every day like Rachel.

"Nix, I can't *breafe*." I didn't realize that I was smothering Rachel. We composed ourselves and bid our farewells with a very manly pounding of our fists and bumping of our chests. My D cups with her B cups. Rachel pulled out a gift, which was flat like a CD case. Rachel and I loved making mixed, well tapes back in the day, and now discs for each other. Sort of like the soundtrack for our lives. She made me promise not to open it until the morning I picked up Bradlame—her new favorite nickname for him was becoming mine.

I waited until she checked in thoroughly with security. She absolutely fumed that she had to remove her designer shoes and jacket, but smiled for the lovely uniformed men and women. Once she hit the waiting area I blew my angel a kiss and headed out. For the first time in a while I felt energized and the sun wasn't even up yet. I had dressed in my work out gear and decided on a run at Seaport Village. On my way out, my Blackberry vibrated. It was Rachel.

"Did you miss me already?" I teased.

"Promise you won't get mad."

"What did you do now?" I stopped walking.

"Promise you won't be mad first." Rachel pleaded.

"I. Promise."

"I wanted to make sure there were armed men between us before I told you this, but I gave Thomas your number and he should be calling you by the end of the day if he's your true love. Love you! Bye!" Before I could register what Rachel told me, I heard her cackling like a mad woman. Then, silence.

Chapter 6

Enter Sandman

I paced the parking lot, but the cool morning air couldn't calm me. I looked at my phone again and a rush of nervous energy coursed through me. Rachel played cupid and with a possible call from Thomas today and the return of my soon-to-be ex-husband in two days, I bolted. I jogged up and down the water way, but the exertion didn't assuage my panic. I tried to enjoy the heavenly sunrise, I really tried. I stopped, I breathed, but Thomas and Bradley's faces entered my mind and all I could see were their silhouettes in the sky flying towards each other in battle like a martial arts flick.

I ran back to my car and pulled out my work folder to check Thomas's schedule for the month. He was off on Fridays. He was off *today*. Butterflies procreated and threatened to burst out of my belly. Maybe I'll just shut off my phone. Simple. What the hell would I say to him? "Hi, I'm Nix and I'm almost divorced and I used to be a fatty and brunette and yes I'm from Guam, but I live here and yes I did an evaluation and you were my target and yes, I think you're hot in an Edward slash Robert sort of way who I'm mildly obsessed with."

I was going to kill Rachel the next time she was within striking distance.

To clear my mind I drove the long way home. Silver Strand was gorgeous, so I pulled into a small parking area. I blocked the impending doom of talking to someone I may or may not have a crush on out of my nervous mind. I decided that now was a good time as any to call my parents. It would be almost ten at night, but I knew their routine enough to know that they would be, *damn*, leaving Bradley's parents house on a Friday night after an evening of playing cards. One of the many activities retirees do. I tried the house phone first and Pharaoh answered.

"Hey dork. It's me." I greeted him in my usual fashion. Pharaoh sounded tired. "Did I wake you?"

"Hey, Nix, no. I just got back from training, watching T.V. Is everything okay?" He always thought something was wrong when I called, and this time, it really was. When I thought of it, Pharaoh and Bradley, being brothers-in-law weren't as tight as I would have liked. That didn't matter now. Pharaoh was concerned when Bradley and I decided to stay in California after college. I invited him to try stateside life, but Pharaoh was too much of an island boy. His reputation was growing in the mixed martial arts realm and he enjoyed where he was rooted.

I took a deep breath, watching the waves roll in. Then, I told Pharaoh nearly everything, using him as a test audience of this news, before my parents would hear of it. He was quiet and listened as I gave him the abbreviated, sanitized version of things. I didn't want to bash Bradley. I really didn't.

"What the fuck happened?" Pharaoh seethed, I heard him breathing. "Nix, what did Bradley do?"

"Why do you assume it's Bradley's fault? It's just irreconcilable differences." I lied.

"That's bullshit. Bradley must have done something stupid. Did he cheat?"

I never took my brother to be so concerned or intuitive. At our wedding, he just wanted to know what was on the menu and how long he had to stay at the reception. I decided to divulge the major highlights, uncensored, since he was an adult, just proven.

"Yeah, he's decided he likes someone from his office more than me. It's done. We're done. We're going to look for a military lawyer to do a clean straightforward divorce." I kept my voice even.

"Good. That motherfucker better not cross my path because I'll destroy him." *Tell me what you really want to do,* I thought. This MMA stuff gave my brother an extra pair of balls apparently.

"Does this mean you're moving back home?" Pharaoh asked, suddenly sounding like a little kid.

I sighed. There were so many reasons to go home and many more reasons to make a life in California work. Before I could give him a definitive answer, my mom's loud voice pierced my inner debate on Guam versus California. But, it was my dad's booming voice on the line first. "Phoenix, everything okay?"

I told my dad and had the same angry reaction as Pharaoh, minus all the curse words. Dad wanted to be sure I was okay. He wanted me to fly home. I told him in a few months. After I told him Rachel had spent a few days with me, he calmed down. He seemed to register my sureness of the divorce. I was so glad he didn't tell me to "work it out." That was something I was positive my mom would tell me to do. After offering me money, I declined and told him that I had enough in savings and would try to pick up more work. My mom's grumbling told me she was waiting in the wings and wanted in on the conversation. Her loud voice on the line now.

"*Fee-nux*. You getting a *da-bors*?" I really missed hearing my mom speak. The nuances of some words and the slaughtering of others were uniquely my mom's.

My one big regret was not learning Korean. It would have made conversation with mom easier. It would have also made my mom proud. I hated when other Koreans shook their heads or clicked their tongues when they found out I couldn't speak the language. Talk about feeling like you let an entire country down.

"Yes, *omma*." I gave her the details of what led up to the problem. She was uncharacteristically quiet. I expected her to interject, question, berate, but her silence was new.

"I *ne-va* thought that my *daw-tor* would go through what I had to go through." What the hell was my mom talking about?

"Nix, mommy was *da-bors* too." I heard Pharaoh in the background. This was obviously a surprise to him too. Then I heard Dad send Pharaoh out of the room. Mom explained that she was once married to a Korean man. She was only seventeen at the time. When she lost her first baby in a late term miscarriage, a girl, she found out that her husband was already married in another province. He had daughters and a matchmaker-fortune teller said that mom would be a guaranteed bearer of a son. Once she didn't fulfill this for this man, he dumped her. Abandoned at the small hospital, mom swore off men. She found work at a restaurant. After many years alone, an Army G.I. aka dad, swept her off her feet and married her. Mom made her journey to Guam and never looked back.

The weight of the fact that dad was mom's *second* husband pressed on me. How would I have coped if who I thought was my loving, caring husband was a fraud? Bradley. Was he a fraud? Was our marriage a fraud? The sorrow I felt for my mom back then and the anger I felt now having to dredge up these memories made me burn. I didn't want Bradley to get off so easily like the bastard who left my mom at the hospital. Yes, we wouldn't be alive if that first marriage panned out for the best, but mom's first husband's actions were cruel. What I was going through now was mild compared to my mom's relationship battle scars.

Bradley tore apart the institution of us and the ripple effect began. I knew he didn't tell his parents about the divorce. I wondered if he just wanted to continue with Barbie leaving everyone on Guam in the dark. After many more reassurances to my family, I called Bradley's mom and dad. I didn't shed a tear with my family and I wasn't going to start with Bradley's. They didn't do anything wrong to me, but they needed to know that I was no longer cast in the role as dutiful daughter-in-law. I would let Bradley clean up the mess my news would bring. I wasn't going to go crazy on good old Brad, but I needed to know my rights. Now that I dropped the news to our families, my next step was military legal. I needed to arm myself.

I discovered that with this divorce, Bradley would have to pay alimony, especially if it was proven that he wanted to dissolve the marriage. I often heard on the news—well, celebrity news, of women suing the mistress for isolation of affection or some crap like that. I wanted nothing to do with Jem and as much as I hated her, she could keep the trash I was about the chuck out.

Bradley would only have to pay for the last year we were married, about half of his pay. What about the previous almost ten years I endured what I thought was a loving relationship? The three years we were married? I wondered for a split second if what I had, emphasis on had, was ever true love. Were our vows before God true in his heart? Were they true in mine? Did we just do what was expected of us? I could never really say Bradley was my best friend or my soul mate. I didn't feel it to my core. And, suddenly, I was strangely relieved by this realization.

.

With time alone, I reviewed my evaluations for the week. Before shutting down the computer, it dawned on me that I didn't bother to check Bradley's emails from the night before. I clicked on the earliest one. Blabber about picking him up in case I didn't get his text. *Delete.* The second latest one was dated three days ago. Rachel and I were doing our salsa class and sweating when he wrote this I thought. He seemed a bit more desperate in this one, wondering what I was up to huh? *Delete.* The one dated yesterday threw me a curveball.

Nix I got yr txt about pckng me up Thnk u I'm not sure if your even reading these mssges I miss you, alot I've been thinking about us lately All this trning and being away from you has made me refocus Can we talk about it please sorry I love you Bradley

I skimmed over the terribly written e-mail. The death of the written word was on our horizon and I was terrified. Sorry, was he? Where did Jem fit in all this? I wondered. The e-mail should have sparked something in me, that desperate me of just a few weeks ago seemed to be dead. I felt numb, immune to Bradley's latest ploy. How could he undo what's already done? He cheated and that was fact. It was marked in the history books.

I didn't bother with any social networks and toyed with the idea of deleting them. The possible phone call from Thomas was in the back of my mind all day.

The condo was quiet now that Rachel was gone. It would be another twelve hours before she landed on Guam. She was due a royal verbal smack down for giving Sir Thomas my number, and how the hell was I going to explain that my name wasn't really

Monica? I kept my Blackberry in hand and placed the ringer on the loudest setting. Maybe, just maybe, I was a bit giddy about the possibility of Thomas calling.

I headed to the bathroom and checked my reflection. The blonder hair made me panic. Would Bradley think I did this for him? I did initially think that it would win him over. I wondered if getting my hair dyed back to brown tonight would make it all fall out. Wasn't I supposed to wait like six weeks minimum between dye jobs?

Just as I dropped my new Victoria *Secretions* undergarments in the hamper, my Blackberry rang. I was ecstatic as well as totally naked. If that was indeed Thomas, he picked a very auspicious moment to call. I rushed to my nightstand and saw an unknown local number. I glanced at my blinds to make sure they were shut, then I grabbed my phone. The Hello Kitty alarm clock showed that it was 7:30, a respectable time of night for him to call. *Answer it already,* something animal in me growled.

"Phoenix speaking." What compelled me to use my full real name was beyond me. Perhaps it was that I was stripped down and exposed, but my best shot at being anything to Thomas was to start with the real.

"Oh, I'm sorry. I must have the wrong number." Thomas's silky voice entered my head and I felt dizzy. He paused, like he was checking the number written on the napkin from the karaoke bar Rachel probably gave him. "I was actually looking for, um, Monica."

"Thomas?" I decided to make this easier for us both.

"Yes!" He sounded relieved and confused at the same time. His voice was more melodic and deeper over the phone and my heart skipped. Would I have our entire conversation naked? Feeling modest, I grabbed my robe.

"Yeah, my friend Rachel gave you this number. She also said I was Monica, but I'm not."

"But, you're the girl who was singing at the bar right?"

"Yes. My name is Phoenix, not Monica though."

I explained the situation to Thomas as best as I could. I blew my cover as a secret shopper and explained that running into him at the karaoke bar was a weird coincidence. I must admit, Thomas was a bright young lad. He kept up with my ranting as I untangled the mess my job and Rachel created. I wasn't sure how he would make me being an evaluator of his customer service. Would he even want to still talk to me since I wasn't officially divorced yet? In my heart and mind I was. I had removed my wedding ring a day ago, with Rachel's insistence, which really meant that she threatened to cut off my ring finger with a dull butter knife. It was very strange to have any feelings for someone new so soon after accepting that I would once again be single. What if he just wanted to be friends? I was getting way ahead of myself.

"Wow." That's all he said numerous times. I wasn't sure if I should tell him that I was the brunette from a few days prior to the hit.

"Thomas, I would understand if you don't want to speak to me. The circumstances are strange and I don't want you or me to get in trouble with the work situation. Your sister might not like that the evaluator sent to assess her brother is even speaking to him now."

"Was the evaluation a glowing one?" *Crap.* He received a 75%. Satisfactory, but not glowing. Hell, the truth seemed to be working for me lately, so I decided to go with it.

"Your sister should be reviewing the report with you by next week." I side stepped his question. So much for laying it all out.

"But, did I do well?" He must have not realized it was me who did the evaluation. He barely caught a glimpse of me when I sang a favorite off his oldies song list. "I mean, what's done is done. It's not like my sister is going to fire me over what you wrote. She evaluates all her employees, family included. She had one done on her husband last month!" He sounded more amused, than shocked.

"In terms of grades, you got a C." I felt at ease speaking to Thomas about this. He wanted the criticism. He owned his actions.

"Great!" *Really?* "I probably failed at not offering you a meal or smiling enough or winking or whatever criteria you have to assess. But, tell me one thing, did you like the sub I made you?"

"I, uh, yeah it was great." The best thing I had had in months actually. I wasn't sure why he was so happy about a mediocre score.

"Enough said. I'm a great sub creator and who cares how the food is delivered. I did it efficiently enough and I got you from point A to point B, no frills. Would you come back to the shop because of me or the delicious sub?" That was a tricky question, because I did enjoy the food, but I enjoyed seeing him as well. Was I going to admit that now? Rachel's little voice popped in my head whispering, *"Let the man pursue you, they like the hunt, leave some mystery—that will keep them coming back for more."*

"The sub." I left it at that and I swear I heard him deflate a bit. I felt bad, but held my tongue. I wasn't even divorced yet and had no business talking to this man—even if he was an Adonis.

"Um, I was actually calling now because your friend, Rachel—that is her real name, right?" Thomas asked sarcastically. "She said you wouldn't have your phone back until after five today and, um."

He seemed rattled. It was darling. I curled my knees to my chin as I sat on my bed and wondered if Thomas remembered me from Tuesday. I'm sure if I told him I ordered under the name, Mufasa, he would make the connection. I decided to hold that tidbit until later. Maybe if we met face to face a light bulb would go off, but there I went again making assumptions about where this initial phone call was headed.

Thomas continued, "I called because I really enjoyed your rendition of the Everly Brother's song. It's one of my favorites. You sound a lot like Linda Ronstadt."

"Yeah, I checked it out on YouTube. I guess I can see why you think I sound like her, but I'm nowhere near as good as her." I expressed modestly.

"I think you're better." *Blush*. "I was wondering if it would be too much to ask for you to have lunch with me tomorrow. I promise it won't be at Bag It, unless you really want to go there."

"Um, you're asking me out based on the way my voice sounded? Did you even see what I looked like? Do you even know when I evaluated you? I know you guys get a lot of customers. I could be hideous!" I was being melodramatic playing devil's advocate, but I really didn't comprehend how the sound of my voice would compel Thomas to ask me out. I pushed this glorious man away because I thought he was being reckless in asking me out on so little data. Was I crazy or was he?

"I guess it does sound weird when you put it that way, but like I said, your voice is wonderful. I saw you in a dark dress sitting at the booth, you have light colored hair. You're human right? I'd like to stick to the same species." I let up and we shared a laugh. Our first laugh together.

"Well, Thomas, did Rachel—whom I will kill on a later date since she's on a flight back to Guam—tell you I was going through a divorce?" From the silence, I could tell that she did not. Was this what I needed to push him away? Why did I want to do that?

"You're Chamorro. I love Guam." It was like I didn't even drop the D-word.

"Thomas, I'm still technically a married, Chamorro woman. Doesn't that freak you out at all? Not to mention, I could lose my job because you know I'm a super secret spy."

"I won't tell anyone I know, if you won't. I don't want to pressure you into meeting me. Heck, did you think *I* was hideous?" *No chance*, I thought. "Rachel said I looked like that vampire character, which I guess is a compliment, but only if you liked what you saw." I did. But, I wouldn't tell him this, at least not now.

"Thomas, it's not that easy. I'm a bit old-fashioned I guess. I literally just took off my wedding ring yesterday. You seem like a great guy and I would love to find out more about your stay on Guam. And, that Sirena painting! I would love to know where you found that. God, I'm talking too much."

"No, I like it."

I smiled, "I mean, typically mainlanders are clueless about my home island or get it all wrong. You, you have those beautiful pictures in the shop and the Guam Sub, I know it's on the menu because of you and you even knew who Sirena was. You sang the song!" *Oops*, that was the brunette me that ordered under Sirena. I could hear the cogs and gears in Thomas's head bring him back to that day I did a pre-emptive strike on the shop.

"Are you? You ordered the Rock Lobster!" He got it. Damn, he was a smart lad. "I followed you out to your car and you said your husband was from Guam! You drive a red Rav4." I wondered how all this new information would affect his invitation

112

to lunch. I so wanted to go. I couldn't understand why I was so resistant. Perhaps it was because having a lunch date the day before my "husband" was due in town was so, soap opera-ish, so wrong.

"You caught me," was all I could say.

"You had wavy brown hair in a ponytail!" Thomas was smarter than the average bear. His attention to detail would make him a great field agent too.

"Yes, that was me. Rachel treated me to a spa day and I had my hair upgraded. I couldn't risk you recognizing me on Tuesday anyway!" Once I said that, Thomas Einstein spread out the pieces and figured out the equation.

"Mufasa?" He began to laugh so hard that I thought he would cough up a lung. It was a very hearty laugh, genuine and cute. "You're hilarious, you know that?"

"Hilarious looking?" I mumbled.

"What? No, you're genuinely funny."

"Is that a good or bad thing?" I asked nervously. I really did want to impress this guy. Did he like the brunette me or the blonde me? Inquiring minds wanted to know.

"Phoenix, Phoenix." The sound of my name from his mouth was hypnotizing. He composed himself and became quiet. I thought our phone call dropped. I looked at the rolling seconds on my phone's screen and then heard, "Do you realize that this is technically my second attempt at asking you out?"

"What do you mean?" I was confused.

"On that day you ordered the sub as *Sirena*—mermaid vixen of the sea, I knew you were from Guam. I wanted to ask what village you were from among other things, but chickened out."

"Oh," was my weak response.

"I ran out to find out if you were really from Guam. I love Guam people, really. I must have been Chamorro in another life. I thought you were cute in your blue suit. I thought maybe you were a flight attendant." He must be joking, until I realized that I did look flight attendant-ish that Sunday. "Your mini Guam flag on the rear view mirror gave me hope and I wanted an excuse to talk to you so I fibbed and said you forgot your meal items. You rejected free food and *me*." Thomas laughed softly.

"I really am on a diet," I murmured more to myself, suddenly excited to know a man who used words like *fib*.

Were the fates trying to propel me to this man? If my karma account was being cashed in, why did I have to go through a marriage with Bradley to find someone like Thomas? *Hold up*, I thought. We weren't talking marriage here. Thomas was fascinating, but I had to keep the reins tight on this, whatever *this* was with this handsome man.

Thomas reassured me that the divorce issue didn't scare him. He did ask if I had kids and sighed loudly when I said that I did not. Was that because he didn't like kids or wanted kids who would be only ours, I wondered wistfully.

I begrudgingly declined the lunch invitation a second time. I explained more about my job and the reason for the divorce. It was a relief to share my dilemma with someone outside of my family and friends. Albeit he was a near stranger, but Thomas welcomed the truth that I offered. He truly seemed interested in me, my story. We spent almost three hours on the phone that first night. If the battery on my Blackberry wasn't about to fizzle, who knew how long we would continue to jabber on. I had the home phone number disconnected because it was an unnecessary expense. A sense of desperation crept into my tummy as I knew our call was about to end.

I never remembered having any conversation for more than half an hour with Bradley. Thomas was understanding of my shaky marital situation. He wasn't jealous at all that Bradley was rolling back into town that weekend, from what I could tell. He did ask, in a shy, adorable way if he could call me later in the week. I liked that he did not pressure me even if I wanted to speak with him tomorrow and the next day. I still had so many questions about his adventures on Guam and this Chamorro roommate he befriended.

Thomas offered his e-mail address and I was hesitant to give him mine since his was straightforward, thomasproberts@bagitsubs.com. He asked for my e-mail again and I sheepishly told him hellokittyguamgirl@hafamail.com. I could tell that he was smiling through his proceeding comments, his tone light. "I like that." He whispered.

I asked if he was on Facebook and he hopped into a tirade about social networks being a waste of time and a simple tool for voyeurs, practical strangers to gawk at and judge your photos and offer unwanted comments. I must be a criminal voyeur then, even though I survived without checking in on the rest of my three hundred friends in the past few weeks.

"God, I'm sorry. You probably have a very active Facebook life."

"Actually, it's slowed down a lot. Don't apologize."

"If you don't mind, can I get your mailing address too? I promise I won't stalk you. I might hang out outside your bathroom window in hopes of hearing you sing though." The psycho killer alert should have gone off in my brain, but since it didn't, I let him have it. He offered his as well and I got a fuzzy feeling in the pit of my stomach when I realized that we lived in the same area. He didn't comment that our zip codes were neighboring districts though.

"So, you're okay about hanging back until I get this mess of a divorce thing finalized?" Thomas didn't owe me anything, but I wanted his promise. Even though Bradley said I should date someone, it didn't feel right. I couldn't have my feet in both the married realm and the dating realm at the same time. I wasn't greedy. I needed the clean break.

"Hey, I'm a fan of your singing for sure. I enjoyed our conversation. You intrigue me to no end and you're as funny as hell. Who's to say we can't just be friends?"

"Yeah," I said, saddened by the idea, "friends for sure. After talking to you for the past three hours, not that I was counting, you've propelled yourself from potential psycho stalker stranger to friend." His gentle laugh made me warm all over.

"So, Phoenix, it was nice to meet you, again and again."

"Goodnight, friend." I added, the beep of the low battery signal threatening to blow up our conversation.

"Goodnight friend—friend for now that is," Thomas almost whispered as the call was dropped. I looked at my Blackberry which drifted off to sleep. Thomas was out there in the next kingdom hopefully not waiting for a response. His voice replayed in my mind, *friend for now*.

Chapter 7

Hello, Kitty!

I don't know how I was able to sleep from last night's marathon talk session with Thomas, but I woke up energized. Thomas's call cracked something in me in a good way. I somehow felt powerful, knowing that someone as beautiful and intelligent as Thomas wanted me, emotional baggage included. I knew I could call him and he would reoffer the lunch date, but I didn't want to rush into this thing secret shopping created. Well, really what Bradley created.

I had a Saturday to do as I pleased. Rachel sparked an adventurous side in me and I hopped on the computer after breakfast to see what fairs or museums or concerts I could crash. The day was mine, Phoenix on a date with Phoenix, and I was excited.

I was forlorn at the thought of passing up a lunch date with Thomas, but I had to stick to my guns on waiting. I jotted down the address to a Halloween costume store, when the door bell rang downstairs. I was dressed in a Hello Kitty tank top with matching shorts, and threw on my robe, my modesty gene still strong in me.

Through the peephole, I saw the largest Hello Kitty in the world! There was a FedEx truck in the background and I opened the door bouncing up and down at the surprise visitor. I didn't realize my robe tie came undone. Before me, the young guy did not look too pleased about delivering this monstrous pussy cat to my door, but when he saw me, he smiled. I smiled back. Brandon, as his nametag read, offered to walk the plush toy into my home. I swiftly tied my robe and told him I could handle it. He had me sign for the gift. I figured Rachel had it delivered as an apology for the Thomas phone number scandal, but I was really happy she did me that service now. Who else could afford this most coveted item?

My Hello Kitty obsession never included the pricey pieces like this two hundred dollar buddy I just snagged. I was quite content with the toys I got from the candy dispenser like gadgets planted by the exits at every Asian supermarket.

FedEx Brandon stood at my door after I signed, lingering. *Was I supposed to tip him?* I wondered. His smile didn't flicker, so I decided to ask him if he knew who sent the item. He looked at his tablet and said the strangest thing.

"My docs says it's from, *uh*, Robert Pattinson." He looked up at me eyebrows raised to high heaven. He scanned me head to toe like he was deciding if I was hot enough for Mr. Pattinson to be sending me stuffed animals. Sure an item like this would be chump change to a successful celebrity like that. From the smile on his face, he seemed satisfied that I would pass. I convinced him that it was just my husband playing a practical joke. At the mention of a husband, Brandon's eyes automatically looked at my left hand. I quickly pocketed my naked finger.

After a few awkward moments, Brandon pointed to an envelope attached to Hello Kitty's bow, the entire stuffed animal wrapped in a thin plastic wrap.

Thankfully, I saw Frances pruning bushes.

"Hi, Frances!" I called over Brandon's shoulder. He finally got the hint and left my doorstep. I locked my door and secured the deadbolt. I made sure Brandon left and ripped open the plastic with fervor.

"Thank you, Rachel!" I said into the air, hoping she would feel good vibes from me in Guam.

I looked at the beautiful script on a plain white index card. It was not my best friend's.

I haven't enjoyed conversation like that which I shared with you. You made me smile and laugh genuinely. You are truly my new, beautiful--FRIEND. I look forward to more correspondence with you. T.P.R.

Thomas. P. Roberts. Oh my God! I removed the rest of the plastic of this pristine and wondrous representation of my love for Hello Kitty. Thomas was a receptive man. I loved this gift. It was a bold statement of his friendly feelings for me. How I would explain this to Bradley? Did I have to explain it to him? Was it bad for me to have a "friend?" I was truthful to Thomas, but I decided to keep mum about this with Bradley.

I brought my new buddy to the office and found her a comfy spot on my reading chair. As she looked at me with her adorable face, sure she was just a compilation of textiles, with plastic eyes placed in such a spot that it would evoke *oohs* and *aahs,* I decided to thank Thomas. I did not want to call him, but chose to write him a heartfelt e-mail. I reread Thomas's card again and placed it in my wallet.

I kissed the giant cat before I headed out to a pumpkin patch. I needed time to think about my Halloween outfit.

I typically didn't costume up, at least not in my teen and adult years for Halloween. The last time was a college party at Rachel's. I wore Pharaoh's old baseball uniform and put on a pair of plastic fangs. The image in retrospect was reminiscent of the beloved thunderstorm baseball scene in Twilight and I smiled at the connection.

I finally found a costume that would be worth paying the fifty dollars for at the third Halloween costume shop I visited. It was an uncomfortably sexy mermaid outfit. A flash of my nightmarish prom dress appeared in my head. Maybe this get up would help me redeem that night so many years ago. My dress was very revealing and without the shimmery tail fins could pass for a belly dancer number. That sealed the deal for me. I had to admit that I had a bit of a girl crush on Bella Donna. I made plans to return to her class, perhaps after my divorce was finalized and my cash flow recovered.

I grabbed a large size out of habit and brought it to the cashier. Two young men stopped what they were doing and watched me intently. I was still not comfortable with the attention I received from the opposite sex. Maybe I needed to pare down my look like Thomas's sister did. I wondered if there was a pair of bottle cap glasses here I could purchase, and my eyes darted around the display of cheap props. Before I could do an about face, the smaller kid of the duo called out to offer his assistance.

"Ma'am?" I imagined hopping over the counter to pile driving the poor lad. Maybe I needed to get over being called ma'am.

"I can help you here!" He yelped enthusiastically. I brought the outfit to Shawn—as his name tag indicated. He asked if I found everything I needed. He looked at the sexy model on the label and I blushed. I hoped he wasn't imagining me in it. Shawn touched the bright orange circle sticker with a bold letter L, and then scanned me up and down.

"Is this costume for you ma'am?" I flinched.

"Yes."

"Ma'am, you're definitely not a large. I suggest you get the medium or small even, depending on the f-f-fit you like. You can try it on if you want." I glanced at the other associate-name tag-Norm. He looked like he was trying to shoot Shawn laser beams from his eyes. Over Shawn's head was a large sign that read, *Packaged Costumes Cannot Be Opened.*

I pointed at the sign, but Shawn quickly reassured me that he would approve the fitting. I did want to see it on me and if this kid was willing to let me try it, I was game. I couldn't see wasting money on something I might not like. He pointed to the single dressing room, which probably saw very little use. He walked a few steps behind me. Why was he following me? I looked back at him. Shawn had his arm outstretched with a size medium and small. I grabbed the medium and nodded. He chuckled nervously and redirected his attention to assist a bone-weary mom and her four demanding children.

I locked the door behind me and smiled into the mirror and waved. I did a quick two-way mirror test with my finger. I also looked above at a dusty vent. The general filth told me that there probably wasn't a hidden camera up there. I smiled at it nonetheless. *Suspicious minds.*

I slipped into the medium outfit easily. I guess I passed as a mermaid. The fish tail was shimmery with jade and cerulean scales. The feathery chiffon fins floated beautifully as if I was really under the sea. The halter top was a tad bit sexier than I was used to, but Rachel unleashed the more confident me and I was actually happy with what I saw. My breasts seemed cartoonishly voluminous, but were covered well under golden clam shells. My abdomen was curvy, with a hint of muscle definition. I typically dreaded looking at my body in store dressing rooms, but I turned around slowly to catch a view of my back. It was lean and streamlined much to my pleasure. No more camel humps! I took a few minutes to admire it. I did some belly dancing shimmies and smiled as I mentally compared my body to Bella Donna's. Maybe I had a career on the horizon as a Chamorrita belly dancer. Elated, I carefully undressed and repacked the costume. Just then, my Blackberry rang. It was Thomas, his name in all caps on my ID screen. Like our first call together, I was standing in the buff. I would have to tell him about these funny coincidences someday, maybe.

"Hi, friendly neighborhood stalker." I joked.

Thomas's laugh bubbled out of the phone and filled the dressing room. I pulled on my pants and fastened my bra quickly. After buttoning my jeans, I sat to give what felt like confession.

"Hi, Phoenix. How's your day going?"

"Great! Got some things accomplished. That's always good right?"

"I agree," Thomas said cheerfully. "I got some things done too. Been feeling pretty inspired since talking to you last night, so I just had to call." I felt the same way, but didn't want to divulge that to him just yet. Keep mysterious.

"What did you do?" I asked.

"Just started some writing again. I'm doing a screenplay." *Impressive.* He didn't mention that the night before. I didn't want to ask him what it was about. I left that to him to share with me.

He explained that his sister wrote the screenplay for *My Dad's Gift* about five years ago. It was a small production with rave reviews at the Sundance festival. He said I should Google it when I had the chance. He joked that he could get me a signed copy if I wanted one. Thomas explained that it was based on their father and it was Tamara's way of dealing with his death. She received some money, but nothing to retire with. She used the money as an investment in her shop. I was in awe to say the least. I never knew anyone who wrote screenplays, now I knew two.

"So, did you happen to have a visitor this morning?" Thomas inquired. For a second, I wondered if he was talking about PMS. I was bloated. I almost forgot about my Hello Kitty doll, well, not really. I was just distracted.

"Oh, you mean Brandon, the FedEx guy? Yeah, he was great. Wanted to come into my condo and everything. Is it customary to tip the FedEx delivery person?" I joked.

"Oh, man. Was he scary? I'm sorry. I specifically asked for a frailest person to deliver the massive Hello Kitty doll to your doorstep." Thomas countered.

"It was beautiful. The best thing in my humble HK collection so far. Thank you, Thomas." I enjoyed saying his name. "Or, should I call you Rob?"

"You're welcome, friend. Thomas will do. I like how it sounds coming from you." There was an awkward pause. "What are you up to now? Now that it's past lunch and you could have been sitting at the library with me." I loved libraries.

"You won't believe me if I told you." I paused. "I'm sitting in a dressing room at Halloween Depot trying on a costume." I wasn't about to disclose what I was going to be this Halloween. I had no intentions of meeting up with Thomas. Bradley would be in town and I had the divorce to worry about. The safe distance of a phone conversation and e-mails offered were fine for now. It was respectable in my eyes.

"Cool, so what did you decide on? Nothing naughty I hope."

"I can be naughty if I want to," I teased. "I decided on the banana suit, but Spongebob Squarepants is really calling to me. Feeling the yellow this year."

Thomas's laughter sent shockwaves down my spine. He asked about my Halloween plans and I freely explained that I had a company party to attend. It wasn't anything major since The Lure Company had ten employees in the office and about twenty five part-time and full-time Field Agents. I was glad Thomas didn't ask where our party would be. I didn't want him to see me half naked, and I adjusted my boobs at the thought.

Thomas said that the Bag It crew was currently planning their party. They did have to work on Halloween, but would be closed by eight. Then I heard a gentle rapping on the dressing room door. It must have been Shawn. I hoped he wasn't eavesdropping.

I bid my farewells to Thomas. He remembered why he called in the first place and thanked me for my e-mail. I blushed, heat making me feel cramped in the dressing room. I finished dressing and fixed the meanest don't flirt with me face on. I opened the door. Shawn's face dropped maybe because I wasn't in the mermaid get up, and he made a comment, perhaps trying on his machismo for size. He said he was hoping I would model the outfit for him. *Blech!*

"Dude, how old are you? Like 18? Why the hell would I model it for you? I'm married for Christ sake. Please, don't let me file a complaint with your manager." I wondered how much longer I could use the married excuse. I wasn't wearing my wedding ring anyway. Shawn was stunned by my comments and like a puppy with his tail between his legs he quickly apologized and retreated to the back. Since getting the job at The Lure Company, I had become very vocal about customer service everywhere I went. I was hyperaware of even the smallest slight.

The one employee left standing, good old Norm waited at the register. He examined the packaging of the outfit and asked tentatively if I was purchasing it. I offered the right answer and he sighed in relief. I threw in a pair of black frame glasses.

Once I got home, I decided to clean up the condo. Although I didn't feel the need to impress Bradley anymore, I wanted the home to match the new me. Clean, polished and untouchable. Everything needed to be shined and put in place. Rachel called in the middle of my living room dancing and cleaning to Beyonce's *Single Ladies.*

"That's my girl!" Rachel said happily as she heard my new anthem in the background. "Just called to see how you've been. I landed safely and it's back to work for the old girl."

"Just cleaning and enjoying my humongous new Hello Kitty plushy from Thomas." I wasn't going to let her off the hook so easily, but I was eager to share the news.

"See, I knew you two would make a love connection!"

"No, Rachel, no love connection." *At least not yet*, I thought. "Thomas is very sweet and so awesome on the phone. Oh, and the handwritten note he sent with the delivery was almost poetic, but no, N-O, we are not an item and don't have plans for that."

"Why not woman?" Rachel whined.

I explained that we were friends. It's unreasonable to fall in love overnight right? I told her about the three hours on the phone last night and the call at the costume shop. Rachel kept insisting that it was more than I was allowing it to be. I drilled in her that I couldn't even think of Thomas in a romantic way until the divorce was final and I figured out my life. She agreed, finally.

Rachel kept it brief and made me promise to torture Bradley again. I finished cleaning up and brought my new toy to bed, the Hello Kitty doll that is. I plugged in my Blackberry by my nightstand and cracked open the latest book I was into. I was more diligent with keeping my phone charged to the max. I didn't want anything hindering my communication with my new friend, Thomas. Just as I thought this, my phone beeped indicating that I had a text message. I figured it was Bradley texting the flight information. Instead, it was a short text from Thomas with an awesome picture of his profile. His honey hair crested backwards, and he looked like he had a bit of fuzz growing on his chin. His eyes crinkled, his smile wide. I wondered if his sister took the picture.

Good night, Phoenix Paltrow. I hope we can go cruising someday, just as friends though—no funny business. Thomas Huey Lewis.

I couldn't stop smiling. I hugged my massive white cat tightly and thought of my new buddy. I saved and set his picture as his caller ID. I set the alarm for five in the morning to get in a jog and pick up Bradley. Even with the stressful thought of Bradley's return. I was ecstatic like a puppy just relieved of her fleas. I had Thomas to look forward to and Bradley to set adrift. In our first day as official friends, Thomas made me laugh and smile and feel wonderful so many times. I drifted into a very peaceful sleep with the image of his perfect profile in my mind.

Chapter 8

Two Coffee Shops and A Boy

The next morning I awoke with a start. Happiness and dread filled me at the same time, leaving me adrenalized. I felt like nothing would get in the way of my new found exuberance, not even the return of my lying, cheating husband.

After my three mile jog and a light breakfast of oatmeal and fruit, I pulled on my pair of dark blue jeans and a flaming red v-neck cashmere sweater. I analyzed my backside for some time. I was still getting used to my new body. It was a bit chilly and I opted for the gray Gucci Janis Tassel boots that Rachel bestowed upon me.

She purchased it when I wasn't watching and refused to tell me the price. I Googled it when we got home, naturally and insisted that she return the almost fourteen hundred dollar boots. *Astro-freakin-nomical.* She told me to consider it an early birthday gift. My 26th birthday wasn't until next spring, but I protested no more. I threw on a knock-off Hermes scarf from the swap meet and looked at my reflection in the full length mirror. The cheap with the luxurious would balance out my financial conscience. Happy with my look, I didn't worry too much about what Bradley might think about my lighter hair. Off to the airport to deal with dead weight.

I found a seat next to the luggage claims area. There were only a few people waiting. I kept my face buried in my book. I wasn't in the mood to play flirt today; I'm never in the mood. I had another fifteen minutes to wait for Bradley.

The small jet from L.A. pulled into the commuter terminal and I watched as the roughly fifty passengers deplaned. I slinked to the glass window, recognizing Bradley right away. He was dressed in his uniform. The siren and lights of the conveyor belt started up and I saw Bradley's large green Army issue duffle bag. Bradley was close to the building now and I had to admit he was looking strong and fit. His face was stone cold. He searched the happy crowd that awaited family and friends. I returned to my seat. I didn't want to give him the impression that I was happy with his return, because I really wasn't.

I watched quietly as Bradley entered and retrieved his bag. In one swift motion, he hoisted it over his shoulder. He marched away from the happy families then paused near me. I stood to greet him, but he glanced at me, half smiled, and then headed away from the waiting area. I blinked a few times before I realized that he did not recognize me. Fifteen pounds and a change in hair color must have thrown him off my scent. I trailed him as he headed to the exit, occasionally scanning his surroundings for me. The old me would have called out "G.I. Joe!" But, my funny bone wasn't on lease to him anymore.

Bradley crossed the threshold and paused outside the automatic exit doors. I cleared my throat to get his attention. The blast of cold morning air blew my hair back and Bradley turned around to finally look at me, for the second time that morning. I couldn't have planned the Hollywood scene any better. The moment when he realized it was me. He stood in place and I remained on the platform opposite him, still in the building. I raised my eyebrows and suppressed my smile. The look on my soon-to-be-ex-husband's face as the slow realization that I was really me was satisfying to say the least. *Screw it!* It was awesome! Everyone should have this experience once before they die.

The double glass doors closed on us since neither of us moved for several seconds. The approach of families and friends reunited with their loved ones snapped us out of the moment. I approached Bradley and his eyes took in my entire transformation. He backed up a few steps and then we both side stepped to let people through. I raised my eyebrows as an invitation for him to say something.

"Nix?" Was all he could ask.

"Yeahhh?" I drew out the word. "Are you ready to go?" I told myself to keep civil and unemotional today. Bradley's mouth was open, but he didn't move or speak. Then a retired military gent who looked to be about eighty years old patted Bradley on the shoulder and welcomed him home. Bradley woke up from his trance and saluted the old man. We watched the veteran shuffle away. Bradley dropped his bag on the pavement and opened his arms. My response was to hug myself. I rubbed my arms to ward off the cold. I guess losing my layer of fat made it impossible to keep warm. Whale blubber be gone! I walked towards the parking lot, leaving Bradley with arms wide open.

"Let's get to the car. It's cold." I stated matter-of-factly over my shoulder.

Several men stopped to let me pass and I took quiet satisfaction as they checked me out in front of *Bradlame*.

"Slow down, tiger." Bradley trotted up next to me, doing his best to demonstrate our togetherness. I quickened my step in answer.

The drive home was reticent. I remembered the gift from Rachel and directed Bradley to open the CD and pop it in the player for me. He read Rachel's handwritten Sharpie label, *October of Your Demise*. I told him it was a mixed CD from Rachel and he gave me a knowing smile.

I offered to get Bradley breakfast at a drive through, as *Never Again* by Kelly Clarkson blared. Bradley was distracted, well aware that the harsh lyrics were directed at him, so he pushed the button to play the next track, *Hot and Cold* by Katy Perry blasted. **Click**. Then, the infamous cheating song by Carrie Underwood. **Click**. Pink was the last straw for poor Bradley. He got the point and asked if Rachel made the disc for me or for him. I smiled slyly and noted that I needed to spank and thank that girl. I ended the torture for Bradley and clicked the stereo off.

After several minutes of heavy silence, I was acutely aware that Bradley's gaze returned to me every ten seconds. I expected him to ask about my hair. I wondered what he thought about the whole situation, the whole me, the better me. I wanted him to know my transformation wasn't for him, it was for me.

I drove home blissfully, thinking of Thomas.

When we got to the condo, I headed straight to my office, keeping the silent treatment going. I wanted to research the upcoming visits for coffee shop evaluations for my work week. On Sundays, I typically did my prelim visits, which were suggested but not required by the company. I didn't care. I really needed a reason to keep away from Bradley. I grabbed my keys, sunglasses and purse off my desk. I petted my Hello Kitty and jumped at the sound of my name.

"Nix. Headed somewhere? I just got here." Bradley stood outside my office door, freshly showered. A towel wrapped around his waist drew my eyes. His body was considerably more defined. I averted my eyes and fought the urge to feel anything for him. Bradley pranced around half-naked on purpose. It didn't matter how clean he got, the fact remained that he dipped his married stick in someone else. He wasn't going to get the welcome home lay he was expecting.

"Got work." I said.

"Nix," Bradley whispered. "Can we talk, please?" The smell of his soap and shampoo invaded the office. It invaded my head; it was the same scent he had for the last ten years. Although the familiarity of his smell was albeit home, it wasn't a home for me anymore. I wasn't going to get lost in a reverie about him now.

I stood behind my desk for a few moments, like it was a shield. His eyes were curiously focused on the large Hello Kitty in the room. "Talk about what?" It was my effort to avoid questions about my new office mate.

"First off, about us." Bradley stuttered, "Ah-about how you've been doing in general. I mean, um, you, you look amazing."

"Thanks. I'm fine. You're obviously flourishing in your Army career." I kept my voice leveled. "Anyway, we'll proceed with the divorce like you originally wanted four months ago, now that you're home for a long enough period to get it done." I gathered my paperwork and danced around Bradley. His larger, more muscular frame and short Army hair cut were menacing, but the sad bulldog look on his face disarmed me for a second. He planted his left arm on the door frame blocking my exit. His black tribal tattoo quivered from the tension. My eyes flickered to his hand and I saw his gold wedding band still on. I expressed my breath loudly and gave him the sternest face I could muster.

"Please, move. I have work to do." He didn't budge so I ripped off his towel and flung it out the door and it floated down to the first floor. "Mrs. Yamaguchi is home by the way." I pointed to the open view of the next unit. Bradley covered his manly parts and I shimmied passed him. As I gamboled down the stairs, Bradley came to the landing exposed, both hands gripping the faux mahogany rails.

"We'll talk when you get back okay?" I refused to look up at him. I wouldn't give him the satisfaction.

"Fine. You're going to want to call your parents, since they know about the divorce." With that said, I stepped out into my day—still fresh and new.

Rachel knew that Bradley would be home and I figured she would be checking on me, but I didn't quite count on how soon that would be. She had called twice during my thirty minute drive to the Charm Coffee Café. I finally called her back after my assessment. I told her that I had another shop to stake out, the same one we visited by the spa. It would take me another thirty minutes to get back south, but I was glad to be away from Bradley. She did better at not shoving Thomas down my throat, but I couldn't help feeling like a giddy teenager as I told her about his friendly text and delicious picture the night before. While we spoke and I sipped my skinny vanilla latte, I pulled the card from Thomas out of my wallet. I reread his message and smiled.

I was back in Pacific Beach for the second coffee shop pre-visit of the day. I parked near the Diva Spa, keeping my car out of view. It would be nice to get another massage, but the idea of Chazzer touching my body again, especially after his intentions were known was a rancid thought that made me heave. I checked my Blackberry hoping for a text from Thomas when I saw that I had two missed calls from Bradley. He was acting like a hopeless fool. I gave in and called him back. He asked when I would be home. This shift in power in our relationship was like a pair of new, uncomfortable designer shoes that I would have to wear for awhile to break in, but I loved it.

"Bradley, I'll be home by dinner, don't bother waiting," he started to speak and I hung up.

I approached The Drip slowly. I made mental notations of the cleanliness of the store. I observed the outside seating. Two older gentlemen sipped their drinks and smoked. Noted. The smell of coffee and cigarettes, my dad's two vices, made me suddenly miss him. The glass on the doors was clean and all signage was in good condition. I opened the door and the warm, sweet air of the shop enveloped me. I pretended to be on my phone as I did a quick survey of the café. I could typically count the number of customers present in one sweep, and because it wasn't necessary to gather physical descriptions of the patrons—I didn't notice Chazzer and Bret in the far corner.

I lined up behind three customers and scanned the menu board. The door chimed as another customer entered and lined up behind me. I was aware that he or she was a bit too close for my comfort since *Mr. I don't respect personal space* bumped into my purse. I didn't want to make a scene so I half-stepped forward, glanced at my purse to make sure the zipper was zipped and clutched it. The joker behind me stepped up too. If he or she started smelling my hair I was going to do a Tae Kwon Do back kick. Just as the image of a rude person flying through the glass door behind me was playing out in my mind, I heard my name.

"Hi, Phoenix! It's me Chazzer!" It had been a week since this meathead laid his hands on my body. His voice grated on my nerves and I turned to look at him.

"Hey, there kid. On a break?" I asked. Bret observed with a smile from the safety of his table. Chazzer obviously didn't like being called a kid from the way his eyebrows furrowed and nearly connected, but he didn't budge. I stepped forward as the line shortened by one. I begged the barista to call for me. I wanted to shake this dude off my scent.

"Yeah, I was, um, hoping you would have called me by now. I have the afternoon free, being Sunday and all. How about another session, on the house?" This kid must be joking. Saving a hundred bucks did sound appealing though. *Snap out of it, Nix!*

"I've been busy with work and stuff. Thanks for the offer though." I turned my attention to the menu board again hoping he would get the hint. Mr. Stallion didn't.

"You can't pass up a free session by the Chazzer? Come on. You look really tense!" Referring to himself in the third person wasn't gaining him any points. Then, the fool actually placed his steroid pumped hands on my shoulder. I wriggled free and glared at him.

"Please, don't do that again." I warned from clenched teeth. I stepped forward a step and the customer behind me stepped up too by what seemed to be a step and a half. Instantly, Bret was at Chazzer's side and like dejavu, he was pulling on Chazzer's muscular arm. Several customers and a cute barista watched us now. I didn't want to blow my cover before the evaluation. I hated having to disguise myself if it wasn't necessary. Did I have to dye my hair blue this week? I wanted to diffuse the situation, but I wasn't about to accept Chazzer's offer. He knew way too much about my personal life and he probably took note that I wasn't wearing my wedding ring now. He was a good looking kid who wasn't used to hearing no.

I kept my eyes forward. Chazzer was in step with me again.

"Hey, Phoenix, I just, you know, *really* like you and I thought we had some kind of chemistry. You are practically single right? Your friend said that . . ." Was this fool going to broadcast my love life here! And just because someone was single, that didn't mean they wanted to be attached.

A voice I had only heard in person a few times piped up behind me. It was…Thomas? That might explain the awkward closeness. God, I hope he didn't think I did anything to keep Chazzer's heat seeking missile locked on me. Hearing Thomas's sweet voice, I was awash with relief. I wasn't going to ask why he was at the coffee shop I cased. I was just thankful he was here.

"Chazzer, right?" Thomas stated confidently. Compared to Arnold *Chazzernegger,* Thomas was taller, but less dense in the brain and muscle department. I didn't want him to get pounded and have his beautiful profile ruined. "Phoenix is actually with me, so if you don't mind, you're kind of ruining my mojo."

Chazzer looked from me to Thomas, doubt evident on his broad face. Bret tugged on his friend's arm again. To send the message home, Thomas leaned in and took my hand in his. His fingers were cool, but comforting. He intertwined his fingers with mine and squeezed, and Chazzer watched intently to see if I would flinch. I didn't. Bret finally spoke up.

"Sorry, man. My buddy just has a big crush on your girl." Bret whispered and gave a thumbs up to the cute barista. Chazzer clenched his jaw and looked at Thomas again. His eyes pools of hatred for this beautiful creature by my side. Chazzer nodded his head in defeat and gave me one last pleading look. I took a step back and took comfort in shielding myself behind my hero. I pressed my nose into Thomas's sleeve, hiding my face. This time, when Bret pulled Chazzer, he followed.

The front door chimed and they were gone. I unwillingly released my hand from Thomas. I smiled like I just won the lottery.

"So, *friend*, do you come here often?" I asked when I finally caught my breath.

"Oh, it's my first time. My sister suggested I check it out. And you, friend?" He replied with his killer smile.

"If I told you, I'd have to kill you." I whispered. He got the inside joke. We ordered together and Thomas insisted on paying. I passed my twenty dollar bill to the handsome olive skin barista— name tag Jonathan—and enjoyed swatting away Thomas's arm as he tried to pass a credit card to the guy. Thomas held my wrist. His eyes bore into me and I was sure I turned as red as my sweater. Jolly Jonathan must have been a romantic because he giggled at our playfulness, instead of being annoyed.

After getting our beverages, I walked out of the shop and started for my car. Thomas followed closely behind. He suggested we stay and chat and I gave him a knowing look.

"You know I can't. Bradley's back and I need to work on a report." I pointed to my drink. Thomas's joy evaporated and he played with his cup cozy, peeling the edges off as a distraction. I wanted to fling our drinks down and kiss him, but my head knew that it wasn't the time.

"Can I at least walk you to your car in case a muscular masseur named Chazzer is hiding in the dumpsters?" I smiled and nodded yes. I wished I parked farther away, and we stood in front of my car too soon. He smiled when he saw the Guam flag hanging from the rear view mirror. Thomas, like a true gentleman, opened my door.

"Please take this drink for your sister." I said. Thomas's gentle touch sent waves up my arm where we made contact as he pushed it away. "Really, I've had too many today." And after finding safety in my car pointed to the coffee waiting for me. "I hope she enjoys."

Thomas crouched down to peer into my car. For a few moments, we just smiled at each other. I reached over to my Guam flag and gingerly removed it from my rearview mirror. I wasn't sure if the rope would be damaged from being exposed to the sun for the last year. The extraction was a success and it was only a bit faded. I handed it to Thomas. He refused at first, but I insisted. He pointed out his car, a dark blue Prius.

"I can't take this, Phoenix." The whisper of my name had my heart quickening.

"The Guam seal will totally match your car." I said.

"I don't know if I've earned this."

"The drink or the flag?"

Thomas took a long sip of the strawberry slush tea. "Oh, this delectable drink, I'm taking for sure. I earned this getting the muscle guy off of you." He smiled, his gorgeous gray eyes disappearing in a jungle of lashes. "But, this flag must be special to you."

"It's the least I could do for you, for saving me. And, anyway, I have three more at home, exactly the same, still in the plastic. Really." I reached for the seal. "Actually, let me give you a new one, not this old thing." He yanked it away.

"No, I like this one. It's special." *And used, I thought.* "Thank you." He smiled my smile again. I bid Thomas farewell and he stood tall and asked if he could call me the next day.

I knew Bradley would be back to his office to catch up with his real estate world and I gave Thomas a time frame that he could reach me. I wondered if Jem was in the office now or still in training, but I quickly sucker punched that thought out of my head. I had this beautiful friend in front of me. I put my hands on my car door and rested my chin on them so I could soak up all of Thomas. I enjoyed his face for a few more seconds. The sun shone from behind him and his body shaded me. The rays burst through his wonderfully tousled hair. It took major effort to break eye contact with this god, but I sat up and started my car. Thomas reached out and ran his fingers across mine as my left hand still gripped the door. His index finger seemed to feel the indentation in the pale skin where my wedding ring used to be. An electric shock coursed throughout my body. In a perfect world, I would kiss him passionately. My love life was too messy to drag him into right now. I wanted to keep him untarnished, pristine and mint in the box—on the shelf for now.

"Goodbye, Thomas." I said breathlessly. The rasp in my voice surprised me.

He hopped back onto the curb to watch me leave. It was nice to see him in attire other than his work uniform. The dark green plaid shirt hung loosely on his frame and he crushed the sleeves up to his elbows. His dark blue jeans hugged his legs. He wore his usual shoes and the gold necklace glinted in the sunlight. His fingers fidgeted with the Guam flag and I finally found the will to drive away from him.

Chapter 9
Man and Ex-Wife

I didn't head straight home. I wanted some retail therapy so I headed south to an outlet store. It was nearing the middle of the afternoon and I yearned for Rachel to be here to join me in the thrill of the hunt. I blasted the mixed CD and it got me angry about Bradley again. I'm sure that was Rachel's intention, the gift that keeps on pissing you off.

Two hours later and one hundred dollars lighter, I headed home. Even before I entered the condo, I smelled cedar planked salmon, my favorite and a regular dish in the former Farmer household. I dreaded opening the door. I hoped Bradley didn't do anything extreme to win me over. It was pointless, I knew—but I guess he didn't get the memo.

I placed my shopping bags on the couch and tiptoed to the dining room. I may as well see what the evening had in store. Bradley had set out our special plates. Flickering scented candles made me nauseated now, when once it was a welcoming fragrance. Shiny wine glasses were ready to be filled. A salad and three varieties of dressing stood like soldiers on the table. In the middle of the neatly placed dinnerware was a large red gift bag, tissue and all. I took a peek inside and saw not only the Coach wallet that was supposed to be my reward for dropping weight but the matching purse too. Maybe Angelica could use a new designer purse and wallet because I didn't want his bribe.

"Honey, you're home." His pitiful tone was awkward. He sounded like a desperate househusband. I stood at the entryway of our kitchen and my arms crossed automatically.

"Expecting someone? Oh, wait, is Jem coming over, should I leave?" Bradley wore an apron and gloves and was ready to remove the salmon from the oven. It did smell wonderful, but that was beside the point.

"No, just waiting for my wife!" Bradley's voice boomed. His nervous laughter grated in my ears.

"Oh, really?" I bit my lip, willing myself to stay calm. "I'll take my dinner to the office. Thanks for cooking." I turned to walk away, but within a blink of an eye, Bradley had removed his gloves and was by my side.

"Nix, please. I'm trying to salvage our marriage. I know I was a prick, but tell me what I need to do to fix this. To fix us."

I spoke softly without turning to look at him, "You can't fix this. I can't fix this. You set the wheels in motion and our marriage is over. And, besides. I'm not broken."

"Please, no." He pleaded. "I'll go to counseling, whatever you want, please, Nix." How *about getting a scarlet A tattooed on your chest.* "And, I'm not with Jem anymore. I ended it with her." *For the second time*, I thought.

"Did you talk to your parents or what?" I was exhausted from the pendulum of feelings of today, swinging from hate for

Bradley to lust for Thomas. I craved normalcy, but Bradley and me again—that was not normal anymore. I made the fatal error of looking at his face. I surrendered in the name of food and headed to the dining table. I would be civil and give Bradley a sit down dinner with me, his last supper.

I learned that he hadn't called his family. He barely touched the food he prepared. I wondered if he poisoned it for a second, and sniffed the pink flaky salmon at the end of my fork. I waited until he took a bite, and then ate. I kept conversation to a minimum. I didn't engage in small talk about Rachel or Uncle Joaquin's funeral or my job despite the many attempts Bradley made to find out about the new me. I left the gift bag on the table, only acknowledging it with a small shrug.

"With the amount of weight you lost, I figured I owed you more than the wallet." Bradley stated sounding dumber to me than ever.

I enjoyed every bite of my dinner, and I wanted to take a long hot bath so badly. I even offered to do the dishes to get this supper over with. After my third glass of white wine, I excused myself. Bradley said he had it under control and like a lost child, he watched me head upstairs. Good, let him enjoy the sight of my butt as I walk away. *Single Ladies*...played in my head.

I rested my head back on a rolled towel. The warm water was beginning to cool when I heard a light tap on the door. "Nix, honey, I know I'm in the dog house, but could I sleep in the bed with you?"

"*I'll* take the couch. *You* take the bed." I turned up my shower radio and the classical music drowned out the rest of his babble. I felt bad that Bradley did not sleep on a proper bed in awhile, but I wasn't about to be horizontal with the man. When I opened the bathroom door, Bradley was perched on the bed, waiting and watching for me. When did his eyes get so big? A flash of his sophomore class photo, the one that made me fall for him blazed before my eyes. I blinked twice and looked at the floor. Before he could speak, I grabbed two pillows and my blanket and escaped to my sanctuary.

I caught my breath on the bottom of the stairs. I looked up and it was quiet. He didn't follow.

I snuggled into my blanket and built a small fort with my pillows. I grabbed the T.V. remote and without needing to see the buttons, navigated my television to a flick. I caught the middle of the movie *Dogfight*. I realized it was River Phoenix's death anniversary this month. I loved the flick to no end, but sleep beckoned me. The last image I captured was of Eddie dancing with Rose before I drifted off.

I had left my Blackberry on my nightstand upstairs as usual and should have plugged it in next to me. But, I had my single habits to blame for that. An hour into my slumber, Thomas sent another picture and text to my phone. I was the second one to see it that night, since Bradley was in the bedroom when it arrived. I guess my little green monster hopped out of my body and entered Bradley's. And, he rode a jealous wave downstairs.

147

"Nix!" I was yanked to the surface of consciousness, but didn't respond fast enough. Bradley knelt by me and held the glowing screen of the Blackberry two inches from my eyes. "Phoenix Farmer!" I thought I was in a nightmare as the glow of the television set and Bradley's menacing glare greeted me. Once I focused my eyes, Thomas's smile filled my vision. He posed with the Guam flag on his rearview mirror.

"Who the hell is *Toe-mas*?" He said it like we do on the island, "Toe-Mas," and it irked me to full awakening. I realized that I wasn't dreaming and sat up. I dove for my phone, and Bradley and his new military skills averted my attempt.

"He's a friend. Why?" I asked.

"Why is he sending you pictures and texting you?" I hoped Bradley didn't really analyze the picture and see the flag.

"Because. He's. My. Friend. That's what friends do sometime." I explained. Bradley slammed my Blackberry on the coffee table and sat next to me. "Damn it, Bradley! You better not have broken my phone." He muted the television set just as Eddie Birdlace was returning from the war to embrace the love of his life, Rose. That was my favorite part. I continued to watch the television screen reading their lips and savoring the romantic moment.

Bradley's knees hopped up and down as he waited for further explanation. I didn't owe him any, but I also didn't want Bradley to jump out of our bedroom window from depression, so I gave him a minute. I reached for my phone and checked it for damage in the faint light.

"Are you seeing this Thomas guy?" *Wow*. Friend must mean something different to Bradley. But, then again coworker meant sack buddy, didn't it?

"No. He's just a friend. I barely know the guy." I grabbed the remote control and turned the T.V. off. We sat in the near darkness, the only light trickled in through the blinds. I pulled my legs up and tucked my Hello Kitty blanket tighter around me. Bradley's hand lingered near my feet and he looked so dejected as he stared at my newly pedicured toes, a tiny hummingbird painted on my toenails. It looked like he wanted to touch me, and then he sobbed. His body convulsed. I had never seen him this emotional, even when his beloved grandfather died. I closed my eyes to block out his face and I nearly drifted back to sleep.

Bradley's fingers tickled my toes and in a second his hand moved up my leg to my knee. I froze. The familiarity of his touch caught me by surprise. I didn't want to enjoy it, but my body had only known his moves, his hands, his general mode of operation when we got intimate, so I did not reject him quickly enough. Bradley took this as an invitation to continue. I held his eager hand at my thigh firmly.

"No, Bradley." I whispered. Was I trying to convince him or me? I felt a pang of guilt, remembering Thomas's picture. Bradley drew close and his hot breath was in my ear.

"Nix, please. I still love you." He kissed my cheek, then my neck. I felt like I was sinking into quicksand. If I sunk any further, I might surrender to him. I hadn't been touched in so long. I would have to grasp for the surface, a branch or something to pull me out of this gunk and I would be able to push Bradley away. I clutched my phone.

My self-control wavered again and Bradley's hot mouth met mine. I let him kiss me for a few seconds and then shoved him away. He kept his face near mine and his hands started for my robe. He pushed the yellow silk off my shoulder and proceeded to indulge in my neck, my chest and my collarbone. I again made a misstep and groaned. As Bradley became stronger in his will, I became weaker. Before I knew it, he laid me on my back and opened my robe. His familiar hands traced over my bare breasts and his warm palms felt my abdomen. I suddenly became self-conscious like the old me. Bradley's body tensed and his eyes soaked in my body. He seemed to realize my body transformed. He registered the changes, my sculpted abs, my smaller hips, my strong thighs. His dark smile drew me in. I made a useless effort to sit up, looking like a new born fawn.

Bradley cradled my butt and pulled me closer to straddle him. I felt his solid intentions in between my legs as he pressed into me through his boxers. He wasn't wearing his shirt and his chiseled chest was emphasized by the moonlight. I breathed deeply and yielded. My brain and my heart had an internal debate about whether giving in to Bradley tonight was right or not. I would still be laying with him as his wife, wouldn't I? But, my heart was being whisked away in a vibrant blue chariot driven by Thomas. I wanted to be with him already, despite our agreement to remain friends.

"Bradley, please stop. I don't want this."

"Um, are you sure?" He kissed my belly and tugged at my flimsy expensive panty. How I missed my sturdy cotton panties right about then. His rough hands placed pressure on my hips and in one swift motion I was naked aside from my splayed robe. I closed my eyes and let Bradley's mouth have his fill of me. I writhed with pleasure all the while thinking of the last four months alone. I felt the heat of his mouth warm me from within. His darting tongue was different, more expert and as I climaxed Jem's glaring face appeared in my mind. Rachel's voice invaded my moment of pleasure, *"You don't know what he caught from that whore."* Then, Thomas's lingering touch on my hand from this afternoon brought me back to earth. I dove into the water from the crest of a wave. I pushed Bradley's head away from between my legs and ungracefully fell off the couch. Bradley sat back and groaned unpleasantly, tugging on the bulge between his legs. His sneer made me think that he just got away with something.

I ran upstairs and locked myself in the bathroom. I sought refuge in the shower. I'm not sure how long I stood there rinsing the last few disgusting moments off of me, crying in the spiky hot water. I heard Bradley knock twice, but ignored him. I couldn't stay in this house anymore. Where would I go?

I cracked open the bathroom door. The room was clear. I heard the garbled sounds of the T.V. I looked at Thomas's picture again. I knew what I wanted. I needed out of this house. I dressed silently and called my Uncle Tony, my dad's first cousin. It was nearly midnight, but he invited me to stay without question. My clumsy fingers grabbed a stack of clean clothes and I shoved them in my gym bag. I grabbed my laptop and Blackberry and tiptoed downstairs. Bradley emerged from the office and begged me to stay. He didn't follow when I told him I was going to my uncle's. He knew better than that.

My uncle was a retired Marine who would pummel Bradley if given the chance. When I got to uncle's house, he said he knew about my separation from my dad. He had been placed on defcon Phoenix 1 status, his obligation as my Chamorro uncle to not only protect me but to destroy the threat. That threat was Bradley.

I didn't visit my dad's cousin often. I didn't really grow up with Uncle Tony's kids either. His two sons were both in the service. David was currently in Iraq and Ty would return soon. Uncle Tony's wife died a few years prior from cancer. I had attended the funeral with Bradley. After seeing him again, I felt guilty that I didn't make more of an effort to visit my uncle and vowed to do so from then on.

Uncle Tony gave me a tentative hug when I arrived, telling me that he liked my old hair better. He wasn't a man to ever mince words. We shared a cup of decaf and I got him up to speed about

152

my love life, the rated G version. He was extremely patient and surprisingly understanding. He reminded me so much of my dad and I decided to call my parents and Rachel after I bid uncle goodnight. He had offered me the guest bedroom after explaining the set up of the house. He welcomed me to whatever was in the fridge and I promised to do some grocery shopping with him in the morning.

As I lay in David's old room—the designated guest room, my body was still humming from Bradley's touch. I felt guilty for having that encounter with my own husband. I expelled the last of my energy with phone calls to Guam…dad and mom and Rachel.

I pulled my blanket over my head, the only light from my phone. I stared at Thomas's picture and read his message.

You like me, you really, really like me. Goodnight, Phoenix. Thomas

No wonder Bradley was enraged. I lay my Blackberry near my face and drifted off to sleep.

The next few days, Uncle Tony gave me my space. He offered to take me to the military legal office to look into the divorce paperwork too. I passed. This was something I needed to do myself I had told him. I continued with my evaluations for the week and asked Angelica to tell Bruce to sign me up for phone evaluations as well. I could use the extra money and distractions.

Uncle worked mostly to keep himself busy. He was a grounds keeper at a golf course, swapping the mundane work for an employee discount for golf. I didn't see him much aside from breakfast and dinner.

Three days into my stay at my uncle's, I searched for a place of my own. As much as I liked Pacific Beach, I didn't want to run into Chazzer or other beach boys like him. I yearned for a nice, quiet community perhaps with a lot of seniors. Eventually, I decided to base my decision on the quality of the library. By the afternoon, I narrowed my choices to Bonita or La Mesa. I continued my hunt for small studio apartments. I didn't want a condo or an entire house. Luckily for me, it was a buyer's and renter's market. I knew Bradley would be at work so I stopped off at the condo to refresh my supply of shoes and clothes.

There lay a sloppy stack of mail on the kitchen counter. Bradley hadn't washed the dishes it seemed like since I left and there was a funk in the air that I didn't recognize. I grabbed the mail and headed for my office where I found two open letters on my desk. My Hello Kitty doll looked at me, but she wasn't a reliable witness. The corresponding envelopes had the beautifully written script from Thomas. The envelope for one of the letters was with it, but one envelope was missing. I panicked and thought that maybe Bradley read these letters, words intended for me. I channeled Sherlock Holmes and collected my mail. Thomas was in danger. Bradley wasn't expecting me to return to see this. A jolt of fear gripped me.

Who would I call first? Thomas to see if he was still alive or Bradley to stop him from doing anything stupid? I grabbed my Blackberry and dialed.

"Thomas?!" I squealed.

"Hi, Phoenix. This is unexpected. A real phone call and not just an e-mail or text from my dear old friend." He sounded unharmed so I relaxed.

"Where are you?"

"At work, on a break, why? Everything okay?"

I explained the jealous carnage I discovered and how I was worried for his safety. Bradley was a trained soldier now. He never really had a history of violence, but he was a different beast. I begged Thomas not to go home until we saw each other. I knew I had to protect my new friend from my own husband. What a screwed up notion. Thomas didn't deserve this.

"So, you read my letters?" I could hear the smile in his voice.

"Of course not. I mean I want to. I will. I'm worried about your well being, Thomas." I hoped Bradley's years of not ever being jealous in our relationship didn't equate to him being as crazy as a nuclear bomb now.

"Why are you so calm?" I asked finally.

"I've been through worse. This is nothing. Please read the letters and call me later, if you want, of course."

I smoothed out Thomas's letters and folded them neatly with the one envelope. I decided to savor them later and made it my mission to search for Bradley now. He wasn't at the office and his cell phone was off. I guess now was a good time as any to see Thomas's place since he would be at work for another couple of hours. I promised to call him back when I located Bradley. I didn't understand how Thomas could be as cool as a cucumber during all this. He really didn't know the potential danger he was in by crossing a Chamorro man. Jealousy is a strong trait in most.

I drove up to Thomas's condo. It was a newer development and must have cost almost a hundred grand more than mine. Mine, not ours, the idea settled around me. Thomas said he was still rooming with his Chamorro college friend, who attended USD. His name was Tano Dela Cruz. Dela Cruz was a distant relation on Bradley's side, but I never met him or heard of him. *Tano* in Chamorro meant jungle. I had a feeling things were about to get wild.

I saw Bradley's Lexus parked along the street. Number 513 was indistinguishable from the other condos except for the wooden sign that read, "This is a Chamorro home, please remove your shoes, *fan.*"

I knocked. I heard thundering footsteps and a deep, Chamorro accented voice called out. "Yeah, hold on!" Tano opened the door and the familiar smell of barbecue wafted out from behind him. Tano was attractive. He had short hair and caramel colored skin. Tano was a massive islander, with the Fokai tank, board shorts, and tribal tats. He smiled widely. Maybe he thought I was a *haole*. My sunglasses were on and nothing on my persons declared I was from Guam.

"Well, hello there. Can I help you?" His Chamorro accent was notably muted. Yep, he thought I was a white girl. His elevator eyes seemed to appreciate what he saw. He lifted his arm and placed his elbow on the door jamb giving me the full view of his hairy armpit. It was perhaps a pose he used to impress unsuspecting San Diego sorority girls, but I was immune to his native charms. As he did this, I peered around him and saw Bradley's disgusting profile. The fool, seated at Thomas and Tano's dining table was eating. *The coconuts on this man!*

"*Hafa adai*, Tano. I'm Phoenix. I'm here to check on my ex-husband, Bradley." I pointed to Bradley with a nod of my head as I removed my shades. Tano's demeanor shifted and he relaxed, looking like my little brother for a second. He looked over his large brown shoulder at Bradley and then back at me. He seemed uncertain about how to proceed.

"Oh, hi." The reality of who I was dawned on jungle boy. He whispered, "Thomas's friend, right?" I nodded and smiled. "Well, you'll never guess, but good old Brad back there is my third cousin."

"I guess that explains why he's raided your barbecue stash."

Tano invited me in, finally. I removed my ridiculously expensive Gucci boots and placed them by the door. I thought about how many college textbooks the cost of my boots would get

Tano. Bradley finally turned to me and smiled. Machismo was so ugly. I hated his cavalier attitude. I wanted him to choke on the sparerib he was eating. His mouth, the same mouth I allowed on me made me sick.

A thick silence settled in the room, and the only sound was Bradley sucking on the rib. Tano looked at Bradley with a sneer and made an excuse to go upstairs.

"So, do you like reading my mail? You know that's a federal offense." I said.

"Hey, you're still my wife and letters from strangers, well, it's my job to look into it." Bradley stated while his mouth was still full of minced meat and red rice. Tano must be a good cook, since Bradley didn't have an appetite just the other day.

"Did you not understand that Thomas is a friend?" My voice bubbled with anger. "How convenient that you happen to be related to his roommate. Do you plan on harassing my friend in his own home?" My mind began to wonder about the contents of Thomas's letters. They must have been harmless enough since Bradley was calm so far.

For a few moments, I allowed my eyes to take in Thomas's sanctuary. It was definitely a bachelor pad. I saw opened bags of chips on the counter, several kids' cereal boxes aligned on the refrigerator, plastic plates and cups. There were *latte stones,* symbols of our Chamorro culture and pictures of different women underneath Guam magnets on the white stock refrigerator. My eyes scanned the many attractive faces and I was secretly relieved that

Thomas was not in any of them. There was a framed picture of Thomas and his sister, and what looked to be his parents on a bookshelf. He looked barely eighteen. I smiled at how cute he was then and Bradley caught me and he cleared his throat.

"Want some ribs?" Who was Bradley to offer food? I shook my head no and continued to stand away from him keeping the counter between us.

"Bradley. Please do not come into Thomas's home again. I don't care if Tano is your cousin. This is just not right!" I wondered how Bradley explained his way in. Did he recognize Tano right away?

"So, Thomas works at Bag It by the base, huh?" Evidently, he did a lot of talking with Tano. Some friend Tano was to Thomas, I thought.

I gritted my teeth. "Bradley. I've set up an appointment for military legal to draw up the divorce papers. It's set for next Monday. Please. Don't make this difficult."

Bradley's eyebrows furrowed and he stopped chewing. Then he smiled again. A piece of charred flesh stuck in his teeth. I didn't think it was possible for him to be more repulsive.

"Oh, Nix, I don't want to make anything difficult for you. I love you." He said melodically, mockingly. I cringed. "But, babe, the divorce will have to wait. I'm off to training again by next week." It had been almost two weeks since he returned, and it wasn't odd for him to go off to specialized training again. I didn't care what it was for or where, I hadn't planned on keeping in touch, but I needed to reset my target for freedom.

"When will you be back?" I sounded like I was begging. Bradley seemed satisfied and he resumed eating.

"Oh, you know maybe the end of November, but definitely by Christmas. Do you really want to get a divorce before the holidays?" I wanted to get divorced last week. I resigned to the fact that I wasn't going to get my way this time. Another six to eight weeks, I thought. I wanted to be released and open to more, to being me, to knowing Thomas. How long would he be patient with this friendship clause I put in place? Why was I being such a goody two shoes? Bradley promised to stay away from Thomas after I assured him for the hundredth time that we were just acquaintances.

Tano bounded downstairs. He looked at me, maybe trying to read the situation. "Thomas is dating someone anyway." I wasn't prepared for how that would make me feel. I felt like my feet were swept from under me, but when I finally looked at Tano, he gave me a wink. I took a deep breath, relieved.

Bradley insisted on staying to catch up with his "cuz." Tano walked me out and gave me a warm hug. Although we just met, he was from Guam and it was nice to meet him. I just wished it was under different circumstances. Tano whispered in my ear, "Hey, Phoenix, don't worry about Bradley. He's a prick. Thomas is my boy and I know he's crazy about you. I won't let Bradley get near him. Promise." Tano's massive muscles surrounded me and I knew he could handle Bradley if he needed to. It was nice to hear that Thomas took priority over Bradley. I left relieved, with Tano's words echoing in my head, *he's crazy about you.*

There was a tiny, silver lining on this dark cloud. Bradley would be gone, giving me time to stay in the condo, put apartment hunting on hold and keep my tiny budget intact. I had to make sure Uncle Tony was okay if I stayed until the weekend was over and Bradley was on a plane.

I called Rachel and updated her on the latest drama. I also shared that our company party would be at Pass the Mic. She wished she could be there and she made me promise to sing at least one song *on stage* for her. I made that promise to her, why the hell not.

I found myself tingling again as I drove to Bag It. Thomas wouldn't know if I was on a job or not, but I had to see him, knowing Bradley was busy at his condo probably raiding their freezer for ice pops by now. This time I pulled up to a spot right in front of the shop. Relief swept over me when I saw Thomas's car. I knew he had another hour on his shift. I fixed the collar on my white turtleneck sweater and rubbed my cold hands over my black jeans.

Alma smiled like she recognized me as I approached the counter. The lunch crowd had just left and several sailors were finishing up their meals. I thought I heard a lewd comment directed towards me, but ignored it. Thomas was not in sight. Alma scanned me up and down and when her eyes saw my boots she flipped.

"Oh, my god! Are those Gucci boots?" I looked down at my footwear like I wasn't sure.

"Uh, yes." I was about to claim they were knockoffs, but Thomas emerged from the back. He had refill bins in his hands. Alma screeched with excitement as she nearly hopped the counter to get a better view of my boots. That drew Thomas's attention to me and our eyes locked. Alma was at my feet and I thought, *they're just shoes.* Thomas smiled that special smile and placed the bins down, not looking at what he was doing. A silver bin of sliced tomatoes almost toppled to the floor, but he made a quick save.

"Oh, what size do you wear?" Alma's voice broke my gaze. She was one strange little cookie. "You must be an eight, right? I'm a five, but I will pay you ten bucks if I could try it on."

"Alma, why are you harassing our special customer?" Thomas said as he approached the counter. Thomas was in a navy blue long sleeved company shirt. He wore relaxed faded jeans and his black leather belt adorned with a silver Celtic knot buckle drew my line of sight to his midsection. I especially loved how he had his shirt tucked in to show off the bling, like it was a sheriff's badge. Alma's peep drew my attention away from Thomas again.

"Ten bucks? How long do you want to wear them for?" I asked, half-jokingly. Alma's eyes lit up. She seemed to be calculating how many minutes would be fair.

"Ten minutes? I'm going on break and there is a bitch next door at the smoothie shop that I would love to flaunt these boots at!" Right time to come in, I thought. I'm going to make this little girl's vengeful dreams come true, for free though.

Before I knew it I was sitting in an almost empty sandwich shop with Thomas, my Hello Kitty socks in plain view. We watched Alma fly out of the shop.

"So what did I do to deserve a visit from you?" Thomas teased. "Besides piss off your husband with my two part essay entitled, *Why I Love Guam*." Oh, he ruined the surprise. I had to read those letters now.

"I'm here because you didn't get pummeled by my soon-to-be ex-husband; and your roommate slash buddy for life was a great guy."

"Yeah, he called me and told me what happened. I'm sorry about that."

"Why are you sorry? I'm the one with a psycho ex. Mind you he's trained now in weapons."

"Phoenix, we aren't doing anything wrong, remember? Buddies only right?" He raised his clenched fist for a fist pump and I complied. His golden pendant twinkled in the fluorescent lighting and I felt it was an opportune time to ask about it.

Suddenly, the outside world stopped. I didn't notice the sound of traffic or the warmth of the sun shining on my back. The two sailors took their cue and left. Even when Alma came back beaming and got my boots back on me, she stayed away and kept busy in the back room.

Thomas explained that the pendant belonged to his father. He gave it to him before he died. I didn't want to pry, but I put a pin in my mental Thomas Board to ask later. Thomas said it was given to his father by his Irish grandfather. I *knew* it was Celtic. Thomas explained the meaning of the Celtic knot, no beginning, no end. It was an enduring symbol. His sister wore the trinity knot herself. I watched his beautiful face closely as pain would flash there at times. I wanted to comfort him, but kept my hands clasped tightly on my lap.

I gave Thomas an update on my divorce. He seemed a bit upset that Bradley decided to drag his feet on the matter, but he understood. His gorgeous, full moon eyes showed me he understood. I really appreciated his patience. Flowers couldn't bloom in a flash, and I was thankful that Thomas afforded me the time for my heart to bloom again.

"If I was Bradley, I wouldn't want to let you go too." Thomas said, his eyes scanning my face. My body was set on fire and it was a mixture of embarrassment and desire. I wanted to reach out for his hands, but I collected my things and stood up slowly. We had been sitting for almost an hour, and Uncle Tony was expecting me for dinner. Thomas walked me to the door. Several young girls walked in and giggled when they saw Thomas. I knew that giggle, I was once twelve crushing on older boys. He smiled a warm smile, but it was reserved, never reaching his eyes.

It was great to see him polishing his customer service skills, but perhaps it was because I was there. Thomas winked at me and held the door open. If we were together already, I would have given him a kiss farewell. I bit my yearning lips instead.

"Thomas, I'm glad you're not Bradley. I'm happy that you're you. You are really a kind soul. Thank you for explaining the story behind your necklace." I reached out for the pendant. It was heavier than I thought. I let the piece of family history go and it made a tangible sound on his chest. "I appreciate it." I dragged out our goodbye, maybe even marking Thomas as mine to the tweens who were staring at us. The bolder, more attractive girl of the group called out to Thomas for assistance. I took that as my cue to leave. I held my hand out to shake his and the gaggle of girls seemed relieved that I wasn't a love interest. Thomas took my hand in his, not rushing to assist his fans. He smiled my special smile again and his eyes remained steady with mine. He bent down and kissed my hand. I'm sure I blushed like a horny rose bloom. I saw the scowls and rolling eyes for a split second from the mob. I smiled, proud of myself even.

"This is how he bids farewell to all his customers, ladies. Make sure you get *your* kiss on the hand." Thomas laughed nervously and I waved him away. As I sat in my car, I saw Alma arrive just in time to take the girls' orders. Thomas returned to his counter and this time he watched me leave.

Chapter 10

Popeye, My Hero

It was the third week of October. Bradley didn't bother me much aside from the occasional text. He told me his training was postponed and that he would be staying at a friend's. I thought it was mature of him, until I saw him and Jem at the park. I watched them interact, holding hands, looking like any other couple in love. She was the friend he was bunking with. The ache I felt for Bradley was mostly gone and that realization was a relief.

It was the weekend of my Halloween party that Angelica was charged with planning. Only half the Field Agents would be at Pass the Mic.

I had spoken to Thomas every night since I met him at the shop. We reluctantly budgeted our time to one hour in the evenings. Each day I learned more about him and he learned more about me. I enjoyed this friendship we were weaving even if it was in moderation.

As I drove up to the karaoke bar, my mind flashed to the evening Thomas sang with his sister. I wished he was here tonight so I could hear his voice again, but I was really not comfortable with the thought of him seeing me in my barely there mermaid outfit. Modesty was still my bane. I wore a bulky hooded jacket just to get passed my Uncle Tony. My cousin Ty was driving into town that evening, but I couldn't hang around to wait for him, although I wanted to. I asked my uncle not to tell Ty about my divorce. Ty, Bradley and I went golfing when we first got married, just before his deployment. Returning from the middle east, I didn't want him to stress about my drama.

I stood outside the bar and unzipped my hoodie, then zipped it up again. I took a few deep breaths to harness bravery. I finally took off my hoodie and threw it on my car seat. I heard footsteps behind me, but didn't see anyone. I ran, or rather wiggled into the building quickly.

Our group wasn't large enough to reserve the entire bar, but we had a nicely decorated section for us. I wondered what the general public would think when they saw a mermaid and sexy bees and pirates milling about singing terribly. My boss, Bruce had not seen me since our interview almost five months prior. He walked right up to me.

"Hi, I'm Bruce. Are you Ashlee, the new field agent?" I heard Angelica chortle. Bruce didn't flirt, I wasn't sure if he was even capable, which was a welcomed change. He was dressed as a doctor, white lab coat and a real stethoscope.

"Hey, Bruce. I'm Phoenix. Phoenix Lizama, well Farmer. I'm getting a divorce." I said too loudly. "I think I'm your only employee with that name. I'm from Guam? I did the strip club eval with Angelica?" The A-ha moment on his face was evident and he

167

apologized profusely for not recognizing me. I wasn't playing fair by not mentioning I was now about thirty pounds lighter.

"You look, well, you look well! I have to get Angelica to start a photo file for everyone. Well, Phoenix, thank you for your service. Karaoke?"

"Not drunk enough." I said as a Pat Benatar song started.

"Me too. I need another beer then I think I'll look into some karaoke." Bruce smiled and walked off.

Angelica and I found a spot away from our group to enjoy drinks and the sometimes wonderful karaoke. "Here's your treat." I handed her the gift bag with the Coach goodies and explained their origins. She squealed and didn't object. She hugged me tightly, bounding around like she just won a prize.

The overall atmosphere in the bar was awkward, since field agents typically didn't mingle or correspond with each other. We saw each other's names in the mass e-mail blasts from the office, but we really were strangers. Worse off, we were all in costumes.

"Maybe next year we should just have our party at a restaurant." I told Angelica. She was dressed as a she-devil. She came across as cutesy and not sexy like I think she intended. I had been working with Angelica on some weight loss strategies and happily she was a third of her way to her goal weight and now a size 14. Angelica gushed over my mermaid outfit. I was really self-conscious, but my second drink melted some of my nerves.

A husband-wife duo were the first in our group to sing. They were dressed as salt and pepper shakers and belted out

You're the One that I Want, from the movie, Grease. Angelica yanked me towards the stage and we danced.

Bruce shimmied his way to us and offered another round of drinks. His presence stopped our groovy dancing. "Angelica, did you know there's another small company Halloween party tonight?" Bruce asked.

"What?!" She looked around the dim bar. Then, a group of costumed Halloween partiers invaded. There was even a poorly dressed Popeye who walked in with a surfer dude. *Wait*, that looked like Tano. He was shirtless in tight board shorts. He had a white smear on his nose and carried in a boogie board. I looked at Popeye closely. He wore a cotton white t-shirt with what looked to be a sailor's outfit drawn on it with a black Sharpie. His forearms were bulging, and he had very childish drawings on each arm, which were probably supposed to be the tattoos. The muscles looked to be made of panty house engorged with white stuffing. The pair both hid behind sunglasses and approached the stage with purpose. I turned back to the singers, wondering if Tano mentioned that he had a job. I peered at my halter top to make sure my girls were securely covered. Clamshells, *check and check*. Angelica noticed the two men as well and made it all too obvious that she found them attractive. I mean, she twirled her devil hair in her fingers with her smile wide and devious.

"Hey, Phoenix, check out the two studs at six o'clock." Angelica prodded me with her glittered pitchfork. "The boogie boarder is hot!" Angelica knew I was on the road to divorceville, but she didn't know I knew the boarder or the person I dreaded Popeye really was.

"His name is Tano." I yelled over the singing.

"What?" She asked loudly.

"Tano! His name?" The karaoke duo neared the end of their cheesy duet.

Angelica pointed to her ears and gestured that she didn't hear me yet again. *"Su-uhm-mer nigh-igh-ts, ai, aiaiai!"*

"His name is TANO!" And the music ended just in time to have me embarrass myself.

"Oh, that's a cool name." Angelica said and she smiled at the guys who now stood right behind us. I turned slowly and saw Tano first.

"Hey, Phoenix!" He hugged me and I felt Angelica tug on my hair. I introduced them quickly. Tano politely smiled at Angelica, but I could tell he wasn't interested by the way he flashed a fake half-hearted smile at her. "Guess who's here?"

On cue, Popeye removed his shades and sidestepped into view. I pulled my long hair over my clam decorated breasts and folded my arms. Thomas, of course, I smiled despite my effort not to. Tano being ever so receptive and gentlemanly started up some small talk with Angelica, who was all too thrilled.

"Hey there, Popeye. Fancy seeing you here." His smile lit up his beautiful face, which more than made up for his ridiculous costume. I reached out to his bulging faux forearms to take a closer look at his childish tattoos. On one side was an anchor and the other was a very cute stick figure attached to the bottom half of a fish. Under that mermaid tattoo was Thomas's handwriting, S I R E N A.

I smiled and wondered what magical force was placing Thomas in my surroundings time and time again.

"Is Tano your date tonight?" I joked.

"Is she-devil yours?" He countered. Thomas pointed to an open booth, and I followed automatically. It felt natural to slide in next to this sailor, and that wasn't just the mermaid in me talking. This wasn't a date, since we just happened to meet here I assured myself. He ordered a glass of wine for me and he chose a soda. He pointed out the group he was with and then I recognized Alma dressed as a sexy nurse and Tamara and her husband, James as Tarzan and Jane.

"Do you mean to tell me that your company party *just happens* to be here on the same night and locale as mine?" I thought that the chances of that were too fishy. We were having ours a week before Halloween since Bruce was scheduled for some sort of surgery the following week. But, I wondered why the Bag It crew was having theirs early too. Thomas became quiet and looked at the stage intently. Then, he started laughing, guilt all over his face. He revealed that he kept in regular contact with Rachel, *my Rachel*. She kept him informed of my whereabouts with texts. *That girl never stopped*, I thought angrily, but that feeling dissipated and was replaced by gratitude. My own cupid was working her magical powers from six thousand miles away on Guam.

"So, Chazzergate at the coffee shop. She called you?" The mystery dissolved in front of me.

"No, she just texted me."

"Same crime mister." I smiled to show him that I wasn't really angry. "And you just happened to be in Pacific Beach?"

"That was really a coincidence, I was nowhere near there, but my Prius got me up north from Chula Vista pretty quick." He smiled that disarming smile again. I gulped my wine and turned my attention to the song binder. Thomas was pleased with all the skin he was seeing, I was sure because his fabulous smile never relaxed. His lovely eyes drifting from my arms, to my face, to my hair. For the first time, I didn't mind. I probably wouldn't have minded if he glanced at my cleavage, except he didn't.

"Isn't this nice. A sailor and a mermaid." Thomas said. "It took a lot of coercing to get my sister to hold our party earlier than Halloween."

"You probably just made that costume this morning because Rachel, the double agent gave you intel about me." I shook my head and my hand reached out to his mermaid tattoo. "This is the best part of your cheap costume though, thanks."

My wish for Thomas to be here came true. I wanted to hear him sing for me. Would that be pushing it? "So, will I get to hear you sing tonight?" I asked, taken over by the wine and emboldened.

"Only if you sing first." I took him up on his proposal. And before my courage evaporated, I jotted down my selection.

"Something sweet like you." He whispered in my ear, goose bumps erupted on my bare skin.

I had my own agenda. I needed to work out my frustration, so I decided to do an angry Kelly Clarkson song. I blamed my relationship status limbo with Bradley, coupled with listening to Rachel's mix CD for weeks for my song choice. Angry women unite! I drank down the last of my wine and submitted my slip. I asked Angelica to hit the stage with me and we were handed two mics. I guess I wasn't as pickled as I needed to be because I wanted Angelica near me, the classic karaoke crutch. She was a Clarkson fan, and I think she wanted to wiggle for Tano. She handed her pitchfork to him and I somehow made it on stage with my fish fins.

Thomas and Tano found a few seats in front of us. I wasn't nervous because I wanted a shift to happen tonight. I was tired of dancing around my feelings for Thomas. In my heart, I was divorced. I had sung this song a hundred times at the top of my voice in my car. It was my new anthem. I wanted it to end tonight so I could sing a new song for a new man. The angry guitar melody started for *Never Again*. Angelica swayed erotically, while I stood stoic. She began the song off with me. I focused on my expression, my voice.

The music swelled and by the time the crashing percussion started, Angelica stopped singing, and looked at me eyes wide. Nerves threatened to silence me, but I closed my eyes and sang the lyrics burned in my brain. She faded into the background moving her head side to side to the beat of the song. The gravelly sound of my voice surprised me and I felt strong as I pounded out the rest of the words that rang so true for me. I hated Bradley. I could never love him again. And I would never forgive him.

I released my grip on the silver microphone at the end of my song. It was dead silent in the bar and all eyes were on me. I must have been quite the sight. Mermaids gone wild. I took a few deep breaths and looked to Angelica for support. Then there was an uproar from the crowd that made me jump. Cheering, not jeering to my relief. I blushed and bowed and waddled off stage. Thomas stood at the edge, holding his hand out. I accepted and felt like I crossed a new threshold.

The bar chanted, "Mermaid! Mermaid!" over and over again. I sought refuge at the booth. I burned from the spotlight. Thomas slid in next to me. Angelica and Tano joined us. The next person on the mic made reference to me, something about being unable to follow my act, but he was going to give it a shot.

"That was awesome, Ms. Clarkson." Thomas leaned into me. He had his arms around my shoulder and I felt secure next to him, even with his ridiculous forearm. I didn't shake him off. I couldn't stop looking at his gorgeous face. Do I dare feel bold and think that he could be mine? I just had to say the word. I've never had this power before. I chased Bradley in high school, campaigned for his heart. This was different.

Tano cleared his throat, breaking the awkward lull and offered to buy a round. Angelica followed him like a love struck puppy. I was alone with Thomas and I didn't want our time together to end. I breathed him in, his light cologne and the scent of his shampoo with his natural state made me heady. With a slow paced love song by Journey in the background, I made the next move and took Thomas's right hand in mine. He rested his forehead on my hair and inhaled deeply. I felt like he understood the reason for my performance. It was my final act of severing my ties with Bradley. I decided that I had been in limbo long enough and that whether the divorce papers came now or later, Thomas and I could proceed with whatever it was we were both willing to explore.

Tano and Angelica ran back empty-handed. It felt like they were shielding us from someone, they were so close.

"Hey, Thomas, Phoenix, Bradley's at the bar. He's been here for awhile apparently. He wants to talk to Thomas outside." Tano said quickly. Thomas kept his arm around me, his grip tightened.

"How did he know I was here?" I tilted my head to see past Tano and there was Bradley at the bar, seething. Suddenly, my cousin Ty busted through the doors. He confronted Bradley, placing his hands on his shoulders. My cousin outweighed Bradley by about twenty pounds in both muscle, height and brains, and was head and shoulders above him in military experience. But, the way Bradley was pushing against Ty, it didn't seem to matter. Ty pointed at Bradley like he was telling a naughty dog to stay and he scanned the bar. I presumed he was looking for me, so I sent Tano to call him over.

"Thomas. I don't want you to fight Bradley, okay?"

Thomas smiled, "Don't you worry. I ate my can of spinach today." He joked, but his smile didn't reach his eyes. They were instead hard and focused. His typically sexy tousled hair became menacing when paired with the fire in his eyes.

Angelica took a seat across from me and her mouth opened when she spied my cousin. Ty marched to our table. He gave me and Thomas a tentative smile, then looked at and addressed Angelica.

"Hey, cuz. I'm sorry, I didn't even know that you and Bradley were on the skids until my dad told me. By then, man it was too late. Bradley called asking for you." Angelica looked utterly confused, as were the rest of us at the table. It dawned on me that Ty hadn't seen me in a year and a year ago, I was a voluptuous brunette. Angelica looked from Ty to me. He realized that she was confused and looked at me finally. I smiled and raised my eyebrows to indicate that yes I was his blood relation. Out of respect, Thomas removed his arm from my shoulder, but kept my hand in his under the table. I could feel his warm body turn rigid as his eyes darted to the bar.

Tano spoke to Bradley at the bar arms pumping, trying to keep him from approaching us. It looked like they were doing a funny side to side cha cha, it didn't help that the latest song blasting was the 90's one hit wonder, *I'm Too Sexy*.

Ty looked back at Bradley to make sure he was doing what he was told and sat down across from me. He quickly apologized to Angelica and took a second to appreciate what he saw. *Men, geez.* Angelica picked up on this instantly and blushed. She looked at me and mouthed, "Oh my god."

"Damn. Cuz, I haven't seen you in so long. You look so, well, you're doing Sirena justice. I'll leave it at that. No wonder Bradley's going ape shit!" Thomas smiled and introduced himself as my friend. I couldn't believe how calm everyone was when there was a rabid beast at the bar waiting to rip Thomas's throat out!

"That's not why we're splitting, this is not why we're splitting," I released Thomas's hand. "Are we done with the pleasantries? Ty what's going on?" I asked frantically.

"I'm sorry, Phoenix. I told Bradley you were here when he called the house. I thought you two were still married. I guess things change drastically when you're deployed." My cousin was a smidgen cuter than Tano and Angelica couldn't believe her luck as Ty took another appreciating look at her. I had a quick prediction that Angelica would end up with a Chamorro man. Love was all around, so what about the pariah at the bar?

"I'm not going to leave my party because Bradley decided to crash." I said defiantly.

"Dad sent me down here and if he doesn't hear from me soon, you know he's gonna come down here himself." I believed my cousin.

177

"Thomas, maybe we should get out of here." I offered. He smiled and said it was a good idea. We rose united, and Angelica volunteered to explain to Bruce that I was leaving early. I looked around for Thomas's group and they assembled on stage. Tamara kept waving at Thomas, but he gave her the thumbs up, pointed at me and pulled me to the side exit. Ty joined Tano in the efforts to keep the enemy at bay.

Bradley, a quarterback in high school, made a dash for us. Thomas was yanked backwards releasing my hand. Bradley grabbed him by the shoulders and swiveled him around. It was outrageous seeing these two men within striking distance. In the blue corner was the man that I was leaving and in the red corner was my future. Thomas was lithe and fair and god-like compared to Bradley who lacked in everything. Why did it take me so long to figure that out? I had a lot to thank Jem for ironically.

The two men didn't say a word. Thomas was a lion, fists clenched on each side of him. The bulging forearms weren't so comical now. Bradley was drunk and he met Thomas's eyes, albeit a good five inches taller than his with an equal intensity. I grabbed Thomas's hand and wanted to escape with him. Tano and Ty were breathing hard and ready for anything. Ty placed his hands on Bradley and Tano tried to wiggle his way in between his cousin and his best bud. The testosterone overload was overwhelming.

"What the fuck are you to my wife, hah?" Bradley addressed Thomas. Ty yanked Bradley's arms back. The poor owner of the bar was a tiny Korean man who knew better than to engage the attention of anyone in this pack of growling men. I reached out for Thomas's hand again and Bradley's eyes flickered angrily to me, he swatted my arm away with violent, angry force and I spun around finding myself suddenly facing the stage. The music was still playing, but all singing ceased, eyes on the developing drama.

Thomas put himself between me and Bradley. "You touch her again and you're history."

Bradley guffawed. This time Tano became overprotective of his buddy and shoved Bradley. Good, I thought, but I hoped it would end there. Bradley gave his cousin a hurt look for a moment. Why couldn't Bradley just let me go? He threw me out four months ago. Ty urged Tano to keep it cool. Finally, the bar owner got on the mic and clamored on top of his bar counter, "If you *doh lib* now I call *polish* man!"

The electricity in our group dropped a notch and everyone did a double take at the miniscule bar owner. I was the lone person who could translate his words, recognizing that he was Korean and spoke English like my mom.

"He's calling the police if we don't leave." I stated quickly. I saw Bruce craning to see the action and I worried about how my boss would view this disaster. I prayed they wouldn't see this fracas. I didn't want to lose my job.

Ty suddenly put Bradley in a submissive hold and forced him out the door. I stayed safe behind Thomas, but a tiny part of me felt like I was betraying Bradley. Tano snapped Thomas out of his intense rage and we headed to my car. Ty shoved Bradley in his truck, being in no condition to drive. Tano agreed to drive Bradley's car back to their condo. I thought this was a bad idea, because I didn't want Bradley to have an excuse to go back to Thomas's place.

"Cuz, I'm going to drive Bradley home and have a talk with him. Can you call my dad and let him know what's up?"

"Jem! Take me to Jem." Bradley spit on the ground.

"Who's Jem?" Ty asked me.

"Long story, but she's the reason for the split. She lives in Poway. He'll be fine there." I whispered. Ty hugged me and shook Thomas's hand. Tano bid us farewell and grabbed the keys to the Bradley's car.

"Thank you, Tano. And, welcome home cousin." I called after them. Thomas held my shoulders, his touch surprised me and I turned to look at his face, softer now that the threat was gone.

"Thomas, I'm sorry about all this. This whole scene is so immature. I never thought Bradley was capable of such childishness. And," I wanted to continue, but I was spinning my wheels. I wondered for a second how Bradley felt, sitting at the bar drunk, listening to me sing such an angry song. It was painfully obvious to him and anyone who knew my situation that Bradley was the target of my hatred.

A moment ago, before Bradley created such a spectacle, I was so sure of my feelings for Thomas. It felt like the exact moment I decided to invite Thomas into my life, Bradley was there to shut the door on his foot. I felt again, like moving on was happening too soon. I didn't want to lose Thomas. These past few weeks unraveled so quickly. My love affair with Bradley occurred over time, it was a slow burn. And, I was certain that the last ember of my love for him finally cooled. My experience only taught me that love is developed over time. I didn't have any other experience to draw from otherwise. Watching romantic comedies don't count.

With Thomas, the escalation was impossibly quick and I wasn't sure if dousing our feelings continuously would kill anything between us altogether. Would it be fair to ask him to wait again? Was I worth the wait? I guess I could only offer him the truth and wait and see. I needed to get myself in focus and if I had to wait another two months to have the divorce, Thomas would have to be patient too.

"Hey, Phoenix." Thomas placed his hand under my chin and raised my face to his. He was quiet and patient as I mulled over these thoughts. Thomas watched as the two cars drove off with three variations of colossal Chamorro men. Ty was smart enough to drive Bradley away from where Thomas and I stood. As the anger and shame began to settle in me, I became aware of how brisk the night air was. My mermaid costume was not a good barrier from the cold. Thomas tuned into my discomfort and he reached out to warm my arms. I let him.

"Want to wear my forearm warmers?" Thomas joked.

"That's okay. I should get back to my uncle's house." I kept my eyes just past Thomas, looking at the gift I gave him dangling from the mirror in his car. Maybe I shouldn't have given him false hope by giving him a token of my affection so soon.

"You'll be okay, Phoenix. I won't let anything happen to you." Thomas reassured me and I believed him. I knew that despite this outburst, he felt we made progress tonight. I didn't want to disappoint him, but I didn't know any other way to proceed.

I looked up into his gorgeous eyes and fought back tears. It was so hard to deny this beautiful creature what he wanted, but I had to. I had to make the journey of being a wife to being available intelligently. My marriage to Bradley was still intact, until we both signed the paperwork. I couldn't enter Thomas's life with the stench of Bradley on me. It wouldn't be fair.

"Thomas. I'm not sure we should," I didn't know how to explain my decision to him since his eyes conveyed such longing. Finally, a tiny, tragic smile appeared and he nodded his head like he understood. Why was he being so nice and making this easy for me? It made me want him all the more.

"I think I get it. But, Phoenix. Tell me. Are we still friends? I mean, can we still continue being friends, I don't think I could just stop being a part of your life." And there he went, he just made this harder.

"Of course, Thomas. Friends. But, let's just give each other some space until I get this divorce thing settled." I knew it was me who needed the space more than Thomas. He dropped his eyes to the ground and began to peel the stockings off his forearms. He looked up at me with his doe eyes and it took all my power not to embrace him, and his next request was exactly what I wanted, but not what I needed.

"I've wanted to kiss you for awhile now. Would it be too much to ask if you gave me that treat tonight?" He smiled expectantly. I bit my lip in response, no, I couldn't do that. The rational side of my brain knew it was a bad idea. I wondered often what his mouth would taste like and feel like against my lips. My body warmed up again and I shook my head, denying his request. Head won over heart.

"That would be a *really* bad idea right now," I whispered.

"Okay, um, how about a hug between friends?" I conceded and fell into his arms. I rested the left side of my face against his hard chest. The warmth emanated from him and calmed me. I allowed myself to encircle his back and I squeezed him tight. Thomas responded in turn with additional pressure on his hold on my hips and back. He moaned with contentment and I savored the moment.

I wasn't sure who let go first, but it was probably me. I felt like home in his warm embrace, and it tore me up to let him go that night. I drove away with the realization that our lives would only be connected by our mutual friendship for each other. Driving to Spring Valley, I cried so intensely, feeling like I missed my chance with Thomas; embarrassed to death of Bradley. Rachel's visit marked a point where I felt like I was in the eye of the storm. Now, things were adrift again. My life was being propelled into the air in a thousand different directions. I prayed for the storm to be over, so I could feel like myself again. I wanted to find all the pieces and rebuild. I tried too soon to clean up and now I was being punished with the tail end of the typhoon causing chaos in my world, yet again.

Chapter 11

Karaoke Therapy

It was hard to forecast my life when the wind whipped debris all around me. I needed to anchor onto something so I wouldn't get swept up in the man drama. Rachel agreed that I should focus on two things: myself and my work. I was on a ship alone in the night, bouncing around in the choppy ocean water, with a beacon of light ahead. That was Thomas. But the vast space between us made refuge from the storm hard to envision.

Thomas gave me space that weekend. I headed back to the condo after Ty confirmed he took Bradley to the airport. My home minus my soon to be ex helped me breathe again.

As expected, the house was a disaster area and I spent the week cleaning his caveman carnage. It reminded me of the funk I was in after our break up, when it took energy just to get dressed. I pitied him for a tiny second.

Bradley was the highest speed bump ever erected, impeding my journey to self-discovery, self-recovery and self-satisfaction. I took comfort in the fact that I had two months to enjoy my home.

Bradley tried to visit me once after the karaoke scene. His mission was aborted when Uncle Tony dictated to him how the next two months would play out. Under duress, Bradley half-heartedly agreed to sign the divorce docs before Christmas. An angry retired Marine Colonel who could render you unconscious with his *men who stare at goats* skill would make me yield too.

Ty packed Bradley's things into boxes expertly. The boxes collected in the dining room like a Tetris game I wasn't enjoying. I continued my search for a new home. My parents begged me to fly to Guam, but I wanted a life in California, I dared to dream about graduate school or owning a business.

Bradley had already secured a renter for the property for the New Year. This was progress. I didn't ask him where he would be moving. Northern California, *I hoped*. Without me, *I knew*.

I was preoccupied with getting the condo cleaned and requesting extra work from The Lure Company, that I didn't realize it had been a full week before Thomas made contact. I wondered if he was writing or working during our break, but I had time to debug my mind.

I prepared for a day of bank evaluations, a crew run as we called it in the business. Bruce didn't think less of me despite the sleazy talk show brawl he saw. Naturally, I asked Bruce to keep me off Bag It duty.

Thomas's text was a welcome distraction. It read,

Hope you are doing well, Sirena. I have missed my friend. I've been busy with my screenplay with a trove of inspiration to draw from. Please open your door and find the treasure by your orchids. T.P.R.

A thousand ants marched up my spine and I raced for the door. Thomas was great at surprising me, something Bradley didn't master. I grabbed my purse and work folder, slipped on my boots and hustled downstairs. The purple orchid plant in a brown glazed pot served the purpose of reminding me of Guam, my mom specifically. I knelt and found a plain brown paper bag tucked behind it. I expected food, being hungry, but no savory smells wafted from the bag. I surveyed the parking lot, thinking that he might hang around to see my reaction. I did my Ms. America smile and wave for good measure.

In the bag was a bouquet of nearly fifty Hello Kitty pens and pencils. They were wrapped with crunchy pink and purple tissue paper, clear cellophane and an explosion of curly white ribbon. A myriad of tiny plastic Hello Kitty faces looked up at me. I was a kid in a toy store. Thomas might have borrowed the idea from Nora Ephron, but I was still grateful.

I decided to take my lunch at Bag It, since it was in the vicinity of the credit unions and banks I evaluated. Really, I was compelled to see Thomas. He baited me with Hello Kitty after all.

Bag It was packed as expected. I pulled a yellow Hello Kitty pen out of my bouquet and I wrote a thank you note to Thomas. It was nice that I could patronize the shop without having to work it.

Thomas's text and gift that morning fanned the quiet flames in my heart. I wanted Thomas, but if something was worth waiting for—I wanted to do it right. I kept my note light and friendly.

Hey, Popeye, thanks for the excessive gift. I loved all 50 pieces. Should I call you Tom Hanks now? Hope you had a great week. Your friend, Sirena—I'll take a Rock Lobster sub—extra onions, easy on the mayo--just a snack-- please. Chips and drink for real this time.

I folded the note and entered the shop. Scary Halloween décor greeted me inside. Someone was into zombies here.

I stood in line for ten long minutes and Thomas hadn't noticed me yet. Alma did. She smiled at me warmly and her eyes checked out my new black, non-designer boots. She looked back at Thomas, Tamara and a new kid working diligently on the sandwiches.

"Mufasa is in da' house!" Alma announced.

I chuckled, but ducked behind two muscular Navy Chiefs. It was fun to see Thomas smile and glance at the line every so often.

188

I wore my professional attire that day, dark gray wool bootleg pants and a fitted, blush colored long sleeved blouse. I proudly wore my gold Guam Seal pendant, but made a note to discontinue doing that because several bank tellers commented on it and asked me about Guam or shared stories of someone they knew from there. I kept my hair in a loose ponytail and curled the ends. I missed my natural curls, now working hard with a curling iron for the first time.

Within reach of the counter, Thomas whispered something to Tamara who glanced up at me. She smiled, almost looking like Thomas for a second and took over completing the sub he left abandoned. He threw his disposable gloves in the trash bin and skipped over to the counter. Before he could speak, I placed the handwritten note on the counter and slid it to him. I brought my finger to my glossy lips and gestured for Thomas to keep quiet. He cracked a crooked smile and placed the note in his back pocket. Alma, all the while watched us amused, like we were elementary kids. *Check yes or no.* Thomas had promised that he would be the only one to ever make my sandwiches from then on and Cohle shrugged his shoulders when Thomas sent him back to the prep counter.

"Your name, ma'am?" His voice warmed me like an old blanket.

"My name is Kelly, my order is on that note." I said. Thomas chuckled and wrote my name for the day on an order slip. I joined the long line of hungry patrons. I hoped Thomas wouldn't try to have my sub hop the line. I didn't want to take time away from those serving our country because I was playing proverbial footsy with my buddy.

With brown bag and the baked chips in hand, Thomas approached the counter. Alma placed a cup of lemonade beside the order.

"Kelly Clarkson. Sub for Kelly?" Thomas said it loud and proud. As expected, all patrons looked around. It was easy to pluck out the few women at The Great Wall of Hunger. All eyes zeroed in on me, the civilian. I smiled brightly, passed Thomas a five dollar tip in addition to my payment, and grabbed my food.

"See you next week!" I teased.

For the next several weeks, I stopped by the shop every Monday. It was the same routine, passing of notes from me with the humorous name for the week. Thomas would squirm when he called out "Rose Bush" or "Ella Vader" or my personal favorite, "Emma Royds."

Thomas and I didn't get to sit and chat, but we at least we got to see each other. My sandwiches grew larger, packed with extras. Thomas placed his own silly, *just friend's* notes in my brown bag, never asking about whether my divorce was finalized or not, much to my relief.

Angelica and I blew off steam on Friday nights at *Pass the Mic.* I knew that Thomas and his staff usually went on Sundays, so there was no chance of running into him there. I kept my Friday night escapade to myself. Rachel was on strict orders not divulge my whereabouts to Thomas anymore.

Ty and Angelica began dating, so it was understandable that he would join us on one or two or all of our Friday karaoke nights. I didn't, however, expect to see Tano.

Ty and Tano had become fast buddies, fused together by Bradley's blow out several weeks ago. The fact that they were islander boys didn't hurt.

"*Tao Tao Tano!*" I teased. Meaning *people of the land.*

"Hey, Bruiser!"

I never got a chance to thank Tano for serving as a bouncer against my own husband.

"Drinks are on me." I said.

Tano filled me in about Thomas's checkered romantic history. It was the "potential girlfriend" version, but I gathered that Thomas dated a lot. I soaked up the information like a thirsty sponge—he liked women from every walk of life.

"I hope you don't think my boy is a player. He didn't sleep with half of the girls he dated. He was a space cowboy on an adventure."

"I'm so mixed up, it would be like dating all those women in one. He should run for the hills." Tano's toothy grin told me that he saw past my ploy.

"Hey, Phoenix. Or, do you prefer Nix? I never asked you that." I embraced the use of my full name more each day. Being called Nix reminded me of my old life. Ending my marriage with

191

Bradley was like trying to scrape fresh gum off of my shoe. It was never completely gone.

"Phoenix is fine. Um, is Thomas going to be joining you?" I tried to keep the excitement out of my voice, but by the pleased look in Tano's face, I knew I failed. Tano explained that Thomas and Tamara took a drive north to Oceanside and Huntington Beach to scout out new locations for Bag It. I panicked for a second, thinking that they were moving the business out of San Diego. Tano reassured me again, in tune with my feelings. He said that the siblings were just branching out. Tamara wanted to cater to the Marine population in Oceanside and try her hand at the L.A. scene too.

"He'll be busy helping his sister set up the new shops. They want to open by next February. Thomas should be back by Sunday morning," Tano added for my benefit. "That guy is still really into you, just so you know." I smiled.

The night was pleasant, and the crowd was very energetic. I took a shot at one song that evening. I decided on The Corrs, *Leave Me Breathless*. I felt it was safe to sing that since Thomas wasn't in the audience. I was secretly pleased at the standing ovation. I had a lunch date offer, which I of course declined and a drink offer, which I also refused. My heart, although in limbo was already on layaway for someone else.

"Hey, Phoenix, you know that I'll be back here with Thomas and his sister and coworkers Sunday night if you want to check us out." Tano was well aware of the friendship clause Thomas and I had in place.

"Thanks, but you know." I smiled.

I received a short text from Thomas on Saturday. He too tried to invite me to karaoke on Sunday. I texted my no immediately. I didn't disclose that I knew where he was and what he was doing. I left it to him to share what he wanted. It was nice to be able to look through the window into Thomas's life. I was content with that for now.

My weekend dragged, despite my attempts to keep busy and entertained. After church on Sunday, I put in a good workout at the gym. I wondered if that went against the religious notion of one day of rest. By the evening, as I sat and watched terrible reality T.V., I was painfully aware that Thomas was at Pass The Mic. Before I could stop myself, I dressed in jeans and a large hooded sweatshirt. I put on my raven wig and no make up aside from a coat of lip balm. I didn't want any male attention tonight. My intent was not to make Thomas aware that I was in the bar. I wanted to sit back in a dark corner, in the hopes of hearing Thomas sing.

It was almost ten o'clock when I got to the bar. Thomas's car and Tano's motorcycle were parked side by side. I entered by the wayward door and made a beeline for a booth in the corner. I kept my back to the stage and sunk into my seat. A new waitress took my order and I kept it cool ordering a diet soda and nothing more. I spied Tano and Thomas at the bar. Tamara and Alma were on stage singing something by Veruca Salt. I hummed along as I surveyed my surroundings. My secret shopping gig helped me practice the art of invisibility. I buried my nose in the song binder and started to take notes on a sheet of paper for songs I wanted to sing next Friday. I was happily surprised to see Eddi Reader, Haim and Marina. I wrote the corresponding disc and song number along with about twenty other options when I finally heard Thomas on the mic.

The audience of Sunday regulars really knew Thomas and his sister. Perhaps they came every weekend just to hear the pair sing. The applause boomed for the two. I wished I had spy glasses so I could watch him without having to turn around. I pulled out my Blackberry and used the record notes app for the first time. I wasn't sure how long I could record for, but my finger was hovered above the button ready to go.

"Thanks." Thomas said shyly into the mic. Hearing his magnified voice made my heart flutter. His music was cued up and I recognized the guitar introduction right away. It was a Jason Mraz song, *If it Kills Me.* The audience was silent. Even new people walking in from my secret entrance, stopped in their tracks to watch Thomas. I lost myself in his beautiful voice, rifts and whispers done just right. His voice evoked so much longing and as egotistical as it may sound, I knew it was for me. I felt like ripping off my wig and running to the stage to embrace Thomas. It took me a lot of power to stay put, but the feelings I had for him were just as intense and I began to tear up.

The explosive applause woke me up from my reverie. I stood abruptly and thought it would be a good time to make my escape. I turned slightly and took Thomas's vision in. He was on the stage staring out at the main entrance, looking melancholy. I backed up a few steps and bumped into a very large man. I apologized quickly and stormed out. I had parked my car further down the street in the darkness, probably not the smartest or safest thing to do, but I didn't want to get caught.

I continued to make my Sunday visits, leaving as soon as I heard Thomas sing once. Week after week, every Sunday evening, Thomas sang a song full of longing on the topic of unreciprocated love. I became cognizant that there were hundreds, even thousands of songs like that out there, and it was like Thomas spent his week researching just the right one to portray his feelings. I didn't record his singing after that first time. I didn't even listen to what I recorded since the feelings and the lyrics were burned into my memory.

I filled my weeks as an almost single woman with work from Tuesday through Friday, a combination of crew runs or phone evaluations. I even joined a Tae Kwon Do class twice a week and I was able to drag Angelica to it. I was rusty at first, but muscle memory helped me remember my forms and kicks and punches in no time. I started at a white belt, even though on Guam as a child, I made it to my blue belt. Dad and mom wanted us to study something of the Korean culture and Tae Kwon Do was the perfect niche. I hated it for the first few months, but enjoyed having Pharaoh to kick around and not get scolded for doing so.

I enjoyed my karaoke Fridays tremendously. It was typically just Angelica, Ty and me. Once we dragged Uncle Tony but he was a fish out of water. Like me, he sang a song he knew from heart from our booth. I watched him closely thankful for his support and missing my father fiercely.

That evening, I thought of Thomas, so I texted him. He finally informed me of the business's expansion north and stated that he would be out of town all of Saturday. I fought the urge to invite him to karaoke. Next year, I thought—after my divorce was done, *finito!* I sent him a text wishing him a great weekend from the bar, without telling him where I was. I got on stage and awaited my Eddi Reader song, *Dolphins*. I silently dedicated it to Thomas.

I would later find out that Thomas was doing secret missions of sneaking into the bar on the Friday's when he was in town to hear me sing. That very evening, as I sang that song for Thomas, he was there to hear it first hand.

After thanking the audience for their kind applause, I asked Angelica and Ty for their drink orders and headed to the bar. The bar owner, Mr. Kang, warmed up pretty quick when I spoke to him in Korean a few weeks prior. I had to back track when he went off into an entire conversation in Korean. I explained that I really only knew how to say *hi, how are you* among other basics. He favored me after that, sometimes offering me and my group free drinks. I knew he also bumped up my song requests, since I never waited more than three songs even on a crowded night. He forgave me for the minor melee at our Halloween party and was relieved to know that Bradley would be out of town until Christmas.

"Hi, Fee-nux!" Mr. Kang beamed, sounding very much like my mom.

"Just a glass of white for me and two Buds, please." Angelica had taken to drinking beers with Ty. I knew she hated beer and usually liked fruity drinks. I fretted that she was drinking in all the calories she lost at Tae Kwon Do.

"Sure, on the house!"

"No, *kamsahamnida, ajasi,* but I can't keep getting free drinks. Please. I want to pay." He refused my money yet again. I would have to order drinks from the waitress next time.

"You know you singing bring me good business on Fridays! Like, you friends, Thomas and Tamara, on Sundays!" I didn't realize that Mr. Kang knew of my connection to the Bag It crew, specifically Thomas, since besides the party, I made it a point to not be here with him.

"Thomas just left, by the way."

"He was here?"

"*Nae*! He order a soda, stay for ten minutes and left." He pointed to the booth, *my* secret Sunday booth. I instinctively looked over to the empty booth. I wondered if he was still in the parking lot. I was suddenly mad at Tano. How else would Thomas

197

have known that I was a Friday regular here? I wasn't sure how I would handle this new revelation. I didn't want to run into the parking lot.

I returned to Angelica and Ty, in the middle of their kiss. I felt awkward as they finally realized that I had returned with their drinks. I told them what Mr. Kang told me and for a split second they didn't seem surprised. I began doubting their innocence in all this. It couldn't have been Rachel because she was on lockdown from texting or calling Thomas.

"You two better tell me what you know. Why was Thomas here?"

I raised a cardboard coaster and threatened to fling it at them. I had mad ninja skills. Angelica smiled and she pointed at Ty.

"Cuz, it's not me. It's Tano. I know you told him not to tell Thomas, but he let it slip when I went over there the other night. They were picking up a huge screen T.V. and needed the extra muscle." With that said, Angelica caressed my cousin's large bicep and I shivered with sisterly disgust. "Tano asked me, while he thought Thomas was outside, if we would be here tonight."

Crap. I felt guilty that Thomas had to find out that I was doing other things, fun things, that he as a friend should be invited to. Should I call him now? I felt hypocritical because I was doing the same sneaking around. I figured it was for a few more weeks only. I really wanted to enjoy his company, but if not for the inconvenience of still being married. Deciding on remaining mum on the topic, I warned Ty and Angelica to put Tano on notice. The rest of night was doused in my disappointment, so I headed home early.

Chapter 12

Yes, I'm from Guam

November turned into December, and I missed my parents a lot over the holidays, especially on dad's 60th birthday which fell on Thanksgiving. I spent turkey day with my Uncle Tony, Ty and Angelica. Thomas noticeably kept his distance.

I wasn't sure about my Christmas plans. That would be answered for me soon enough and in a way I never expected.

Thomas and I carried on like we weren't spying on each other, hiding in the dark during karaoke nights. I was aware that a hooded man, sitting in the spy booth was present. Even Mr. Kang played along with me and gave me the okay sign when he knew Thomas was there. Mr. Kang was on my side, so even though Thomas asked Mr. Kang to keep his visits a secret, he was none the wiser. I decided to make him squirm. This karaoke cloak and dagger game was fun.

I selected the same Jason Mraz song Thomas sang weeks before. I stepped onto the stage boldly. I wore a pair of black linen pants and an eggplant colored cashmere sweater. I playfully held my wine colored pearls and locked the heels of my black boots on the bar stool ready for this rollercoaster ride. I told Angelica that I would be singing Thomas's favorite song. From our table, she gave me a wink. When the familiar guitar melody started, I could see Thomas shift his body sideways. His face was still hooded, but I had his attention. I watched his knee bob up and down, double time to the beat. I shooed my nerves off like they were flies and imagined that I was auditioning for Thomas's heart. He didn't know that that was my motivation, but I had to throw the guy a bone or something. I didn't want to lose him. The New Year was on the horizon. I was about to go from Nix Farmer back to Phoenix Lizama.

"This is dedicated to a dear friend of mine. I miss him so much. Thomas." My voice started low and soft, then swelled. My heart was going to burst as the song escalated. I kept my eyes closed for most of the song, imagining Thomas's beautiful face as the sun shone behind him. I surveyed the near distance for him and he stayed where I last saw him. I almost lost focus when I glanced at Mr. Kang behind the bar clapping out of sync with the beat of the song and swaying side to side which was reminiscent of my mom's dancing.

At the last few lines of the song, I clutched my pearls dramatically with my left hand and sang from my gut.

"I want to be your Thomas!" A guy at the bar yelled. I was more accustomed to the applause and then curtsied.

A small movement in the dark beyond grabbed my attention. Thomas stood now at the rear exit. I made out his lean silhouette highlighted by the street light. He had his hood off now and looked like he wanted to be desperately noticed by me. I averted my eyes and exited stage left. I saw his retreating figure and after telling Ty and Angelica where I was headed I grabbed my clutch purse and made chase.

Thomas must have parked away from the bar like I typically did. I looked up and down the street and saw nothing familiar. The chilly night air slapped me into reality. Had I lost him for good? I summoned *the force* and walked briskly north on 5th Avenue. I had to find him. The synthesized melody of a Foreigner song faded as I got further away from the bar, left with only the staccato tapping of my heels. I could have called out for him, but I didn't want to seem desperate or draw attention to myself. Inhaling the cold night air, my body warmed up in my sweater.

It was too quiet and dark, and the little hairs on my neck prickled. *Let's not get crazy and get hurt*, I could hear my parents' warning. I gave up my search to return to the bar, but I stopped in my tracks.

There was a figure in the distance, veiled in the darkness. The shadows played tricks on my eyes and I believed it was Bradley and I froze. I knew he was out of state, but my mind translated this menace as my ex. The dark figure moved. The sound of his shuffling feet became louder. He made his way in my direction. I was aware that the streetlights on the path I chose weren't on. *Stupid move, Phoenix!* I instinctively removed my long string of pearls, imagining this fiend choking me with it. I could possibly use it like a weapon, testing its weight in my hands. I straightened my posture and walked with purpose. Criminals only attacked women who looked meek and easy to subdue right? I clenched my fists and readjusted the angle of my path. I didn't want this man, who was about ten feet away now to think that I was scared.

I strengthened the hold on my clutch purse. I only had a fifty dollar bill if the fool was going to mug me. The purse also housed my Blackberry, and instead of worrying about the purse or cash being stolen, I worried about my recording of Thomas's singing. Thomas's first hand written note tucked in my Hello Kitty wallet was also a treasure. I had been carrying it around like a security blanket for the past two months. I panicked when the dark figure adjusted his walk towards me. I picked up my pace, breathing quickly, prepping my body for the possibility that I would need to start running. I decided to look the man in the eyes and scowl. Hopefully that would scare him off. No dice. I kept my purse on the right side of my body away from his view, but I saw his line of vision and either he was checking out my pants or looking for my purse. I called out to Ty, knowing that he wouldn't be able to hear me since I was a good fifty yards away from the side entrance. The menace stopped for a second and looked at the direction of the bar. I took that opportunity to make a run for it. I had only mastered walking in designer high heeled boots recently, and running was a bit more complex. Hell, I probably looked as graceful as a moose running in steeltoe boots. I found it humorous how quick my priorities shifted from wanting Thomas to wanting not to be killed, mugged or raped.

I was close to the side entrance because I could smell the stench of the dumpster. I heard this huntsman's quick pace behind me and braced myself, in case he decided to yank my purse or throw me into the large metal container.

Just as I was about to round the corner and find safety, two large, strong capable hands grabbed both my arms from behind. I yelled as loudly as I could, but unless someone was entering the side like what I or Thomas had been doing, no one in the bar would hear me.

When they say your life flashes before your eyes right before you die, it's true. I had images of my dad and mom and baby brother. Bradley weaseled his way in there. Even dark chocolate made an appearance. Rachel would be pissed if she found out that she came after my vision of my almost ex-husband and my biggest vice. That led me to Thomas and his smile. Would I get to see that smile again? My pulse thundered in my head and then I collapsed.

Before I realized it, my back was on the pavement, the wind knocked out of me. A dull pain radiated on my skull from where it thudded on the ground. The beast straddled me and I continued to clutch my purse. He placed his forearm on my neck, but luckily I pressed my chin to my chest before he could choke me. As he sat on my hips, I was repulsed and bucked. This guy was heavy. If he wanted my purse, he didn't reach out for it or demand it. Did he want me? To do foul things? I freaked and shook my body to no avail. I decided to hit him on the head with my purse, but the less than two pounds of leather didn't do much but irritate him. The pearls! I did my best Wonder Woman lasso reenactment but it only swatted his ear. He grabbed the weak weapon and flung it to the where the light bordered the darkness.

"You are sooo hot," the jerk growled near my face, he was the most pervy, dirtiest devil I had ever encountered. His grimy teeth were so close to my face, I gagged. I quickly assessed his physical traits in the dimly lit area where we played twisted twister. He was Caucasian, about 40 years old or more, looked to be green eyes in that unshaven face, alcohol on his breath and brown or black hair. A name tag would have been convenient now. He wore an old Padres baseball cap and a Member's Only jacket. *Really?*

How could I even think of laughing at this moment was beyond me. A minute had probably passed, but if felt like so much longer. I lifted my pelvis in an upward thrust suddenly and let's just call him *Kaduku* man, which means crazy in Chamorro, fell off me to his side. He was probably only 5'5" and 170 pounds. I was taller than him and I wished I could do some fancy *Jet Li* moves. I pressed on his stomach and tried to get to my feet. I called out for help again. Nobody. *Kaduku* couldn't get up quick enough so I took the opportunity to kick him in the face. *Hard.* Real hard, with my boots. *Tae Kwon Do hard.* I heard a crunch and his nose spewed blood and then his whimper turned into a roar. He spat curse words and spit sprayed and before I turned to run, he reached into his back pocket and pulled out a switch blade. I backed up and just my luck I hit the dumpster. Why didn't I run? I took five seconds too long to congratulate myself and enjoy the byproduct of my kick.

I apologized and pleaded with him. He demanded my purse then. I held it close to my body. He wasn't going to get it. It wasn't the money. It was the mementos of Thomas that I couldn't part with. The jerk lunged after the purse. I sidestepped and the *Bruce Lee* in me used the single aversion move Pharaoh taught me. His momentum landed him in the dumpster. He hunched over grabbing his head, knife still in hand. Stupid me, I should have started running, yet again, but I so wanted to kick him in the nuts. So, I did.

Kaduku buckled forward, but took a swipe at my leg and cut my pants. Darn, that was a hundred bucks wasted. This time, maybe his survival instinct or male pride kicked in, so he leapt to his feet and lunged at my purse again. His knife cut through my sweater and slashed my flesh. Fire erupted on my body from the spot I was stabbed. The heat of my blood trickled down my leg and *Kaduku* looked stunned at his work, almost sorry.

My right hip was cut, I wasn't sure how deep, but all of a sudden *Kaduku's* knife clanked to the ground and so did he. I grabbed my side and ran, finally, well more like limped to the side entrance. I kept pressure on my cut and was mindful enough to move my purse to my other hand. Didn't want it stained by blood.

My attacker didn't follow and I staggered into the bar, stunned. Mr. Kang was the first to notice me. I sat at the booth, breathing shallow, taking stock in how I felt. Was I going to pass out? Tano and Angelica looked in my direction when the person on the mic saw me enter and stopped singing, and yelled, "Holy Shit!" I told Tano that the attacker was outside by the dumpster. He ran out to find him despite my protest. Meanwhile, Angelica was on the phone with 911.

I would later find out that Thomas had been driving by when he saw me being chased. He was the one who brought the attacker to the ground. Tano helped in detaining the bastard for the cops. By the time the ambulances arrived, one for me and one for *Kaduku*—I had to explain which injuries were from me and which happened when he was being *detained* by Thomas and Ty.

The rest of the night was a blur. As news crews showed up to the bar, Mr. Kang was all too quick to provide details of the crime. I lay back in the ambulance and cried. I could have been killed tonight and I finally wanted to be with my mom and dad. I wanted to go to Guam.

"Fee-nux. That her name," Mr. Kang stated, butchering my moniker. "She from Goowan." Poor guy was making me sound like an alien from another planet. The reporter was confused to say the least, so Tano and Angelica jumped in to set the record straight.

Bulbs flashed and a camera man was outside the ambulance door. I averted my eyes and covered my face with my beloved clutch purse. "I'm with her." I heard Thomas's frantic voice. "Her name is Phoenix Lizama. I'm her boyfriend for Christ sakes!" After hearing his last declaration, I tried to sit up and regretted it instantly. The medic held my shoulder down and ordered me to relax. She kept pressure on my wound as Thomas hopped into the ambulance. He looked spent and disheveled, but still rewarded me with a smile. His eyes glistened with tears.

On the ride to Naval Hospital, he filled me in on his heroic deed. I scanned his body for cuts, but he was unscathed and more gorgeous than ever. His cheeks were flushed bright pink and his constantly furrowed brow was oddly sexy to me. Us both being alive was sexy.

I suffered a three inch gash on my right hip, to the bone, so luckily no internal organs were punctured. Thank you child-bearing hips. For a split second, I thought if I was still thirty pounds heavier, it would have only been a paper cut and less serious. *It's amazing how the dumb, old me still crept up in my thoughts.* My leg was fine, but doctors wanted to keep me for a few days to observe the concussion I apparently suffered when I was knocked to the ground. I didn't know how I would explain this to my parents, but to my relief, my Uncle Tony did the talking for me. He arrived with Ty and Angelica just after I got my cut cleaned and patched. Painkillers, a marvel of modern medicine got me through it.

Throughout my grogginess, Thomas stayed by my side holding my hand when I requested his. He assisted the cops with a witness statement. He had been driving by when he saw me kick at the assailant. He left his car running and ran over. He had tears in his eyes as he looked at me and then back to the officer when he explained that he couldn't get there in time to stop the guy from cutting me, like it was his fault. I spoke to my parents, keeping my voice strong and steady. I assured them that I just had a small cut and I was fine. Dad didn't seem convinced. I didn't tell them that I needed to stay in the hospital for a few days. They didn't need the added stress.

Ty was interviewed by the local news and proudly said he was my cousin. He gave the reporters my maiden name and added that we were from Guam. I didn't want to be interviewed, but it got out there somehow that I had busted the jerk's nose and did a number on his frank and beans. The next morning, ten large bouquets of flowers later, I saw the footage for myself. I cringed as my professional picture from The Lure Company employee profiles was pasted on the T.V. Now, that wasn't smart. Would have to find a new job? *Cover blown*. I had to remind myself to kill Angelica, since I knew she had direct access to the photos. I'm sure Bruce didn't approve the leak.

Once it hit CNN that a San Diego woman, formerly from Guam, averted a robbery and possible sexual assault, my parents called constantly. After my brother was reassured that I was okay, he gloated that his big sister was an ass-kicker. He said I could come home and become an ultimate fighter like him. *Right*.

"Did you really break the asshole's nose?" He asked excitedly.

"Yes." I stated plainly, suppressing a smile.

"Awesome! And did you bust his nuts." My laugh was cut short by the dull pain on my hip. I was even afraid to sneeze, cough, pass gas or get constipated. Pharaoh heard my groan and dropped the questions. He did ask if I would be coming home and I really didn't know. Was this trauma going to send me packing to the island home that was ten times safer than here? I had a lot to think about, someone special to consider. I looked over at Thomas, who was catching up on sleep in the single chair in my hospital room. He had stubble on his chin, and his hair uncombed. But he was still so beautiful to me. My hero.

Pharaoh had never said he loved me, although he showed it often. But that day, he told me twice. And so did my mom and dad. I just about lost it, since we met our quota of *lovey dovey-ness* for the next year. We weren't a family of *I love yous*, and I was happy that that was changing now.

Thomas canceled his drive up north with his sister. He reassured Tamara that I was fine and would recover. She had meetings she couldn't miss. She visited me once with a bouquet of white carnations. Our first official meeting in a hospital was not how envisioned it.

After another assessment, the docs were satisfied that I didn't suffer a brain injury. Thank goodness. I would hate to ruin any memories I had, especially of Thomas. Bradley was another story.

Thomas had gone to my condo and brought back clothes and toiletries. It didn't bother me that he would be in my home without me there, it bothered me that it had to happen under these circumstances. I read over the wound care documentation. I felt fine except for when I moved suddenly. There was so much to think about with this story going national and the prosecution side of things. It wasn't the way I wanted to start December.

I begged Thomas to get back to work, or do whatever he normally did on a Monday. I felt bad that he lost his weekend to yet another drama with me. He smiled my smile and said warmly, "Phoenix, *you* are my business."

Thomas was set to drive me home. It was a good thing his Prius was low to the ground, so I could just use gravity to get in. After signing a few more documents at the nurse's station, Thomas grabbed hold of my wheelchair. It was a distance to the lobby and he still had to get his car from the parking garage practically three cities away. He rolled me quietly to the elevators, sometimes playing with my hair, or keeping his hand on my shoulder. Thomas bent over to whisper something to me, when the silver elevator doors squeaked open. Bradley stood in the metal box, hat in his hands, the Farmer stitched nametag as plain as day on his uniform. He looked thinner and older and his vacant stare flickered from anger to confusion to shock as he took in the sight of me in the chair and Thomas intimately at my face. Thomas stood and became still. Bradley held the elevator doors open as they creaked to close.

"Going down?" Bradley asked with a scowl.

Thomas pushed me into the elevator, cutting through the tension our triad created. Bradley remained in his corner. I hadn't expected him back until the following week. A surge of fear coursed through me when I realized how destructive it could have been if Bradley went to the condo to find Thomas there.

Bradley cleared his throat and spoke in a weathered voice, sounding tired and stressed. "How are you, Nix? I mean, it's all over the news and stuff."

"I'm fine. Just a small gash, no brain injury, so all is good." I reassured him, glad to break the awkward quiet.

Thomas was quiet and did not make physical contact with me.

Genuine concern danced across Bradley's face. "Where were you cut?" I touched my hip gently. "Have you been discharged?" I'm pretty sure I knew what he really wanted to know. Was I leaving with Thomas to his place?

"Yes, I'm going back to Uncle Tony's. I just want to get rest and heal."

"Is *he* taking you home?" Progress, I thought. He acknowledged Thomas's presence.

"Yes." I looked up at Bradley, irritated.

"Well, Sergeant Reynolds is downstairs and can give us a ride. He drove me straight here from the airport." The recruiter must have told Bradley about the emergency.

"Did he arrange for you to get home?"

"Well," Bradley hesitated. The elevator doors opened. Thomas pushed me into the fresh air. "Actually, Jem told him."

"Oh." I didn't know if this was good or bad. But I left it alone.

"Yeah, so. We can take you to your uncle's."

"Doesn't Sergeant Reynolds have a Hummer?" I stated with exasperation.

"Yeah, so?" Bradley was really dense. I had to explain that I wasn't about to climb into a tank, and risk having my wound open up. I had a deep enough cut that I got dissolving stitches internally then dermabond, basically crazy glue to seal the cut shut. Bradley finally realized my dilemma.

Bradley waited with me while Thomas ran to get his car. I knew it would be about ten minutes of hell, even though the wintry winds were chill. Thomas reminded me that he parked at the furthest structure, this hospital was extremely busy. By the speed of his run, I almost thought he *was* a superhuman vampire.

Bradley had texted me several times during this last training cycle. I had only responded to the ones about the house or bills. I decided now was a good time as any to ask for the divorce again.

"Bradley, how long are you in town for?"

"Why?" He tried to sound ignorant. Maybe he was.

"You know why." I countered quickly. "I've got the divorce papers drawn up. You just have to agree and sign. Irreconcilable differences. It sure beats adultery, right?"

"Are you doing this because you're with Thomas?" He asked sadness dripping from his voice.

"No. I'm doing this because we were never a perfect fit. You cheating," I brought my voice down, "and this Army reserves thing, that's irrelevant, really. I'm a different person. You were the catalyst for that and I should actually thank you."

Bradley crunched his eyebrows together, confused, I was sure. I wanted him to see the positive of letting me go.

"Did you tell the news that your name was Phoenix Lizama and not Farmer?" I wasn't getting through to him. I actually felt sorry for him. He had his pride and that was preventing him from seeing the bigger picture.

"That wasn't me. This whole attack has been blown way out of proportion. Slow news day in San Diego, that's it."

"Well, I'm glad you're safe. I'll be here until after the New Year. Sarge pulled some strings for this emergency and I was able to leave training and complete it the next cycle."

"Will you be deployed anytime soon?" I was genuinely concerned. It was a relief to be able to speak with him like an adult. He said that because he needed more training, he wouldn't be deployable until maybe the end of spring. Bradley actually looked forward to heading to war. I was surprised when he shared that he was thinking of joining the army active duty. I thought, *whatever makes you happy, as long as we get the divorce finalized.*

"Maybe we shouldn't divorce yet since if I die in Iraq or wherever I'm sent, you—still being my wife would get a ton of money." I couldn't believe he was joking like that!

"Bradley, that's not funny." Thomas finally drove up and exited his car. I saw Bradley smirk. He thought hybrids were for pussies, *his words*, not mine. Bradley asked me if it was okay to speak with Thomas. He said this loud enough for Thomas to get wind.

Thomas looked from me to Bradley and nodded. I guess they had some man things to discuss. Their conversation was briefer than I thought between the man from my past and my friend from the here and now. It ended with Bradley offering his hand to Thomas. They shook firmly, but didn't smile. The mild standoff was over. The tension in the air dissipated.

Bradley approached me and Thomas waited by the open passenger door keeping his lovely platinum eyes on me. His face was relaxed, a small smile danced on his mouth. Bradley knelt in front of me and looked me square in the eyes. He had tears in his own eyes and I stopped the compulsion to want to comfort him. That wasn't my job anymore. To passerbys, it might have looked like Bradley was proposing to me. I finally got him to kneel, but the circumstances were so ass backwards. When I was proposed to, his mother did it. She slid a ring to me, her mother's ring. It was a simple barbecue dinner. She said, "Here, use this. It's special and then you don't have to spend money." Bradley smiled, mouth full of food, "So, will you?" And that was how we started our journey to be husband and wife. Now, I was about to be released like a wild animal and I couldn't wait to run.

"Thomas seems like a good kid. I'm sorry for how things," a rush of quiet tears streamed down his face. He sucked it up when Sergeant Reynolds's Hummer rounded the corner, making his presence known with the obscene rumbling. Thomas's Prius looked like a toy car next to the monstrosity. "I'm sorry for everything I did and whatever I didn't do. I'm happy for you, really. Shit. I always knew you were hot stuff. At least I can say you were my first wife, right?" I was going to get my wish. He finally agreed to divorce me and I was at a place in my life where I accepted that with both arms, wide open. Thomas turned his head away when he saw me lean over and give my soon-to-be ex-husband his last kiss on the cheek.

"Thank you, Bradley." I whispered.

Bradley rose, "We'll always have Guam, right?" And then, his face returned to a stone cold soldier.

He was right. Bradley wheeled me slowly to Thomas. They shook hands again looking almost like friends. Thomas took my hand as I negotiated getting into his car. He closed my door gently, smiling the whole time. We both were. We drove off, leaving Bradley on the curb with my empty wheelchair.

Chapter 13
Our Two Dads

It took a week to feel normal physically, and two weeks more for the divorce papers to be filed and official, helping with my emotional healing as well. In that time, Thomas and I met up without hiding, the friendship clause still intact. As much as I wanted to strip him down in all senses of the phrase, I was too busy doing work from home and healing. I also had to deal with being recognized as the girl from Guam who kicked her assailant's ass. It was nice, but I never wanted that kind of attention. Mr. Kang even named a special on his menu for me, *Phoenix Fried Rice*—a *kimchee* fried rice dish. My mom would have loved that, and Rachel too.

The last straw in this whirlwind of attention was when I stopped by Bag It and a group of uniformed men recognized me. They bombarded me with questions. I answered each inquiry curtly, but then someone made a vulgar comment about my skills in bed and I froze. A strong fight or flight debate raged in my brain and I suddenly found myself in my car. Enveloped in its safety, I focused on my breathing and closed my eyes.

Thomas knocked on my window gently, but I hopped in my seat. I guess my nerves were still rattled from the attack, in fact, I knew it. Hands in the air after reading my reaction, he apologized and asked to sit in the car with me.

"Are you okay?" He rubbed my shoulder. He hadn't heard the disgusting comment and when I told him he grabbed the door handle, ready to confront. It took some convincing, but he stayed by my side. I twisted my rearview mirror to check my eyes when I noticed my hair. The caramel blond color of my hair had grown out and my roots revealed its truth.

"I really need to get my hair back to brown. Brunettes don't get attacked as often as blondes, right?" I said this more for me than for Thomas—but I felt I was withdrawing into a shell and I didn't want to.

Thomas had been patient and even though my divorce was official, he didn't ask about it. I really wanted to jump his bones, taste his lips for the first time, but *Kaduku* broke my spirit. I recoiled on life, but I didn't want to lose sight of Thomas as this happened. He anchored me to reality somehow.

The evening I sang for Thomas, the second time I attempted to let him into my life turned out tragic. Were the heavens trying to dissuade me from being happy? Like Dorothy in the Wizard of Oz, I felt like my house was about to land after a twister and hit me squarely on my thighs, which no longer rubbed, mind you—but, was I the witch in my own story?

It didn't help that in another week I would have to find a new place to live. Thomas invited me in a round about way to stay with him and Tano, but I knew that was a bad idea. As much as the feelings I was having for Thomas were becoming I dare say, love, I didn't want to jump into a situation again where I was so attached to a man—even a man as glorious and intelligent and kind as Thomas.

Thomas pulled out his phone. I must have been so lost in my funky thoughts, sitting in silence, that he let me be.

"Hey, sis, it's me." He smiled at me and I felt a wave of comfort lift my spirits. "Tom-Tom of course. Yeah, I'm in the parking lot." I looked at his gorgeous profile, studying the details as he ran his long fingers through his honey hair. I marveled at how his smile could ignite the beauty of his face. I stared at his lips as he spoke and for me time stood still.

"All clear. Let's go."

"Huh?" I got lost in my reverie that I didn't catch what just happened.

"Where? What?"

"All clear from Tam. I've got the afternoon off." Just then the men walked out of the shop. Thomas's face turned dark, his eyes menacing. I saw them in my peripheral vision and instinctively buried my face in his chest. I breathed in slowly the luscious scent that was Thomas. He stroked my hair so softly that I thought I dreamt it. The boisterous chatting of the men faded away and I felt his tension dissipate. His breathing slowed and his heartbeat followed. I wanted to fall asleep in his arms. I felt the lightest kiss on my head and looked up at him. His face transformed, his eyes large and serious. A slow smile danced on his lips and I responded in the like. Thomas stroked my face gently, his hands warm. "Let me drive."

His words were like magic setting me in motion. "Where are we going?" I was suddenly in the passenger seat, nerves and giddiness shooting me forward in time.

"I'm taking you to find yourself."

"What?"

"The Divas. They're going to take care of you this fine afternoon." Before I could object, we were on highway 5 headed to Pacific Beach. I cringed at possibly meeting up with Chazzer again. Thomas took care of that by going in to scope the area. Chazzer was off, by the graces of the Spa Gods. Thomas spoke to the stylist and got me an immediate appointment. I later found out that once he said my name, my recognizable maiden name, the young lady accepted the walk-in without question.

"My lady?" He held his hand out for me.

"Thomas, what are we doing, a massage?" I was about to argue that my injury was still tender.

"No, let's bring back the Chamorrita side of you." I smiled widely when I realized that I would finally see my brown hair again. That should ward off unwanted attention from guys, I hoped.

Thomas entertained my request to get himself a pedicure. He was so amazed at how awesome and smooth his feet turned out, that he asked me why I didn't tell him about this chick secret sooner. The girls in the salon were thoroughly entranced by my friend. I didn't mind that there were three beautiful salon divas fawning over Thomas—like Bradley, the green monster that sat in me divorced me too.

The colorist leaned into me and after complimenting me on my *girl-power-kicking-of-the-jerk's ass* at the bar, she asked to see my scar. Feeling like Harriet Potter with an awkwardly and sexily placed scar from *Voldemort*, I obliged. Thomas craned his neck and got an eyeful too. *Good thing I wore my pretty panties*, I mused, as I gingerly pulled my pants down past my hip bone. The almost "S" shaped scar was raised, still pink and angry. Cyndi—as her nametag indicated complimented me on my "boyfriend."

"You do realize that your boyfriend is a dead ringer for Edward Cullen." She whispered.

"You mean Robert Pattinson? No. Nope. Don't see the resemblance." Cyndi's eyes opened wide and she guffawed. Thomas smiled as he pretended not to hear. "He's more, hmm, a young Nathan Fillion."

"Now, I know that guy and I love *Firefly*." Thomas said.

After all that primping, I actually felt normal. "Thank you, Thomas." I said as I reevaluated my image.

"You look beautiful." At his compliment, the girls made a collective sound like you do when you see a cute puppy.

Awwwww. And he treated too, someone added. I looked at Thomas in disbelief as I reached for my purse.

"Thomas, you didn't have to do that."

"I know. But, I wanted to do that." He smiled and winked.

"Okay, coffee for the next three months on me." I said.

"I'll take that deal, if I can hang with you for the next three months." He offered his elbow and I accepted like we were about to embark on our prom. Thomas's warm body pressed into mine as we left he salon. I paid for our coffees and we sat for a few minutes in the car. I enjoyed the warm cup as I gazed at Thomas.

"So am I?" Thomas asked, breaking our easy silence.

"Are you? Are you what?" I smiled.

"Your friend or boyfriend?"

"Um. Why do you ask? I mean, you're my friend and you're a boy, right?"

"I ask because when the Diva said 'your boyfriend,' you didn't correct her."

"I didn't?" I guess I didn't correct her, or the idea of Thomas as my boyfriend was gelling more and more in my mind.

"It's okay. I'll take that non-protest of the word boyfriend any day." He blushed. "Shall we..." and he leaned into my face, a flicker of mischief there... "karaoke?"

I won't lie. It was a kissable moment, but he was a man of honor. *And, when did "karaoke" become a verb*, I wondered. I hadn't been to Pass the Mic in two weeks. And, despite the attack, I heard business was booming from Ty and Angelica. I wouldn't be surprised if Mr. Kang had Angelica frame my mug so he could place it behind the bar for all to gawk at. I wrangled up my fear, tucked it into a bag and decided to go for it. I deserved some fun with Thomas, didn't I? Karaoke wasn't a kiss, but it would do for now. "Let's karaoke." I finally said.

I invited Ty and Angelica, it was Friday after all. Thomas said he would call Tano and the girl he was currently dating.

It was going to be a great party.

As we cruised, I did another bold thing. I pulled out my phone and cued up Thomas's song. Yes, the illegal taping of the Mraz love song. We drove in happy silence, then I hit play. He heard the singing, which didn't do hearing it live justice.

A wry smile on his beautiful face, he said, "What the heck was that?" He didn't sound angry, but amused to my relief.

"I have something to admit." I started. "I'm a Thomas-o-holic and I've been getting a hit every Sunday for the past few months." *God, that sounded lascivious,* I thought. "I mean, your karaoke, your singing, not you, of course."

Thomas laughed and placed his hand on my thigh. I took his hand in mine and kept it there. I explained that I was going to the bar incognito just to hear one song every Sunday. I told him every song he sang in order from the last six weeks. He blushed bright red and shifted nervously in his seat. As he raised his right hand out of mine to sweep away the amber strands of hair from his eyes, he asked nervously if I had a recording for every week. He breathed a sigh of relief when I said it was just the one. Thomas reached into his jacket pocket and pulled out his IPhone. He asked me to find track 10 on his recordings. I had a sinking feeling, and then, I heard *me*. I sang *Dolphins*. There was a lot of ambient noise, but that was me. He had the whole song recorded start to finish. I punched his arm and he whimpered, then his laughter boomed in the car. I joined him without jiggling too much since my S scar wasn't too happy. My singing didn't sound too shabby, I thought to myself. Maybe I could indeed hold a tune.

It was almost eight o'clock when we pulled up to Pass the Mic. The bar wasn't at capacity and I was able to walk by Mr. Kang unnoticed with my new coffee colored hair. I loved how it felt and the lightness of having five inches chopped off felt great too. Thomas complimented me to no end when it was done, saying he liked chocolate better than caramel anyway. Mr. Kang hugged me tight enough to make me cringe. Thomas my protector, swiftly asked Mr. Kang to lighten up, already undoing his arms around me. After ten apologies, Mr. Kang patted Thomas's back. "She look good. You do this?" Gesturing to my hair. "She look happy and you look happy. We all happy, no?" Mr. Kang made me miss my dad and mom.

We practically had the bar to ourselves, so after our first round of drinks and my trademark fried rice. I reminded Thomas that he owed me a song, now that he knew I was there in the audience. He didn't hesitate and passed a slip written with the number he already memorized to Mr. Kang. The rest of our party would join us after nine, so it was nice to be sitting dead center by the stage, ready for Thomas to sing, just for me.

A familiar melody started and Thomas cleared his throat. *He can't be nervous*, I thought, but maybe he was. *Angel Eyes* by Jeff Healey was a beautiful, romantic way to start the evening. I swayed with his singing and wasn't self-conscious when he made eye contact and gestured cheesily to me throughout the song. During a guitar break in the song, I glanced at Mr. Kang and he held up a lit match and moved out of beat. The match burned to his fingers and he flung it on the ground and started stomping. Thomas and I shared a giggle and then he finished the ballad.

I gave Thomas a standing ovation and Mr. Kang hooted and hollered at the bar. Several college students walked in and now the audience grew by seven. My song was next and a light veil of nervousness fell over me. I wanted to retreat to the booth I first sang at for anonymity, but I reminded myself that I was going to sing for Thomas and him alone. I handed my song slip to a smiling Mr. Kang.

Thomas put a chair on the stage. I wasn't going to be belting out a song anyway, opting for a subtle song. Alana Davis's *32 Flavors*, started with the lyrics right away. Any song about Phoenixes was automatically a winner in my book.

I maintained eye contact with Thomas and felt the song until the end. Angelica and Ty arrived and sat at our usual booth while the applause started. I beamed as they all stood and applauded me. I tipped an invisible hat to them and took a small bow. I smiled knowing that this was my family.

The fun night stretched into the wee hours of the morning. We bid our farewells to the couples and Thomas and I walked side by side to my car. If this was a romantic movie, I guess it would have been acceptable, heck even expected for us to kiss passionately and end up in bed at his place. He stood at the passenger side door and I gave myself a hug because of my exposed arms. I hadn't expected to be out so late and I didn't bring my jacket. Thomas wrapped me in his brown leather jacket, then kept his hands in his jean pockets and fidgeted side to side. We were like a pair of nervous teenagers about to have our first kiss.

It was strange to think that at a quarter of a century in age, I had only kissed one other person in this world. In this vast interesting world of seven billion people. Being one of the many blessed to be from Guam with a population of 180,000, I chose one to latch onto—the wrong one. Only to travel to California to find THE One.

"Cold?" Thomas's teeth chattered.

"Yes. Cold." I agreed. He opened my door. Our chance to seal it with a kiss was thwarted by the weather. I hid my infamous clutch purse under the passenger seat, a new habit I formed after being assaulted. I immediately checked my Blackberry for the time, just as Thomas got into the driver's seat. Three A.M. and I had five missed calls in the last three hours, and three texts. I checked my voicemail, a different type of cold fell down my spine.

One after another, it was the frantic voice of my mom to call Pharaoh's cell, or my brother himself in a gruff voice demanding that I call home. I noticed distinctly that my dad did not call and my fingers couldn't work fast enough on the tiny keys as I dialed home. Thomas watched me quietly and didn't ask questions knowing I had no answers yet.

"Phoenix!" Pharaoh's voice was a squeal. "Where the hell have you been for the past three hours?" Thomas started the car and turned on the heat. I braced my heart for bad news.

"What's wrong, Pharaoh? Is it dad?" My brother went quiet, providing the answer I needed.

"Are you home? Are you driving? I don't want you freaking out."

"Tell me already!" I could hear my mom in the background speaking in Korean. I had no idea if they were home or at a hospital.

"Dad, he, um he had a massive stroke tonight." Pharaoh's voice cracked and it reminded me of when he was a toddler and upset over a broken toy. I suddenly regretted not going home. Maybe I would have seen him and the turmoil of my divorce and the mugging would not have added to his stress levels. There were a lot of maybes running around my head. For Thomas's benefit, I repeated the news. Dad suffered a stroke after dinner at home. Mom was there, called Pharaoh before the ambulance. I wasn't sure if that was wise, but I wasn't going to be upset with her for that.

"Is he at Memorial or Naval?" Worry had me on the edge of panic. "Is he conscious?"

"Memorial, yeah, but his left side's affected. The docs said it was good that mom crushed aspirin and forced him to eat it. He collapsed in the bathroom when mom found him."

The vision of my dad on the cold white tile on the bathroom floor started my tears. Thomas rubbed my back. "Dad didn't want me to call you and worry you." Pharaoh continued.

"That's bullshit." I whimpered. "Thanks for calling anyway. I want to come home." I looked at Thomas and his serene understanding face was a comfort. He caressed my cheek and wiped away my tears.

My mom got on the phone and was emotional as she repeated everything Pharaoh just told me. I listened patiently, hearing it a second time made the grave situation more real. I thanked mom for taking care of dad and promised that I would be on the earliest flight home. Mom was about to argue for dad's sake. Dad didn't want me traveling, perhaps thinking I was still healing from the attack. No one in my immediate family had major medical problems. Now my dad and I have made hospital visits within the same month. It's not something I wanted to have in common with him.

"Thomas, can you please drive me home." I wasn't sure how he would be getting home himself, but I did more of the drinking and I wasn't in any condition to drive, especially with my emotions running high. I had a lot to plan for and needed to start right away. If ever I needed Thomas's patience and understanding, it was now.

"Let me go with you." Thomas said.

"Okay, home? Yes, can you please drive me home? Then, you can take my car home with you or the shop or whatever."

"No." He turned my chin so he could look at my face, my horrible puffy eyes. I understood him finally.

"Oh, Thomas. I can't ask you to do that. I can't ask you to follow me home, to Guam. I mean, I really need to focus on my dad." And how would I explain this beautiful creature to my family, I thought.

Thomas nodded, looking so dejected. Score another one for Phoenix. He was quiet all the way to my condo.

I didn't have much experience or knowledge about strokes. After securing my ticket, I researched. I had to know if dad would make it out of this. I couldn't imagine my mom without my dad. A pang of guilt ran through me because my parents were banking on Bradley and me providing them grandchildren. I went two steps forward and three steps back in that department. I thought of Thomas and wondered if my dad would ever meet this stellar man.

My flight was scheduled for Sunday morning, which would give me a day to pack all my stuff and put it into storage until I could get back.

I received regular texts from Pharaoh about dad. I even e-mailed Bradley, since he was visiting an uncle up north in Whittier for the weekend. It was more of a way for him to give me space since the divorce dust was settling. He had a right to know nonetheless.

Thomas had called twice already. He usually didn't pressure me, but I understood how he was feeling since I was leaving the next day. I needed to talk to him, probably more for his sake than mine. I had so much on my mind and this blooming thing with Thomas was on the back burner yet again. I'm not sure if I was extra skeptical about romance in general or freaked out by the fact that every time I made a decision to go for it with Thomas, something tragic happened.

First, it was the almost brawl. Second, the stabbing and third, my dad had a stroke. It was all tied to the Pass the Mic karaoke bar too. I loved that place, but after three incidences I was getting superstitious all of a sudden. There were too many coincidences for my taste. When did my life become such a soap opera?

"Hey, Thomas."

"Phoenix. How are you? And your dad of course?" Thomas's kind voice floated through my phone and calmed me. My daddy laid in a hospital bed and it wasn't fair for me to be playing Who Wants to Date a Hot Sandwich Slinging Screenwriter.

"I'm fine. He's stable and I fly out tomorrow. I really want to hear his voice, but," I got choked up.

"I know, Phoenix. Did you need me to do anything for you? Tamara has unlocked the shackles for the weekend." Thomas was enthusiastic.

"No. I'm meeting Ty and Angelica to get my stuff into storage."

"Why didn't you tell me?" Thomas's anger was palpable. "I can be there to help too."

"Oh, well, I really thought you were heading north for the weekend, with the new shops and stuff." I lied.

"No." There was an awkward pause. How many times have I made Thomas feel like he was just on the outskirts of Phoenix town? It really wasn't fair, but I felt strongly that I wasn't able to move on with him, at least not just yet. Bradley had offered his life and love to me on loan, it wasn't an unconditional gift. I feared I was doing the same to Thomas.

"Thomas? You still there?" I knew he was, I could hear him breathing rhythmically. Soft music played in the background and I wondered for a second where he was.

"I'm always here. You know that." He sounded like a whimpering puppy. And I felt like the jerk who kicked that cute puppy.

"Thomas. I, um, I don't mean to make you feel put out. I just need to wrap my head around my dad's situation. I mean, you understand, losing your dad and everything."

"You're right. I can't be forcing myself into your life when you aren't ready for it. But, Phoenix, just know that." He paused, desperation dripped from his voice, "Please, just know that I feel…I care deeply for you. Okay?"

"I know. I appreciate it. Really. If all this wasn't happening I would be treating you to a massage and pedicure right now. The Diva girls miss you, I'm sure." Thomas finally let up and laughed a bit.

Thomas shared his dad's story and how he passed away. I found myself gripping my shirt over my heart like one would when watching a movie. Thomas was a stellar storyteller, pausing for effect and emphasizing certain points with dramatic flair that made me see the scenes in my head. It seemed so effortless for him. I knew he was the same type of writer. I was hungry to read his screenplay.

"My father died when I was a sophomore in high school. I just got my license and it was supposed to be an enthralling time in my life." I thought about myself at that time, starting kissy games with Bradley. All the while, Thomas was going on a tragic journey with his dad's illness and his older sister's rebellion. "My dad's name is, was Daigh Thomas Roberts." It is pronounced like the word, day.

"It's a beautiful name." I stated mostly for myself. I didn't want to interrupt the flow of his story. I knew this must have been hard to tell. It had been ten years since his father's passing. Thomas said his father was a hard worker in construction, but he really wanted to open his own restaurant. His father was given a death sentence when he finally got sick enough to go to a clinic. Thomas and his father had to deal with the terminal illness alone, since Tamara was off in college and disconnected. Liver cancer. This explained why Thomas shunned alcohol for the most part. Thomas said that his father drank heavily after his wife died. Thomas was only seven when he lost his mom. Combine that with the fact that his father contracted Hepatitis C; cancer was inevitable.

"So, who was the woman in the picture with you and Tamara and your father? It looked like you were about 17 years old." I wondered referring to the seemingly happy family portrait in his condo.

"That was my *almost* stepmom. She, she left my dad when she found out he was sick. Tamara kind of spiraled out of control after that. She really loved Moira. I was only fifteen in that picture." He explained.

Tamara was a college student and off wild. She was never close to her father and their like personalities and temperaments made for a lot of drama in the Robert's home. Father Roberts merely wanted to see his only daughter succeed and she wasted her college money on parties and drugs. I couldn't see Tamara as a party girl, but again that was almost ten years ago. People change.

At his deathbed, Father Roberts only had Thomas by his side. Thomas stepped up to care for his father and the home, all the while maintaining his grades in school. His high school years were wrought with stress and pain and loss and Tamara was not there to assist. She didn't even go to the hospice, despite knowing that her father had a short time to live. Thomas said his father had accepted his fate and was at peace. Thomas was not. He was a witness to his father's decline every day, every hour. Tamara was not.

The night before Father Roberts died, he had given Thomas his Celtic knot pendant and told him where to find his late mother's pendant for Tamara. To the end, even with a wayward daughter, Father Roberts loved her unconditionally.

Thomas wasn't angry that his dad died, but only angry at Tamara for many years. Even though she signed for guardianship over Thomas for the next two years until he was an adult, Thomas was in many ways already an adult.

In college, Thomas stayed away from Tamara. Their last contact was when he flung their mother's pendant at her, tears in his eyes and disappointment in his older sister. He studied hard in college, but also found interest in the opposite sex, finally being allowed to because for once he only had his happiness to worry about. Thomas admittedly dated many, which verified Tano's stories.

Thomas said he never found love. Never found someone to motivate him to do for himself. He reconciled with Tamara after she graduated from college with a master's degree and wrote her screenplay. She mailed the entire document to him as a peace offering. In tears, he met with his sister, who was just starting her business plan. She completed her master's degree in literature because that was her promise to her father—finish college. But, she chose to open the shop because that's what her father always dreamed of doing for himself. The movie detailed that story.

"I'm so sorry, Thomas. Your father sounded like a wonderful man."

"Everyone sounds more wonderful than they are after they have passed," Thomas stated bluntly. "My dad had imperfections. I was orphaned, but I moved on with my life. I didn't become a victim of my past, and luckily I have found family again in Tamara. She has evolved so much in these last five years alone." He sounded like a very proud brother.

Thomas asked if he could see me one last time and suggested that he stop by my condo in the evening. My immediate answer was no. I knew with my misery and worry and stress, something we might regret would take place. I hadn't even declared my love for him and I didn't want to get physical with Thomas because of ill circumstances. He began to make me feel like I might lose him.

"I don't know Thomas. Please. Understand, this is really a case of it's not you, it's me. It sounds trite, but I have so much to do and I'm afraid that things will get out of hand if you come over."

"I see. I wanted to give you a gift and just see your face before you leave." I felt terrible after hearing his sweet, innocent reason. "I don't want to be a jackass and ask when you'll be back. I know you have to look after your family. I'm doing my best not to jump on the plane with you." He offered a nervous laugh.

"A gift, huh? I don't think I deserve it." I tried to lighten the mood too.

"Well, I'm at your condo now. I'm thinking of taking your orchid so I can think of you and care for it. It reminds me of Tano's house in *Asan*." That was actually a good idea. I was tickled that Thomas was outside of my home, well the home I would have for one last day.

I was instantly excited to get home from the storage unit. A huge ring on the concrete by my door was the proof that Thomas was there. He did take my orchid and I smiled, absolutely fine with the thievery. I checked my mail slot right away and saw the DVD. Thomas had placed a copy of the movie his sister wrote in my mailbox. It was indeed signed by Tamara. The cover art was very minimalist with simple pendants on gold chains on a patch of green grass. I recognize the Celtic knot pendants right away. Side by side was Thomas's father's pendant and his mother's.

I settled in with a bottle of wine to enjoy the show. I was glad Thomas was not next to me, since I was basically watching his sister's journey from the time her father died to her attainment of goals. I don't want him to suffer pain of any sort. And, there were many painful flashbacks and I began to see Tamara in a new light. She was a fully developed woman. A woman with dark and light to her soul. She lost her father, but worse off, left him to die without reconciliation of any sort. I felt akin to this scenario except

I was on my way home to see my father with the hopes that he would make a recovery. I ran through half my tissue box by the time the movie ended.

Once I composed myself, I called Thomas to thank him. Thomas picked up on my distraught.

"Phoenix? Hey." Thomas must have been asleep, his voice was deep and gravelly and for a second I wished I was next to him.

"I'm sorry Thomas. I just had to call."

"Oh, no. Is it your dad? Is he okay?" He seemed more conscious now.

"No, no, no! Sorry, it's more like *your* dad. I just finished the movie." I could hear Thomas sigh in relief. I wondered how he slept. I tried to envision him on his bed. Was he in PJ's? Did he sleep in his boxers? Then, I got my mind back on track. "It's a very beautiful movie, Thomas. I wish I could have time to take your sister to dinner and pick her brain. She definitely has evolved. Why doesn't she write more?"

"She says that her small stroke of genius was a one time thing. I think she's a talented writer, but my sister seems fulfilled with her family and her business. Tamara really is a simple lady. She must have used all her wild and crazy tokens in college."

"And, you love her very much."

"I do." He added plainly and truthfully.

"The actor who played you didn't do you justice." I shared and Thomas chuckled.

"There were a lot of unknowns. I kind of agree, but Tamara had very little say in the actors."

We spoke for another hour about our fathers. It was nice to get his advice. On one hand, Thomas reassured me that my father should be fine. On the other, he added that if I found myself without him, that life would go on, that I could move on and grow, as he did. I didn't want to face a life without my dad. I felt like I was still his little girl, with a lot of growing up to do.

"Phoenix. Please keep in touch while you're on Guam as much as you can. I understand that I may not hear from you everyday, but an occasional e-mail or text will help keep my hair from graying."

"I will." And I hoped that I could.

Chapter 14

Humid Homecoming

After a last minute scan of each level of the empty condo, I stood at the doorway and took stock of my life. If I really wanted to, I could stay on Guam and leave California and my divorce here. I could put my experience as a secret shopper on my resume as a bullet item. I could keep Angelica and Gerard on my Facebook friend's list and nothing more. But, I would miss Ty and Uncle Tony. I would miss Angelica and I secretly hoped that she would marry Ty and be my official cousin-in-law. I would even miss my work as a Field Agent. I danced around the thought that I could be in love with Thomas. Could I leave him here so easily? Would he move to Guam, where life moved at a slower pace just to be with me?

"Adios!" I called out to no one. My voice sounded foreign as it echoed through the empty dwelling that was once my home. I locked the condo for the last time and didn't look back.

Uncle Tony waited in his car with Ty. My cousin had been such a godsend these last few weeks. He was going to drive me to the airport and take my car home with him. As far as anyone here was concerned, I was coming back to San Diego. As far as my new found friends and family were concerned, I was merely visiting Guam to see about my dad's health. As far as I was concerned, *I wasn't so sure*. I would deal with the material things I leave in California later. Thomas was the one thing binding me to San Diego.

The second leg of my flight home after leaving Los Angeles went faster than I thought. I had a good book and my laptop to keep me occupied. As much as I'd like to sleep on a flight, I never could. The ambient noise of the jet engines and the constant activity of the flight attendants kept my eyes peeled.

The final leg from Honolulu to Guam reassured me. I already recognized almost half the passengers—the girl who went to elementary school with me, the cashier from the local market with her family, the bank teller I thought was cute from the Bank of Guam, my auntie's ex-boyfriend. It was odd that no one really recognized me. I liked it, but I also felt removed. I didn't have to explain myself in the way you have to explain yourself to anyone from a small town. Guam is essentially a small town with the same mentality. Everyone was in everyone else's business and I was happy to be above the fray.

Pharaoh was set to pick me up at the airport. I wondered if people thought I would look like the image on CNN, fair-haired Phoenix who dropped a ton of weight. I had been in my clothes for almost a full day and aside from seeing my dad right away, I just wanted to take a hot shower.

After retrieving my two luggage, easily identified with the purple ribbons I tied on the handles, I headed out into the humid Guam evening. I scanned the awaiting crowd of family and friends, recognizing every other person. I had enough sense to wash my face and freshen my make-up. A dab of perfume as well, in case a random acquaintance or family member expected a hug.

Then I saw Pharaoh, hairless and massive. He looked menacing, but he still had his baby face. He held up a cardboard sign that read, "Phoenix L—A**Kicker!" There were three other massive Chamorro boys flanking him. They must be from his gym, *Countershot*. I got teary-eyed when the real purpose of the visit home gripped my heart. I hugged Pharaoh tightly, not caring what other people thought. Then a few flashes from someone's expensive camera caught my attention. I recognized the photographer from the local paper and the woman next to him had a notepad and pen in hand. They both went to my high school, like I said, Guam is small. I looked at Pharaoh questioningly. He shrugged his shoulders indicating that he was as clueless as me.

"Hi, Phoenix! My name is Jan Cruz and I wanted to ask you some questions about your visit home and your recent attack in California." Did she have to be so loud? I didn't greet Jan with a smile. I realized she was just doing her job, but I had to get to my father. I wondered who called the media about my return and figured it was one of my brother's goonies. My eyes raked over the three faces, the muscle bound group of cage fighters. My sights landed on the guy avoiding my eyes.

"Hey, did you call them?" I asked. *Busted.* Pharaoh grabbed him by his gruff and yanked him aside to have a word. I didn't want to be perceived as a bitch, so I gave her a nibble.

"Jan. I'm here for my dad and I *really* need to get to GMH right now."

"Oh, I totally understand, but perhaps you can give me a brief summary of the ill-fated night in San Diego?"

"No. I can't, and it really wasn't ill-fated since I'm alive. Correct?" Pharaoh returned and growled at the poor girl. I placed my hand on my giant brother's arm and looked at Jan again. "If we can set this up for some other time, I should be able to give you a proper interview, but really, I miss my dad and I have to see him. Now."

That seemed to do the trick and Jan offered her business card. I asked her to give me until the end of the week to get over my jetlag and settle matters with my ill father. I hoped she wouldn't write anything up yet. I didn't want to be misquoted. And, I wouldn't want to have to visit her, or worse yet, Pharaoh. She trotted off and I flicked her card into the trash when she rounded the corner.

Leaving the airport, the humid air felt like someone dumped a giant circle of uncooked pizza dough on me. I sweated instantly. Pharaoh and his hanger-ons managed my luggage and Hello Kitty backpack with ease. Pharaoh still drove his old white Toyota truck. It was nice that some things didn't change. His friends piled in the back of the truck. W*as that still legal on Guam?* I wondered. Pharaoh and I retreated into the air-conditioned comfort of the cab.

"Sorry, about Ken. He's a dough-head. He just likes attention." My brother said. "I think Jan's his ex or something."

"That's obvious, that he's a dough head. Can we just get to dad already?"

"Of course." Pharaoh peeled out once he got a green light. We felt the men shift in the bed of the truck, they cursed loudly and Ken knocked on the back window. My brother and I shared a laugh.

My mother had carefully chosen our unique names. She learned English by watching Sesame Street and had my dad read her Encyclopedias. Those thick brown books, pages trimmed in gold from the 70s? Yeah, we still have our set. My mom always loved the letter P, perhaps because she mastered those words easily. She asked my father for strong things that start with P. He offered her Pewter, Power, Pharaoh, Phoenix, Platinum and Piranha. She chose wisely.

"What's with the bald head?" I touched the sandpaper skin on the side of Pharaoh's coconut head. He swatted my hand away playfully.

"You look pretty fit there big sister! So, how much do you weigh?" It was nice that the athlete in our family noticed. I wore my favorite red t-shirt, which was considerably spacious now, a pair of dark blue jeans and my black Chuck Taylors. I wasn't home to impress anyone, even though a few of Pharaoh's buddies asked him about my availability. They really were numbskulls to think that they would get pass him to me. *My heart was already claimed anyway*, I thought.

"How about I tell you how many pounds I lost. Thirty five. And you never ask a lady how much she weighs."

Pharaoh drove forty miles per hour and was technically breaking the law. Once, we hit Marine Corps Highway, the largest vein of road on Guam, the speed limit was thirty five and nothing more. The pace was excruciating to bear since I knew the hospital was only about five miles away from the airport, if even that. I was so used to moving at warp speed on the mainland. I turned up the rock music and closed my eyes. I hadn't been gone long enough to miss the island and no major changes occurred in the last year, I was sure, so I caught a kitty nap.

Less than ten minutes later, we parked at the hospital. We loaded my luggage in the cab and locked up. Pharoah placed his heavy arm around my shoulders, pointed at his buddies and he walked me in. His buddies hung back, faces buried in their smartphones. I guess by my kid brother's simple gesture they were instructed to stand guard. I needed privacy with my father anyway. He was still in intensive care unit and might be moved to a regular room by evening according to Pharaoh. Mom saw us walk by the cafeteria and raced after me.

"Fee-nux! *Aigoo*! My girl! Oh, you look so good! But, too skinny." We embraced tightly. My mom was always a superb hugger. She was both soft and hard and I felt like a little girl every time she hugged me even if I was almost a foot taller than her. Her smell was familiar, a mix of her flowery perfume and lots of garlic. It was distinctly my mom and I loved it. She told us to wait for her while she grabbed the cup of coffee she abandoned at the table.

"Oh, how was *you* flight?" She asked, even her bad grammar was welcoming. I smiled, but I didn't want to exchange pleasantries. I wanted to see my dad. I held her hand and kept her in step with my pace.

"Mom, how is dad?" She explained his ordeal from the start, but I kept my frustration with redundancy at bay. Mom finally said that she believed he was getting better. I hoped she was right, but I wanted to hear it from the doctors. I felt like a zombie and I eyed my mom's coffee. She always drank hers black and I wasn't that desperate. We arrived at the ICU, which was a cluster of rooms locked away from other rooms—the rooms with hope. We had to be buzzed in. Mom drank the rest of her coffee quickly, complaining about the heat.

The smell of the ICU hit me first. It was the bitter smell of dread. I held my breath outside dad's door. I really didn't want to see my dad in any other way than the way he was last year. *Strong, robust, happy*. Pharaoh held the door open for mom and me. I walked in and looked at everything but my dad. A tray full of medications, machines, wires, blinking lights, tubes. All attached to the blanketed man who was my father. I finally looked at his face. His sad, helpless face. His eyes were closed and sunken in. His gaunt face rocked me to my core. He looked like the shell of the man I knew. My dad's brown and gray hair wasn't combed to the left like it usually was and for a split second I was mad at my family for not grooming him. Dad's mouth was wedged open by a clear tube that entered the side of his mouth. If this was dad improving, it didn't look right. I kept that thought to myself.

I knew dad had an Ischemic stroke. The more common kind, but I wasn't comforted by that truth. I wondered if stress caused it. Dad never told me about his health problems, and we never asked. Maybe dad had high blood pressure and bad cholesterol and diabetes. I didn't really know. What kind of daughter was I? Rachel's aunt had a stroke several years ago, but she didn't suffer many adverse effects from it. I was hoping for the same for my father. I wasn't that confident though, since being in ICU was pretty serious.

"Is he sleeping?" I whispered. I wanted my dad to wake right up, jump out of bed and give me a hug.

"Yes. You daddy sleep *a lot*." Mom spoke loudly. I walked to his side. The room was so cold and smelled of rubbing alcohol and something repulsive that I couldn't identify. I reached out for dad's hand pierced by a large IV needle. I stroked his hand and traced the IV line to the source of its feed. I took his cold, bony fingers in mine cautiously and squeezed. He didn't move. I desperately wanted him to know that I was there. I began humming, the tune emerging from me like a sorrow call. I sang his favorite Everly Brothers' song.

I whispered the song to his ear. When I finished, he squeezed my hand. It did the trick. Dad's eyes popped open and he searched for me. He smiled, then grimaced. I saw that the right side of his lips did as commanded, but the left side of his face rebelled and stayed in place. I began to cry softly and I kissed my father's bony cheek.

"Hey, Nix, my princess." I looked away. Tears flowed without pause now, because I had never heard my father call me his princess. I was always his tough girl, his tomboy, his ass-kicker. I smiled at him. I didn't want to upset him and if he wanted me to be his princess, I would. Dad slurred and the sound of his deep, strained voice broke my heart.

I kept my eyes on his and whispered, "Hi, daddy. I'm so glad I'm here with you."

"You. Look. Good. How. Are. You?" I was thankful that I could understand his slurred words even if it was slow coming and measured.

"Thank you, daddy. I'm doing great, but I think we need to work on you, huh?" Dad chuckled. As he attempted another smile, tears soaked his pillow. I used my fingers to smooth out his hair to the left. I desperately wanted him to look his usual self. To be healthy, to be normal again.

When dad finally fell asleep, I left the room and felt completely drained. My cup was emptied and I wavered between calling Rachel or Thomas. Rachel was in Japan and would get to see me by the weekend. I didn't want to bother her. I decided to text Thomas while I waited for the doctor.

I made it safely to Guam. I hope you are well, Thomas. My dad is as good as can be expected now. Waiting for Doctor Octopus to give it to me in laymen's terms. P.R.L.

Less than two minutes later, I received a response text from Thomas, but before I could read it. Doc *Oc* appeared. I wanted to speak to him without my mom trying to interpret or question him. I love her, but it would just delay the exchange of information. Pharaoh understood and took her for a walk.

"Phoenix Lizama?" A young Filipino doctor addressed me. He looked like a teenager and I was concerned about his qualifications.

"Hi, Doc." Doogie Howser I really wanted to say.

"Please, call me Gene." He smiled widely. The doctor was a bit too chummy for my taste. I might just lose it if he asked about my attack in California.

"Nooo. No first names, I would be more comfortable calling you Dr.? What's your last name?" His badge covered by his clipboard. I folded my arms and my small smile faded.

"Pallid. Dr. Pallid." He sounded defeated.

"Can I get your prognosis for my dad's recovery please?" Doctor Pallid described my dad's current condition. He said that it was a good sign that he could speak, but he would need extensive physical and speech therapy. He recommended a smaller clinic in another village for the recovery. Once an opening was offered, dad would be transferred. God, how long would that be? I thought if he needs it, he should get it, right?

I thanked the doctor and deflected any attempts from him at small talk. Aside from my dad's recovery, Thomas was on my mind. I later took Pharaoh aside to explain that I wasn't on the market even if I was unattached. I didn't really want to share Thomas with my family yet. Pharaoh knew not to advertise me as available to his friends or Doctor Talksalot.

I finally read Thomas's text.

Hey Guam girl. I miss you. Thank you for checking in with me. I yanked out the one gray hair that sprouted since you left. T.P.R.

Chapter 15

If We Took a Holiday

It took two days before dad was transferred to the skilled therapy clinic in the village of *Barrigada*. He was sitting up and eating soft foods, finally. To see him sitting, smiling and joking made me feel tons better. His daily physical therapy involved walking with his IV stand in hand. Gross and fine motor skills practice and speech therapy would also be tackled.

No one was allowed to stay overnight with dad. We could be at the clinic as early as eight in the morning and stay until seven in the evening. My poor dad shared a room with another patient, only separated by a curtain.

"Phoenix. Can you get me a small CD player? I want to listen to my music here. It's so boring." A few days of recovery and my dad was speaking clearer and quicker. I could totally sympathize with him. I wanted to make him as comfortable as possible. He wasn't at a point in his health to be home and receive therapy from a visiting nurse. There were no television sets in the rooms too, so I made a note to get a portable DVD player as well. A good Eastwood or Bronson flick should cheer him right up.

The days bled into each other and a routine was set. For a week, it was much of the same. Mornings were usually with mom and dad and me, with breakfast that we snuck in from wherever dad had a craving for, Denny's, Kings, McDonalds. I would buy him a big breakfast as requested. He barely ate more than three bites of his food. Mornings when he finished one over easy egg meant that he would be strong. Other days, the rest of the family ate his leftovers.

The multiple prescription drugs dad took for various conditions were crazy. My last count was at ten different medications. I wasn't a doctor, but I'm sure his organs were being taxed, I barely touched Tylenol. Pharaoh always showed up by lunch to finish off dad's extra restaurant food and he would stay until his next college class or training.

Thomas would send me an occasional text, sometimes with a picture of him being sad, or a lengthy e-mail about his screenplay or the progress for the new Bag It locations. He said he was a third of the way complete with his writing project, but he wouldn't tell me the title, let alone the basic storyline. This was fine; I had other things on my mind.

Christmas and New Year's was celebrated together at the therapy clinic. Mom didn't want to decorate the house with anything Christmasy, even when dad and I insisted. She brought a miniature tree for his room instead. The clinic held a luncheon with all the fixings. More than half the dishes on the table were bad for the patients, but this was Guam. Our lives centered on *fandangos* with salty, fatty, flavorful food. We piled my father's plate with everything he craved, spinach in coconut milk, fried fish, turkey, red rice, spicy *finadene* sauce, and barbecued pork ribs.

"So, where's your veggies, dad?" I joked. He pointed to the onions swimming in the salty soy sauce, a common condiment called *finadene*. Just as I thought, dad left his plate mainly untouched. Pharaoh had no problem polishing off dad's food.

The best gift, aside from my dad's continued improvement was that my divorce was final.

I began to lose touch with the world around me, Thomas included. I focused so intensely on my father. He made progress everyday, and then the fall occurred. I wish God would just cut my dad a break.

Dad fell during his walking practice. I knew he was weaker from not eating well and the constant flow of medications in his body. He probably dropped another fifteen pounds since I arrived. The blood thinner he took made the bruise on his hip and thigh speckled like zombie skin. It got to the point that the excess blood in his leg pooled and caused swelling. Dad's therapy was halted and he was placed back in the hospital. A two inch incision was made to gruesomely drain the dead blood. The open wound was reminiscent of my own trauma a month earlier. I was surprisingly at ease helping my father. Even dealing with taking care of his urine bag and changing his adult diaper were no sweat. When you love someone, you love them through the good and the not so good. My mom was the same way, but poor Pharaoh was in hell. He loved dad, but as tough as he was, my baby brother was easily grossed out. And, I think he was feeling like his hero, his dad who was strong and mighty was indeed frail. Human. Mortal. It was scary for us all.

Rachel offered me a sanctuary when I needed a change of scenery. I would head to her shop on some mornings after situating my mom at the hospital. Dad would have to be there until his leg healed and the swelling went down. Therapy would continue at a slower pace. My family hoped he could be home after the New Year.

"So, how's pops?" Rachel asked. She placed her soft perfumed hands on my cheeks.

"His leg is pretty messed up, but it's healing okay. He's on so many meds it's crazy!" I felt like a hot kettle letting off steam, whistling and whining. Rachel responded by hugging me tight.

"Run into any old friends? Other family?" Rachel continued to chit chat, distracting my brain to think about other things.

"Actually, no. Thankfully, no I should say." I was content not running into anyone I knew. My crowd really was just Rachel. I knew Rachel wanted intel on Thomas, but my focus was my dad. She knew better than to ask. I had no desire to go to our old haunts either. The most retail therapy I had was going to the grocery store.

"Do you have time to meet me for dinner or lunch or anything?" Rachel asked in a tone that told me she understood my dilemma.

"Maybe next week. Dad might come home." Once dad was settled at home I would be more inclined to go around the island. I thought of taking pictures for Thomas.

"How long are you staying?" I really couldn't answer my best friend's question. Would it be another two weeks, or two months?

Rachel gave me two size 6 tops right off the rack that she saw me eyeing.

"This is for you." She swiftly placed it in a large lavender bag marked with her frilly font, S.P.T.

"No, Rachel, I can't just take things off the rack." Rachel showed me her star tattoos. I counted five more and congratulated her. "Japan?"

"*Hai*! Five stores in Japan now carry my line." Rachel beamed.

ShinyPurpleThread was a bustling store. Most of her business was from tourists who kept our economy afloat. Rachel required at least one sales associate on hand who spoke conversational Japanese and Korean.

Rachel shoved the bag into my chest again. "If you don't walk out of the shop now, I'll call security and tell them you shoplifted!" I knew she would, so I thanked my bestie, hugged her quickly and promised to call her at the end of my day.

I stopped for a caffeine boost and the warm cup of coffee reminded me of Thomas. I finally called my friend. It had been weeks since I heard his honey butter voice.

"Hello." Thomas answered without realizing it was me. He sounded like he just awoke from sleep. He probably didn't check the caller ID or he just wasn't expecting a call from me.

"Hey there, Thomas Patrick Roberts. This is your conscience calling." I said animatedly. Along with his cute chuckle, I heard some shuffling and then some really loud clanking.

"Shit, sorry Phoenix! I dropped the phone."

"Are you that surprised to hear from me? I'm sorry it wasn't sooner." I suddenly missed San Diego and him.

"Actually, yes. I miss your voice, Phoenix. How are you? How is your dad? Your mom? Your brother?" I giggled. I loved that he was always inclusive.

"Fine. Seen better days. Hanging in there. Massive and deathly afraid of blood and bodily fluids." I knew Thomas would be able to figure out the answers.

"I'm glad you're fine. Your dad seems stable for now and your mom is a tough cookie. Your brother is not cut out for nursing and his bulging muscles would look ridiculous in scrubs. Sounds about right?" He laughed heartily and it washed over me leaving me warm and bothered.

"You always get it right. How are you?"

"Backache. Tummy ache. Headache. *Heartache*." My silence the only response. *Heartache? For me?*

"Wh-where are you?" I asked.

Thomas explained that he had been crashing in a sleeping bag on the floor of the Oceanside shop. They were going to open in another week and he took it upon himself to paint and work on fixtures.

"I didn't know you were such a handyman!"

"I'm not. I've got Youtube constantly running with do-it-yourself tutorials on my laptop. I've done the track lighting and painting so far. My Sunday is looking like more Bob the Builder B.S., but I love my sister *that* much."

"That's sweet. I can't wait to see the shop. Will it look like the San Diego one?"

"For the most part. Guam photos included. I wanted to ask you to get some new shots of the island for me, but I know you are way too busy with your dad." He was right, and I was happy to hear that the new shop would maintain the simplicity of the original. I wondered if I wasn't on Guam, if I would be at the shop spending evenings with Thomas and helping him renovate. I thought it was better that I didn't share this thought out loud with him.

"Make sure you're taking care of yourself. You must be freezing!" I teased remembering San Diego in winter—sunshine, but chilly at night. Guam basically had two types of weather, sunny or rainy, sometimes both at the same time. If it was 85 degrees out, that was a normal day. January to December.

"It's chilly here, but not because of the weather." He said. I smiled to myself. "How's Rachel?" He asked and I grew suspicious.

"She's dandy, but remember our agreement." I warned.

"Yes, ma'am. She does not text me at all."

"That's good." His usage of 'ma'am' didn't faze me this time, maybe I was easing into my ladyhood.

"Anyway, I've got an open line of communication with you now. Right?" He asked.

"Right." If he meant the open line on which I kept a tourniquet fastened, then sure.

"I really do miss you, Phoenix."

"Um, I know." I looked at the clock on the dashboard, thoughts of my father pulling me away.

"Do you?" I wanted to share my concerns about my dad's mortality with someone who had been through it, but I was scared that if I uttered it out loud something bad would come to my father. "Phoenix, are you okay?"

"Oh, yes. I was just thinking of my dad." And, I wanted to get off the subject of Thomas missing me. I wrestled with the idea of telling him the same, but the truth was—I was too preoccupied with my family and being home, that Thomas was really a small blip in my thoughts. Well, okay he was more like streaming classical music that played softly in the background every minute of my day, but my heart and mind could only focus on dad now.

"Thomas. Thank you for being my friend through all this."

"Stop. You don't need to explain yourself or feel guilty. When I say I missed you, it's true. It's not like I expect you to say the same back to me. I get it. You have bigger things on your plate right now. I'm okay being just the decorative parsley on that plate." His melodic laughter filled my head. "I've been there, remember? I'm just happy we had some time to actually talk, okay?" Thomas always knew how to make my life easier and I guess I was beginning to love him for that.

"Well, Dr. Feelgood, you set me straight. I'll take two pills and call you in the morning." And I told myself that I would.

"Have a good rest of your afternoon, *Sirena*."

"You have a good day, *Builder Bob*."

I smiled as I drove to see my dad, energized by Thomas's affection.

After Pharaoh arrived for his hospital duty, mom and I headed back home to clean the house for dad's return. I knew my dad would be excited about sleeping in his own bed again and being amongst his things. As mom and I headed to the parking lot, Bradley's parents were checking in with the security guard. They were asking for my dad's room number. Mom intervened. I stayed back a few paces. I hadn't spoken to my former in-laws since the day I told them about the divorce. I loved them like a second set of parents since Bradley and I became a pair almost ten years ago. It wasn't odd for them to be visiting my dad. My parents and Bradley's parents were friends in their own right, but mom said that since our official divorce and dad's health issues, she hadn't seen or spoken to them lately. I always loved how Bradley Sr. and Rosalia treated my mom, like she was local—like she was Chamorro at heart. I didn't want to address my ex-in-laws as mom and dad, but I felt like I had to. After a few short words with my mom, they both looked at me. Quiet, still, and then walking towards me with urgency.

"Oh, Nix! You look wonderful, how are you baby?" Rosalia broke through the force field I tried to create around me. I'd have to work on that.

"I'm fine, thanks." I stepped forward and gave her a hesitant hug. Bradley Sr. kept his distance and I felt like he had shame in his eyes. I felt bad because they really didn't have anything to do with the reason for our divorce, but I wasn't going to discuss that in front of the people in the lobby. I opened my purse and pulled out a black ring box. I was half-expecting, half-hoping to run into my former mother-in-law. I returned her mother's wedding ring, my ex-wedding ring and didn't say a word. Rosalia opened it and a grimace flashed across her face. She placed it without incident into her purse, smiled meekly and resumed her conversation with my mom.

"Hi." Was all I could say to my ex-father-in-law.

"*Buenas*, Nix. When did you get back?" I was surprised that they didn't know from Bradley that I had been on Guam for weeks. Bradley knew when I left and I also e-mailed him every few weeks about dad's progress. Although I loathed Bradley, he still was a big part of my family's lives. Dad worried about him despite the infidelity. At first, I was angry at my dad, but I couldn't be mad at him for anything now. It's not like they would take Bradley in. Mom was another story. She hated Bradley and made occasional comments about her disdain for her former son-in-law. When she ranted in Korean, I wondered if she was cursing him.

"I've been home almost a month." Bradley Sr. looked surprised. I later found out from mom that Bradley's father stopped talking to my ex-husband, his own son after I called about the impending divorce. He wanted things to work out between Bradley and me. Rosalia told my mom that Bradley's father's last comment to his only son was to never get married again and that he didn't want another daughter-in-law. It shocked me how loyal my ex-father-in-law was to me and I regretted not hugging him now. I would show him more gratitude and respect next time.

The rest of the day, I shined up the house in preparation for dad's return. Mom's standards of clean far surpass my standards and I felt like I was in Mr. Clean boot camp. I just wished I had pads to save my knees on the hard Italian tile.

It was a quiet Sunday when dad was discharged. Pharaoh cradled and lifted dad off his wheelchair. In a warped role reversal, Pharaoh carried my father like he was the child. Although we insisted that dad ride in mom's low riding Tercel, he refused. He asked Pharaoh to go through the tourist village of *Tumon* and to take his time heading home to our home village, *Mangilao*. Mom and I followed the men in her car.

"*Fee-nux*, you have boyfriend now?"

That came out of left field. I looked at my mom, and shook my head, "No! Why?" I shot out my response, but she studied my face and smirked. I was told by a nosy aunt once who had asked me if I was dating Bradley back in tenth grade that because I denied it so quickly and vehemently, that I was lying. Mom must have the same belief.

"Oh, my darling. You can tell omma." She teased.

"Why, did someone tell you I did?" Rachel's cackling laugh filled my head. "Do you *want* me to have a boyfriend?"

"That's up to you. *You adult*. I just want you be happy." Mom stated earnestly. She removed her right handed death grip on the steering wheel to pat my leg. That was a huge gesture from my mom.

"I *am* happy, mom. I'm happy to be here and helping with dad."

"Mmm." Mom stroked my cheek and hummed. It was a melodic tune she usually hummed to herself when she was busy around the house or thinking. It was nice to be near my mom's healing and cleansing essence. I couldn't however, share my budding enthusiasm about Thomas. That was mine for now.

Thirty minutes later, with four Happy Meals in hand, our complete, whole family entered the Lizama home again. I had been restored to my previous state before marriage. It was odd to be home, but also comforting. My parents left my bedroom the way it always was, only selling my bed and placing a computer desk in the room. My stuffed animals, mostly pandas and Hello Kitties, still lined my small bookshelf. My hardcover books were left untouched, no one in my family sharing my obscene love for books. My favorite movie posters still lined the walls of my closet, where clothes from middle school could still be found.

This guest room slash office was my space again. The futon couch was suitable, but I missed my high quality, semi-firm mattress. Bradley had been nice enough to let me keep it. I sprinkled holy water on it of course, well just *Febreze*, to excise all the evil marriage demons and sexual memories. I wrapped the bed and tucked it into expensive storage. My parents' home was noticeably void of all photos of Bradley. Our framed wedding portrait sat in a box on the top shelf of my closet.

That evening, I created a schedule for dad's now twelve prescription medications. I was disoriented, having to take over what the nurses did so effortlessly. I made a chart on excel to mark the times and dosages for each medication. There were things like iron pills that would luckily be completed in a week, since dad's bleeding subsided. Other pills that would prevent a seizure, one to keep his blood thin seemed more crucial. Dad remained in his room, glued to the television set. He caught up with all his police dramas and history channel documentaries. His appetite was still very suppressed and that evening we would have a battle about his meds.

"How many pills?" Dad asked, agitated.

"You need three at dinner and then four by your bed time." Dad groaned. He pulled his sheets up and still had trouble grasping with his left hand. This frustrated him and as I reached out to help, dad looked up at me. The stern look in his eyes was a mixture of determination and hurt. I withdrew my hand and let my father do it for himself.

"I hate those pills. My stomach hurts and my mouth is like cotton. I'm never hungry too, but I want to eat." Dad said this series of sentences slowly, trying to emphasize each word. To someone not knowing his condition, dad perhaps sounded drunk. I focused on the dusty religious statue icon near dad's T.V. Mother Mary. It was there since I could remember, smiling through the layer of dust. I choked down my tears with her help.

"I know dad, but they're suppose to help you get better. And, you do need to have food or milk in your belly when you take most of the pills."

"Bah!" He grunted. *Humbug*, I thought.

The first day home, dad did as he was told. But the following days were wrought with rebellion. Dad didn't want to eat or take his medications. Only when mom cried and begged him, did he take the pills that didn't make him feel groggy or nauseated. Pharaoh was home less and less and I felt that he was feeling relaxed now that dad was out of the hospital. He didn't see what mom and I had to deal with for most of the day. In an effort to get my brother more involved with dad's recovery, I tasked him with calling the at-home physical therapist. Dad needed to have physical therapy from the day he got home, but because of some hiccup at the insurance company, the therapist was never scheduled.

"Sis, can't you do it? I'm training for an upcoming match."

"And dad can't walk without a walker!" I made sure we spoke outside. I didn't care if the neighbors heard me, but I didn't want dad stressed.

"I know, but" he whimpered.

"But, nothing. Pharaoh, just because dad's home, that doesn't mean he's out of the woods. When he's well enough I'm going to offer to take them back to California with me so I can help out." Pharaoh looked shocked. Life without me was one thing, but without the entire family was another.

"Why can't you just live here? You're divorced now. What's so important in California?" Pharaoh protested. Thomas's beautiful smile flashed in my mind.

"Medical is better for one thing. And, I happen to enjoy living out there. I've been toying with the idea of opening my own secret shopper company. You can come out too you know."

"No way. I *happen* to enjoy living on Guam." Pharaoh was a big fish in a small tank here.

"Well, tomorrow morning, I expect you to call the therapist and get dad on a regular schedule." Pharaoh nodded in agreement and I handed him the business card.

Changing the subject, I pinched the purple hickey on Pharaoh's thick neck. "Got that from training?"

He checked his reflection in the window and blushed. "No, from a girl I met."

"In training?" I joked.

"No, in my psychology class."

"I don't remember hickeys being part of the psych curriculum?" I teased. Pharaoh and I had an easy conversation that afternoon, one of our last.

The next morning would mark dad's first full week home. Typically, I would hear dad's T.V. blaring, but my eyes popped open to an eerie quiet. The brightness of my room told me it must have been past eight o'clock. I tiptoed to my parents' room and pushed the door open slightly. Our home was always a home where bedroom doors were never locked. Mom was not in the room, but I could tell that already from the savory smells of breakfast wafting through the hall. Dad was still. I stood over him to make sure he was still breathing. I felt a wave of overwhelming relief when he snored loudly.

In the lonely kitchen there were two pans of fried rice on the stove top and a pot of fragrant coffee. Mom had made a large batch of her delectable *kimchee* fried rice and a smaller batch plain, not spicy garlic rice for dad.

I knew mom was outside tending to her orchids or watering the lawn. I reviewed the meds dad needed to take that morning and decided to let him sleep for half an hour more. I looked outside and sure enough, mom was pulling weeds, close to the earth in her classic Korean squat. Mom was like a hummingbird, fluttering around from one thing to the next, always keeping busy.

I sat with my bowl of rice and steaming sweet coffee. A note written on a napkin from Pharaoh caught my eye, *"Had to get to class, I'll call dad's therapist after lunch when I get home."* I dropped my spoon with force on the table. I hated that Pharaoh put things off, especially when it came to dad. I had seen enough of the physical therapy exercises that I decided that after dad had breakfast, I would run him through the paces. I opened the newspaper, then heard a crash from my dad's room. I ran in to find that dad had awoken and attempted to go to the restroom. Medication bottles and colorful pills peppered his floor. Dad groaned, his walker upended next to him.

"Dad!" I raced to him. He looked like a beetle turned on its back. I lifted him easily off the floor, his frailty scared me to my core. Panic and dread drenched my heart.

"I wanted to go to the toilet," dad slurred.

"You could have called for me." My voice came out shriller than I expected. My parents' house was small enough that if you called from one side of the house it was heard. "How's your side? Did you fall hard?" I shook with anger. I had even put our board game buzzer by his bedside for him to summon someone when he needed us. Granted mom or I were typically in the room with him, but now I felt like crap for not taking my breakfast into his room.

"I think. I'm okay." But as dad said this to me, I pulled down his pajama pants and saw the fresh bruise. It was bright red and ran along the side of his right hip and thigh. Dad's adult diaper had also unfastened. It was obviously full of urine. This time, dad's pride didn't stop me from doing my nurse duties. I heard mom's humming and the door slammed shut.

"*Fee-nux? Yobo?*" I heard her sing from the kitchen.

"Help mom." I kept my voice just below a panicked scream. Mom's quick steps echoed in the hall.

"Oh my God!" She burst the bubble and my mouth went dry.

Mom helped me hoist my dad's long, slender legs onto the bed. She pulled his pants down and asked me to leave.

"I do it, *Fee-nux*." I wanted to protest, but obediently left into the hall. My mom gasped at the sight of dad's fresh bruise. Then, mom became hysterical. "*Fee-nux!* Oh my God! *Fee-nux!*"

I bolted through the door and didn't care if I saw all of my father, mom had thrown a blanket over my dad luckily. On the floor was dad's drenched adult diaper, one he wore in case he couldn't make it in time to the toilet. It was varying shades of orange and bright blood red. Not normal or healthy by any means.

I carefully picked up the gruesome evidence of dad's failing health and showed it to him. He twisted his head to the wall, not wanting to see.

"Dad! This is not normal! Please, look." He squeezed his eyes shut, like he was about to stare at the sun, but turned to look. The realization and fear in his eyes were evident. Dad had not been eating well for the last month and Lord knows what havoc the medications were wreaking on his insides. Dad had gone from a 6'3" stocky man at 200 pounds to a waifish 140 pounds. It was shocking to think that I was even within the same weight range as my dad. His muscles had gone soft and his bones jutted out everywhere. I didn't take any pictures with my family since I had come home. I didn't need to. Dad's current visage would remain burned in my mind forever. I thought of Thomas just then. How did he handle his father's deterioration? I wasn't sure I was strong enough for this. I couldn't lose my father, not now.

"*Yobo*, you need to go doctor, go hospital, please." My mom now joined in verbalizing what I was already thinking. I felt like I failed at caring for my dad this past week.

"No." Dad said defiantly.

I brought the blood soaked diaper closer. If dad was in any pain, he wouldn't have told us. He was so adamant about coming home. I felt tricked by the hospital, my dad, God. He wanted to come home to die I finally realized.

"Please, dad. Let me call an ambulance. I love you too much to let this slide." Finally, dad's eyes softened. He reached out for my hand. Mom discarded the diaper in a plastic bag and set it aside for the paramedics if they needed it to gauge the seriousness of what I figured was an extreme bladder infection. As I held my father's hand, my mom held the other. I dialed 911, *then* called my brother. I didn't care if he was at school with the latest girl of his dreams.

Pharaoh arrived just as the paramedics pulled into our driveway. I gave the paramedic whose name tag read Torres, a synopsis of the morning. He did indeed want to see my dad's bloody mess. As they maneuvered my father onto the stretcher, mom grabbed her purse and followed. I told dad and mom that we would be right behind them. The other paramedic-name tag Guerrero- recognized my brother from his mixed martial arts notoriety, his attention on Pharaoh.

"Hey, my brother, aren't you Pharaoh Lee?" My brother's professional name was Lee, carrying my mom's maiden name. The medic had stars in his eyes as he saw my brother up close. I watched him assess my brother from a few feet away and the medic probably thought he could take Pharaoh.

"Yeah." My brother barely looked at the medic, keeping his eyes on my dad. It looked like my brother's biggest fan wasn't going to let up and as he began to speak again. I felt my face flush.

"Do you *freakin'* mind if we *not* talk about this right now?" I gestured to my father. Medic Guerrero turned his attention to me and his scrunched together eyebrows relaxed. A flicker of recognition on his face when he looked at me made my blood boil.

"Aren't you Phoenix Lizama? Oh, shit! Yeah, you two are brother and sister!"

Before I could verbally pounce on the unprofessional prick, my brother turned his full frustration on the uniformed jerk. He stepped to Guerrero who seemed to take in the full massiveness of my kid brother. Pharaoh didn't say a word, but his stare and pulsing biceps did the trick. Medic Guerrero cowered and grabbed the gurney to maneuver dad from the bedroom, finally.

As they wheeled my father through the living room, my dad looked at me, uncertainty in his eyes, and in a strained whisper said, "I love you, my princess."

"I love you daddy." I fell into my brother's arms after the ambulance left. He didn't say anything. But his body shook with emotion like mine.

Pharaoh drove, silent. I called Rachel and let Pharaoh figure out what happened as I explained it to her in between sobs. Rachel cried with me, telling me she would meet me at the hospital. I begged her to stay at work and wait for my update. She finally agreed. I wanted to call Thomas too, but I didn't want to intrude on his workday, calculating the time difference between Guam and the West Coast.

"Nix, I'm sorry about not calling the therapist first thing." Pharaoh's voice was hoarse.

"Whatever. Dad's really sick anyway. He must have a bladder infection."

"Was there a lot, like *bula* blood?" Pharaoh shivered with disgust.

"Yes." I was curt, bigger things on my mind. It was an enigma that my brother was afraid of needles, hospital and blood when he pounded the guts out of guys in the cage for pure joy. Maybe it was just the blood of family members that made him quiver.

Pharaoh caught up to the ambulance holding my father and mother, my lifeline. I stared at the vehicle, praying quietly for my dad's recovery.

"Sis? Are you okay?" Pharaoh rested his large hand on my shoulder.

"No. I'm afraid, Pharaoh."

Within fifteen minutes, we were at the ER. My mom gripped my dad's rolling bed, her little legs hustled to keep her near her husband. We were directed by a nurse to wait outside. Pharaoh and I kept to ourselves, although several waiting family members of other patients eyed us too much for my comfort. My brother and I had been mistaken as a couple in the past, and we were united on the front that that was extremely repulsive.

My phone pinged. It was a text from Thomas.

As I hang the Guam pictures in the new shop,
I am thinking of you friend.
Hope your dad is well. T.P.R.

Fresh tears flowed and I really wanted to hear Thomas's voice and his reassurances. But more importantly, I wanted to hear from the doctors that dad was fine.

"Who's T.P.R.?" *Damn.* Pharaoh had been looking over my shoulder.

"Nosy much?" I said sarcastically, as I buried my Blackberry in my pocket, and wiped my face with a rough fast food napkin excavated from my purse. "He's a friend."

"Why is he *thinking of you*?" Pharaoh nudged me, nearly knocking me off the concrete bench. I didn't have to answer the rest of his inquiries since Pharaoh knew the medic who just pulled into the circular ER driveway. My brother stood and waved his friend down. A warm breeze raced up the hill lifting leaves into the air. It refreshed me and I felt hopeful. I hated sitting in the stuffy waiting room inside, even if it was air-conditioned.

When Pharaoh returned to me, I became painfully aware that his medic buddy watched me. This was confirmed when Pharaoh asked if I planned on dating again.

"I told you no. Never. Why?" I already knew the answer, keeping my eyes on the ground. "We have bigger things to worry about right now." Guam boys were relentless. You could get picked up at a funeral around here.

"Well, my buddy over there—Vince, he went to high school with me." I didn't let my brother finish.

"That's nice for you both." I watched the door for my mom or the doctor or someone to update us on dad's status.

"He's a good guy. Younger than you, but that would make you a mini-cougar right?"

"Is this your attempt to keep me on Guam?" I punched my brother on the arm. "Anyway, I left my heart in San Diego." Pharaoh raised his eyebrows, comprehending. Mom appeared suddenly, her face gray, serious. We ran to her.

"You daddy is in ICU again." She whimpered before collapsing into our arms, sobbing. Everyone turned to look at the three of us. Pharaoh held mom up with ease and Dr. Pallid approached us tentatively.

"Hi, Phoenix." He nodded. I was surprised he remembered my name. He looked around, then stepped closer to us. He kept his voice to a whisper, which I appreciated. "I'm sorry. Your dad seems to be having renal failure, well kidney failure basically. We need to put him in ICU. Running more tests. At this time, he's unresponsive and we've given him morphine for the pain." In retrospect, I knew my dad was in extreme pain these past three days. He just never let on how bad it was, but I remembered his groaning in the night, my mom's whispers of comfort. I thanked the doctor and he lingered uncertain when I started crying. We all knew where to go and like zombies we shuffled to the ICU.

Being in the ICU was a death sentence for many patients. Dad escaped it once, but many people do not. The weary look on these families' faces mirrored ours as we walked down the long hall. Mom was buzzed in and Pharaoh and I were asked to wait again. We sat together on the cold tile floor, the only space available. I rested my head on his shoulder and my brother and I wept quietly together.

Chapter 16

Funerals Suck

"I never regarded myself as 'Daddy's Little Princess,' but many of you have told me that that was how my father, Sterling Thaddeus Lizama, spoke of me. You may have known my father fondly by his nickname, Thad. I will forever miss conversations with him. His comedy, his wit, and his undying love for family didn't just make him unique, but the combination of all these characteristics embodied in one man defined my father. His generosity and limitless love can be seen in my mother, Sun Lee Lizama. Dad's strength and protective spirit carries on with my brother, Pharaoh. In me? Well, in me is my father's song." The microphone magnified my frail voice.

My tears overwhelmed me now, reading this eulogy. I held on to the cold marble podium. The small sea of family and friends watched me patiently. I cleared my throat and took a deep breath. I fixed my eyes on my dad's silver casket adorned with white and red roses. I sang the chorus to the Everly Brother's song dad loved hearing me sing, *All I Have to do is Dream.*

Everyone in the church melted away and my father's smiling face filled my head. I closed my eyes and finished the song, as if I was only singing it to him. I never wanted to sing my dad's favorite song again and the idea that I could never talk to him overwhelmed me, but I finished strong. I braced myself as I stepped down to my dad's casket. I draped my body over it and whispered, "I love you daddy." My mom wept loudly, and several aunts and cousins joined in. I felt naked suddenly, realizing all eyes were on me. Hearing my mother's wail helped me regain consciousness. I had to finish the eulogy before my knees gave out. My shaky knees brought me back to the podium.

"On behalf of my mom and brother and the rest of the Lizama and Lee families, we thank you for your support in our time of sorrow. And to dad, we love you and," my voice broke with emotion, "daddy, I will always be your little princess." I left the podium and fell into the arms of my family.

My father had died two weeks into the New Year. He was 60 years old.

Funerals on Guam are an all day affair. After nine days of evening rosaries and service of food at our home, I still didn't want this day to end. I had made it through the mass without breaking down again. The long procession of cars were about to caravan through the Guam roads to my father's final resting place at the Veteran's cemetery. The church was only two miles from the cemetery, but many family and friends wanted to give their kind words as we exited the church. It wasn't expected for everyone in attendance to follow us to the burial site. That group would be headed to the church's social hall, where there was a catered luncheon, a never ending buffet. Immediate family and friends would dine after the actual burial.

I had Rachel by my side and Bradley even flew in from California. It was awkward to have the Farmer family there, but Guam is so small that their attendance was expected despite the divorce. Pharaoh even put aside his anger at Bradley for the day. The solemn funeral director drove my family, Rachel and me to the cemetery. I rested my head on Rachel's shoulder and held my mom's hand.

I knew Pharaoh was having a lot of guilt with dad's passing. He wondered if he did enough to help dad. The evening dad died, Pharaoh lost it. It was hard to see him so fragile. I reassured my little brother that he did his best. It was something he would have to deal with in time, much like Thomas's sister, Tamara.

Thomas. God. I had left him out of all the latest developments. I could only hope he would understand. I didn't feel that he should feel obligated to worry about me. He didn't know my father after all. My father's funeral should not be a reason he should return to Guam, as much as Thomas loved the island.

Mom's cell phone rang and shattered my thoughts of Thomas. Mom received a call from our Korean relatives who flew in from Seoul. I closed my eyes and tried to comprehend what I could of their discussion in Korean. They got lost in the shuffle of cars and needed directions.

"Phoenix?" Rachel called to me quietly. We slinked along at ten miles an hour with about thirty cars behind our van and my dad's hearse. It would be another fifteen minutes or so until we reached my dad's final destination.

"Hmm?" My eyelids were so heavy.

"Promise me you won't get mad." Oh, no. I never liked it when Rachel prefaced her declarations with this comment. I opened my eyes, the sun shone brightly illuminating Rachel's pretty face. "I know you didn't want Thomas to know about dad's passing, but I had to call him and at least tell him to call you. He was very persuasive and shook it out of me." She whispered as she described another act of defiance.

"Did he?" I was too tired to be angry or to choke my bestie. "How does one do that from 6,000 miles away *and* over the phone?"

Rachel explained that she called Thomas two days ago when she saw that I was too preoccupied with arranging the funeral and handling my dad's affairs to even mention his name. I'm not sure if I blocked him out on purpose, because he was indeed the one person I wanted to talk to during all this. He had his life in California, and for some reason I didn't feel like I was an official part of his realm. I couldn't imagine him flying out here, just for me. He was fervent about our friendship and yes we had some almost romantic moments, but did that define us in any other way other than friends. Were we even *good* friends? I was quietly relieved that he knew, but I felt guilt for not sharing this news personally. It was like I refused to blend with him, being oil in his water.

I didn't want Pharaoh or mom to hear our discussion about Thomas, so I patted Rachel's leg as a promise that I wouldn't do her more physical harm and remained silent. She kissed my cheek and whispered, "Please don't kill me."

The white canopy erected over a large hole in the ground marked the spot where my dad would be buried. I swallowed hard, the ever growing lump of despair threatened to turn me into a crying ball of crazy. I had been to so many funerals in my life, but this was the first time it really mattered. This was my father. This place in the earth, here on our island would be his final resting place. The only image I wanted of my father was not of him in his coffin, or buried in the warm soil. I wanted to imagine him always in his favorite chair, watching his favorite show and with a glass of iced tea in his reach. And my mind knew my dad was gone—in heaven, in limbo, in a parallel universe, but my heart worried that he was still suffering somehow. Was he watching us? Was he proud of me? Was it selfish for me to be relieved that he no longer suffered physical pain?

Mom cried softly as we walked arm in arm. Being dressed in black, the island sun's heat magnified our pain. This would be a day I would never forget. Rachel and I almost matched in our skirt and suit jackets, hers in lace and mine in linen. I twisted up my long hair and as if Rachel could read my mind, she offered me a hair clip. Irritating wisps of layered bangs floated around my face, snagging in my sunglasses.

Our priest was already waiting under the canopy, Bible and mic in hand. I looked at the parade of cars and knew it would be at least twenty minutes before everyone else joined us. There were three rows of plastic green chairs and we sat in the front row as expected. Mom produced several oriental hand fans from her purse and Rachel fanned us both and I offered Pharaoh some relief. He was sweating even in his stiff white shirt, and he wouldn't be caught dead holding the little fan adorned with cranes and cherry blossoms.

I watched each car and noted the people I recognized. Bradley and his parents arrived. There were a few "aunts and uncles" I didn't quite recognize, and it dawned on me that I didn't have my dad around now to point out who to pay respects to.

Towards the end of the line of cars was a blue Prius, exactly like Thomas's. For a second I thought that it was realistic for him to have had the time to fly to Guam. Albeit, his last minute ticket purchase would have been astronomical at two thousand bucks, but why would his car be here? I pointed at the car and told Rachel, "Look, Thomas made it. Maybe his little Prius transforms into a fast going submarine."

Rachel pulled her Gucci sunglasses off her face and squinted at the car. The lone occupant was a Caucasian man with dark sunglasses. "Yeah, that car has a rental sticker."

"What?" I was shocked. My Korean family rented a large van, so that should have been the only rental car in the caravan. Rachel and I strained our eyes in the bright sun. As the rest of our party gathered around the fringes of the canopy sweating in the afternoon heat, Rachel and I watched the blue Prius. The unknown visitor parked at the last spot away from the cluster of cars. He didn't come out and the priest started prayer. Between "Lords" and "Jesus Christ" Rachel and I would glance at the little blue car. No movement. Maybe it was just some random person visiting a relative's grave. Mom pinched my shoulder when she realized I was staring off into the parking lot and I didn't rise with the rest of the mourners. That was it. I wasn't going to dwell on the mystery person who might or might not be Thomas.

The funeral director, name tag-Hector, passed out white roses to all the mourners. He offered red ones to my family, including Rachel. She glanced at the red rose and then to me and then to the funeral director like he made a mistake. I smiled in confirmation at my one and only sister and Rachel squeezed my hand.

Before dad's casket was lowered into the red earth, my mom and I cried a fresh round of tears. Mom was presented with the American flag. She clutched the triangular symbol of my father's service in the Army and we approached dad's casket to place our red roses. I plucked a petal from the rose and placed it in my jacket pocket. The pallbearers took their turns in removing their black arm bands. They tied it to the bars of the coffin which was customary. As soft church piano music played on an antiquated tape player, dad was lowered into the shade of his plot. Pharaoh rested his large arm around me and Rachel, with his other arm being used as a brace for my grieving mom.

The cemetery hands began shoveling dirt onto my dad's casket, as several mourners walked towards the parking lot to smoke cigarettes. Others conversed quietly in the sun, offering us privacy. It was like someone hit the play button on the remote control and everyone resumed their lives.

The four of us stood quietly and when we finally sat down, a stream of relatives and family friends approached to console us. I glanced again at the blue Prius and in the time we took to say our final goodbyes, the lone occupant was no longer there. I scanned the green grass peppered with headstones discreetly, between hugs and kisses from relatives. I didn't see anyone wandering or standing over the other graves. I drew my sights closer to the perimeter around me and then I saw Bradley in the shadow of a man head and shoulders above him. This stranger wore a sky blue cotton long sleeved shirt. The only male here in long sleeves. It was tucked into a pair of black slacks. I scanned to the shoes and saw black leather shoes. It couldn't be Thomas. I hit Rachel with my elbow and directed her attention towards my ex-husband. She had only seen Thomas in the dark at Pass the Mic back in San Diego. Rachel was mesmerized and I willed this mystery man to turn around.

"I guess that's not him, he isn't sparkling in the Guam sun." Rachel whispered in to my ear.

Could it be? My gut told me that I knew this man. I knew in my heart it was Thomas.

Chapter 17

A Phoenix is Forever

When the crowd grew thin and cars began to file out of the cemetery parking lot, Bradley walked over to kiss my mom. My mom showed grace despite her hatred for my ex-husband. Bradley shook his former brother-in-law's hand cautiously and I was glad Pharaoh kept his bearings. As Bradley took in the sight of my very large brother, his face was comical with a mixture of fear and awe. Bradley used to be the bigger one of the two.

I looked back at the man Bradley was talking to before. He watched the ocean, his lean back still to me. I stood alone with my ex-husband.

"How are you, Nix?" Bradley asked. He wore his formal Army uniform and looked like he aged another five years since we divorced.

"I'm fine, thanks." I looked back again and Rachel strolled away with the not so-mysterious man. Rachel turned to me, and gave me a huge smile and a wink. I should have chased after them instead of standing here in front of Bradley.

"I guess you've seen who Rachel's talking to." Bradley continued. I was relieved that he didn't want to hash up old memories of dad. I nodded, still not fully grasping the idea that Thomas was on Guam for the second time in his life. The second time in a year. "You know, Thomas is sad for you, but also, I don't know. I guess he should explain it to you. Needless to say, he's disappointed."

I squared my shoulders, upset that Bradley would try to get involved with a relationship that didn't exist. "Well, that's between me and him." I kept my eyes on the sweaty men filling in my father's grave. I wondered, irritatingly why they didn't wait until the family left.

"You're right." I looked up at my ex-husband. I wasn't used to hearing those words from him and my eyes met his. Bradley rested his hand on my arm. "You're eulogy was very, um, touching. Take care, Nix." Bradley's eyes darted over to Thomas who was now facing us standing in the sun, several yards away. "You're in good hands."

"Thanks, Bradley." I wanted to hug him one last time, but decided not to. I had been such a jerk to Thomas so far, this would just be another kick in his stomach. I felt Rachel and Thomas's eyes on me. Dad's too in a sense. Bradley shook Thomas's hand and dove into Rachel for a hug. She shoved him roughly and I bit my lips to keep a smile from spreading on my face. Bradley trotted to his parents and Rachel smiled at me and shook Thomas's hand before leaving. I waved feebly at her.

Thomas waited outside of the canopy. His profile was tragic as he slumped forward, hands in his pocket. His wild wind-whipped hair looked almost golden in the sun. His dark blue tie was peppered with white designs and it waved rhythmically in the

Guam breeze. I approached him slowly, keeping in the shade. He stood in the sun, watching the ocean again. God, he was so beautiful. What did he want with me? What could I offer him but misery? He was this rare exotic bird and I didn't want him to fly away, so I remained behind my border in the shade.

"Hello, Thomas." My voice cracked with emotion. I feared that Thomas would be angry with me. He angled his body towards me, but did not look up. I couldn't see his eyes behind his dark sunglasses. His beautiful lips were downturned. "Thomas, I'm *so* sorry I didn't contact you during all this, it's just that when my dad, *uh*," I looked over my shoulder and the men were conveniently on a break, eyes on me. I continued in a whisper, "I was overcome by so much that I didn't think it was right to drag you into my world."

"Phoenix." Thomas looked at me completely now, my name sounding so odd in his pained voice. Shame overwhelmed me and I hid behind my sunglasses. Finally, Thomas moved into the shade inches from my body. He slowly removed the funeral program and my clutch purse from my hands and placed the items on a chair. He took my hands in his and didn't say anything for a few minutes. His hands were warm, his body emanated heat and a delicious musk mingled with his cologne. I became heady and I swear the ground shifted beneath me. I continuously kept Thomas on the outside, and even now, after he traveled on a whim to be with me in my time of grief—I couldn't just say what he longed for. *I want you.*

I began to sob despite myself. How I wished my dad was still alive to meet Thomas. He wrapped me with his body, lightly and maintaining a small distance between us. He let me cry as he rocked me side to side slowly.

My head and arms rested on his chest and my hands were balled into fist maintaining the barrier between us. *Why couldn't I just let him in? Even now?* As I watched the last car leave, with Pharaoh and mom and Rachel, I thought of my father and the many things he didn't get to experience. That family trip to South Korea we were always talking about but never took. The unfinished projects around the house that dad stockpiled materials for. The family tree album he started, but left incomplete for the last ten years mostly because Pharaoh and I didn't show enough interest.

I finally reached both arms around Thomas and held on tight. Now was all I had. Now was all anyone ever had. My dad had a career, a wife and children. He got to see retirement. He walked his daughter down the aisle, for the wrong guy unfortunately. He saw his son finally find his calling. But, he didn't see his grandchildren, and he didn't see his daughter happy, truly fulfilled. As I held Thomas, I wasn't sure if my words could make up for the self-made rift I created over these last three months. I moved my ear to the left side of his chest. I wanted to find solace in the rhythm of his heartbeat. Thomas jerked backward like I burned him. In an instant we were apart again. He stood out in the sun and I remained in the cool of the shade alone. He looked down at his chest, hand wavering over his heart. I heard the cemetery workers shuffle away behind me, finally giving us privacy. I was about to be dumped even before I had Thomas's heart.

"I'm sorry, Thomas." I guess this was his chance to let me have it. He never really lost his cool with me, but I knew I deserved it. I mean, his physical reaction now was to push me away. How could I be the great love of his life, if I wasn't even a good friend to him? I raised my face to Thomas expecting him to be glowering at me. I squinted my eyes in preparation for the onslaught of hateful words. Instead, Thomas was loosening his tie. He slowly unbuttoned his shirt. What the hell was he doing? We were at a cemetery and my dad, rest in peace, was technically in the area.

Thomas, looking like a hotter Clark Kent, stepped towards me again and pulled his shirt open to reveal the left side of his chest. There was an eight by eight white gauze loosely taped on his flawless ivory skin.

"What happened?" I asked frantically. "Don't tell me you were saving another damsel in distress." I joked. *Was he shot? Stabbed?*

Thomas pushed his sunglasses off his face finally. His beautiful iridescent eyes looked weary, maybe from the traveling and jet lag—but I suspected it was because of me. He shook his head no and gingerly peeled off the tape. I'm not sure what compelled me to take over, but I stepped up to Thomas, his chest level with my eyes.

"May I?" I asked Thomas. He removed my sunglasses carefully before allowing me to be Nurse Betty. It was like I was in the Twilight Zone. What kind of injury could he have under this gauze? The sci-fi part of my brain fantasized that Thomas was from an alien planet and now that he declared his love for me, this thing was going to bust out of his chest and take over my body. That would explain his otherworldly beauty, I mused.

As I peeled back the bandage, the skin underneath was shiny. Was it a burn? I continued to unveil what looked like blood. But this wound had a distinct pattern, an art to it. I dare say, it looked like his skin was aflame. Thomas did not move, his eyes remained on my face. It was like he awaited my reaction. On Thomas's chest, right over his heart was a vibrant Phoenix. My mouth dropped open as I gazed at this fresh tattoo.

"When? Why?" I looked at Thomas like he was crazy. Did the airlines have a tattoo parlor on the plane that I didn't know about? My eyes returned to the beautiful red firebird.

"Well, when? The day before Rachel called me. Why? Because. Phoenix Rose Lizama." Thomas lifted my chin so I could meet his gray eyes. "I love you." I let his words sink into my brain and travel through my body. He stood there looking both beautiful and vulnerable. He just branded himself for me and I was hesitating like an idiot, yet again.

The warm breeze whipped around me and it felt like the forces that be were nudging me forward. I took a hesitant step towards this glorious man. Thomas's hands remained relaxed by his side. His palms faced towards me, begging me, reassuring me that it was okay to make that leap of faith. I looked up into his eyes and the tears that rolled down his beautiful face was enough confirmation for me.

I bridged the small gap between us quickly and took Thomas's tragic angelic face in my hands. I pressed my lips tentatively to his. Thomas's desire surged and he swept me up off the ground and pulled me into him. He seemed unaware of the pain on his chest now. Our lips, hungry, continued to discover each other in the balmy paradise weather. My senses were heightened and I took in the heat of his face, the warmth of his tongue and his flavor mingled with the salty ocean air made me light-headed. We came up for air twice before reality got the better of me. I felt like jelly as we continued to embrace. *Finally*, was my only thought. At last, I opened up and Thomas was true. That kiss was a fantasy turn reality.

"Finally." Thomas whispered, echoing my thoughts. "So, Phoenix," his voice was husky and dripping with desire. "Did I have to fly *all the way* to Guam to make you realize that I love you?"

"No, Thomas. The tattoo helps though." I joked. "And, just so you know my mom almost named me Piranha."

He chuckled, "Glad she chose wisely."

I kept off Thomas's freshly scarred chest this time. I turned to face him again. He deserved to hear what I was about to say, instead of just having my kiss, a damn good kiss admittedly, declare my feelings. I made a space between us to look up into his eyes. "I, I love you too, Thomas. It was always there, but I was too chicken shit to tell you. I'm sorry."

"Hey," Thomas soothed me with his voice. "You don't have to apologize. I was all ready to offer my condolences, then chew you out like a jilted lover. But, after the way you just kissed me?" Thomas teased, and I smiled despite myself.

"You did some in return too mister, but we should get going." I had to remind myself that we were in a cemetery and dad was only several feet away from us. I also didn't want my mom to think I was kidnapped or something. "Nice touch on renting the blue Prius, by the way."

"I can be dramatic too." He smiled.

Thomas buttoned up his shirt after I reapplied his bandage, which he made tough between kisses. I helped him with his tie and after a few more kisses, I gathered my things and invited Thomas back to the church social hall.

"Phoenix. Your eulogy was beautiful." I hadn't realized that Thomas was in the crowd. "Would you mind if I pay my respects to your dad?" I smiled at my new man. Why was he so perfect? Did I really get to keep him? I nodded and Thomas handed me the car keys. I walked slowly, willing myself to keep moving forward and give my dad and Thomas their privacy. I sat in the warm car and immediately blasted the air conditioner. I saw Thomas in the distance, kneeling with his head down. A new bittersweet bud blossomed in my chest and my eyes teared up. If I had just opened my heart faster, Thomas would have met my father properly. I guess things have to work out in their own time. But, I felt like my dad lost out somehow in knowing such a good hearted man. Someone like him.

As Thomas made his way back to the car, I took my hair down, which was now in nice waves. I reapplied all my make-up. The humidity on Guam was a killer. I made up my mind that before I left Guam, I was going to make my commitment to Thomas more permanent. I didn't have the energy to figure out how yet. The blackness of the day had shifted to bright white. I wondered if it was possible for my heart to suffer whiplash. It was all so melodramatic for me that the day I buried my father, was the day I admitted my love for Thomas.

Chapter 18

He Loves Me, He *Really* Loves Me

My eyes flickered from Thomas's wonderful profile to his chest. I didn't know where to start, how to ask. As usual, Thomas made it easy for me. He turned up the cold air, held my hand and drove slowly back to the church.

"How are you doing with all this Phoenix?"

"I'm okay, I guess. I'm sorry, Thomas. Sorry for being a terrible friend."

"Stop that!" His raised voice surprised me and I wanted to pull my hand away, but he held it firm. "Please, Phoenix. You are my best friend. You are everything. No more apologies. Let's just be."

I leaned into Thomas, which was easy in the tiny hybrid. "Just be?"

"Yes, Phoenix. And we don't have to make any official announcements about us. Not today. I don't want you stressing about that." He kissed my forehead as we pulled into the packed parking lot. There was still a good number of people at the church. Thomas hopped out of the car and opened my door. If he was jetlagged he hid it well. We walked hand in hand to the social hall for the reception. Thomas's released my hand as we reached the double doors. A rush of longing overcame me and I gave Thomas a quick kiss. Energized by his presence, we opened the doors together. I targeted my mom right away and made a bee line for her table.

Thomas was concerned that Bradley and his family might be put off or feel disrespected if I walked into the *merienda* with him, hand in hand. Thomas told me that Rachel would have explained to Pharaoh and my mom about him.

Thomas walked with me. All eyes in the room were on us. I didn't realize that I held my breath until we finally reached my family and I exhaled.

"Mom, Pharaoh, *Imo*, this is my, *um*, this is Thomas Roberts. He came in from San Diego to be here." I kept my hands crossed in front of me like I was about to get scolded by my mom. I could already feel the eyes of my Korean aunt, my *Imo*, burning into me.

"Oh, Thomas! Nice to meet you. Thank you so much for coming today." My mom was absolutely polite, her grammar flawless this time. And was she swaying as she spoke? Rachel dwarfed by Pharaoh's bigness looked ridiculous with her giant smile. She was practically dancing in her seat. Pharaoh looked like he was ready to pounce on Thomas. He stood slowly and walked towards us. Tension rippled around the table. Thomas remained relaxed and as handsome as ever.

Pharaoh extended his large tan, tatted arm to Thomas. My brother's white shirt rested on the chair and he was in a white wife beater—*always hated that term for the tank top*. He leaned in and asked, "Thomas Roberts, as in T.P.R.?" Thomas smiled and nodded to affirm that he was indeed T.P.R. Pharaoh then pulled Thomas to his body and they did the man hug. "Nice to meet you bro." And I saw Thomas flinch when my brother made contact with his new tattoo, his first tattoo.

We all relaxed after Pharaoh invited Thomas to the extensive buffet for a tour. Mom grinned and my aunt thankfully left me alone. The four of us women kept our eyes on Thomas, who glanced back at us occasionally, offering his God-like smile. It was like a celebrity graced us with his presence. Rachel spoke first.

"So, Nix. How *you* doing?" She laughed sounding like Joey from *Friends*.

"I'm fine." I leaned into Rachel and we spoke in whispers as soon as my mom started up a conversation with my aunt. Most likely talking about me and Thomas. "I won't be banishing you to Coco's Island anytime soon."

"Good. You and Thomas?" She wriggled her eyebrows rapidly looking like Groucho Marx minus the glasses, moustache and cigar.

"Yes. Me and Thomas." I giggled and fanned myself with a paper plate as if I was hot from desire. Rachel stared at Thomas in disbelief when I disclosed the tidbit about the Phoenix tattoo.

"Wow. Wow! Now you're the only one at this table who isn't tatted. Even your mom and *Imo* have tattooed eyebrows!" We laughed and somehow Rachel planted a seed of inspiration in my mind.

I wanted to be sure Pharaoh wasn't scaring Thomas too much. Before I reached the table, my self-declared-sexy and single 45-year old Aunt Beverly and her single 30-year old daughter, Beverory took their opportunity to swoop in on me.

"Hey, baby doll." Aunt Beverly addressed me in this melodic way since I could remember. "Who's that handsome *haole* man? Your cousin here would like to meet him again."

"Meet him again?" I was more curious than threatened. Aunt Beverly and her daughter were notorious for hitting on men. The pair could pass for sisters. They had curly brown hair down to their waistlines. They both wore an obscene amount of jewelry. Today, they wore similar flowing sheer black and white tops and inappropriate black miniskirts. Beverory, whose name was a combination of my aunt's name and my cousin's deceased father, Gregory, hit on Bradley often in the past ten years. She also took a stab at Pharaoh once. Yes, we were only fourth cousins in Beverory's eyes, but that was still a relation to me.

"She spoke to him in the church, *nai*. He said he was from California. He's your friend, right?" I wanted to clamp my aunt's mouth shut with my fingers. And why wasn't my cousin speaking for herself? Oh, that's right, she was hiding behind her mother ogling Thomas and drooling.

"He's actually, my," and I turned to look at the love of my life to remind myself that I wasn't dreaming. It was like Thomas read my mind and he gave me that wondrous smile. My aunt and cousin were witness to Thomas's glory and I heard them sigh. "He's my boyfriend." I continued quickly, ignoring the shock and disbelief in their eyes. "But, my divorce with Bradley is finalized and *he's* free. Oh, and Pharaoh can introduce you to his wrestling buddy, Ken." I offered as I thought of the goonie who called the reporter.

The shameless duo scanned the room for Bradley and made their way to *seduct* him, *their word,* not mine. I couldn't suppress my smile as I floated back to Thomas.

"Hungry, huh?" I whispered to Thomas as I pressed myself into his arm. He had a heaping plate of food, which was normal by Guam standards.

"I took everything that Pharaoh said was *mungi*." Thomas laughed melodically. "Have you seen the size of your brother's arms? Maybe if I eat like him, I'll bulk up too."

"No way, you're perfect the way you are. Let's top your meal off with a diet soda. Guam tradition." I laughed and grabbed a napkin and fork. I decided to help Thomas eat his mountain of food.

"Thomas, where you stay? How long you stay?" My mom shot questions at Thomas like she was a CNN reporter.

"I'm at the Pacific Guam Resort and I'll be here for about a week. Maybe longer." Thomas stated between bites of ham and red rice. He had his free hand on my leg.

"You stay at our house and save your money! Please." Mom surprised me and everyone else at the table.

"Oh, no, Mrs. Lizama. Thank you for the kind offer though." I couldn't see Thomas sleeping on the couch, but then my mom painted a more R rated picture.

"There is a king size futon bed in *Fee-nux* old room, you two can fit!"

"Mom!" Pharaoh and I screeched in unison. Rachel laughed loudly.

Thomas coughed and his cheeks flushed. Mom finally dropped the subject when Imo said something to her in Korean. Thomas answered all my mom's other questions graciously and got to talking about mixed martial arts with Pharaoh. I didn't realize how much he was into it too. It was nice to see Thomas in this setting. All that was missing was my dad.

My mom practically pushed me on Thomas when we left the church. She volunteered Thomas to drive me home or do whatever we wanted to. She was crushing on him pretty hard. We drove to my parents' home and I was excited to show Thomas where I grew up, my humble beginnings. Everyone was exhausted, Thomas included, but the freshness of our declaration of love gave us wings for the rest of the day. I packed a change of clothes and my only bathing suit. Mom brought out a few photo albums from my childhood to keep Thomas occupied and to no doubt embarrass me. Thomas smiled warmly with his cup of black coffee and a large pile of Lizama family memories. Then, my mom dragged me to my old bedroom.

"You love this man?" Mom was blunt and pushy as usual. I smiled at my mom and felt awkward that one moment we were burying my beloved father and by sunset we were discussing my love life with a new man.

"I do, *omma*." I typically called my mom *omma*—the Korean word for mother--when I was feeling especially affectionate for her.

"Well, life short, and you a grown woman. Now, I don't want to see you until tomorrow night for the rosary. And he's so handsome." I was shocked to say the least. Mom emphasized her message by pointing to me like I was a naughty daughter. We had seven more nights of rosaries, just for the immediate family. "You did so much for daddy. You need to relax now, *araso*? Understand?"

I took the keys from Thomas after I hugged my mom again. Pharaoh and my aunt were knocked out cold from the stress of the day. Mom should be asleep soon after. I worried about her that night—but she reassured me that she would get to sleep fine.

I held Thomas's hand as I drove us from my village of *Mangilao* to *Tumon*. It would only take about twenty minutes, which I knew would be too quick. I wanted these little first moments to move like molasses, to stay sweet, and preserved in amber. Thomas seemed content looking from me to the beautiful greenery outside. "Your mom is great, you know. I can only imagine what your father was like." Thomas stated thoughtfully.

"He would have loved you." I added. Thomas squeezed my hand tighter.

He looked very tired and I suggested he take a power nap. He did, looking like a god. The bright lights of the touristy village were overwhelming and Thomas's eyes popped open. Pacific Guam Resort was a fun place to be with waterslides and a great massage spa. I felt a twinge of guilt as I stepped into the large open air lobby, thinking this was not exactly how I envisioned mourning my father.

We walked hand in hand and headed for the elevators. We kept in time with the rhythm of the rolling suitcase. Thomas hit the button for the 25th floor. The premium rooms were there I knew since Bradley had a stint here years ago as a resortmate.

When Thomas opened his door, he let me in first like the gentleman he was. The Royal Club Suite was vast and elegantly decorated. The strong scent of plumeria surrounded me. I waited by the door as Thomas brought my pink duffle bag in. He laid it on the king size bed and returned to the living room.

"Why are you just standing there?" He sounded amused. I removed my shoes like any good island girl would and stepped tentatively forward. Thomas's wide grin told me that his power nap gave him a boost of energy. It felt electric in the room.

"Great accommodations," I teased. "I'm impressed." I wondered how he afforded the suite.

"Well, don't be. It was a gift from my sister. She paid for my air fare and room for the week." He ran his long fingers through his hair. "She's just trying to spoil me after all the guilt she had over dad. She's been doing that for the past five years, remember? My Prius was my college graduation gift."

I made my way to the balcony and enjoyed the view of the glassy ocean. The sun was setting and the warm breeze felt refreshing. Nerves caused my pulse to pound loudly in my ear. I thought about being here alone, divorced, single and hungry for Thomas. Time seemed to move so slowly before that point and my head was still spinning from the last six months. It was like I was brought to this moment at warp speed.

The setting sun blazed over the blue waters, the beauty sent shivers up my back. I felt underdressed in my black tank top and cargo shorts for such a wonderful milestone in our relationship.

Thomas excused himself to the bathroom and I remained anchored to the balcony, my nerves settled by the orange wash of sunset. I made a quick call to Rachel. She was ecstatic for me, making a vulgar comment about finally getting "*sumthing, sumthing.*" She wanted me to call her with details as soon as I woke up the next morning.

My dad's smiling face danced into my memories. I gripped my phone and worry made me call home. My mom sounded surprised to hear from me. After she reassured me that she was okay, she told me to have a nice time. She made Thomas's presence easy. A good cry later with her, Thomas appeared. He reached around from behind me and gave me a hug. When he kissed my cheek and tasted my tears, he braced my hips and turned me around.

"You okay, Phoenix?" He was wonderfully concerned.

"Yeah," I tried to laugh it off. "I was just thinking about my dad, had a quick talk with my mom."

Thomas's solid, long arms entangled me into his body. The smell of the soap on his skin was calming. We spent several minutes kissing and it was as phenomenal as the first time.

"What did you want to do for dinner?" I asked trying to dampen the flames that were erupting around us. Thomas's eyes looked dreamily at me. His smile grew and it felt like his body was humming happily. He kept me close to him and a billion butterflies played bumper cars in my stomach. He placed his hands on my hair and swept it off my face. Thomas looked like he stepped out of a J Crew catalog. His white unbuttoned shirt flowed beautifully in the wind twenty five stories above ground. My fear that he was just a mirage and would evaporate into the sky resurfaced. He seemed so relaxed in his khaki shorts. His hair, still damp, danced playfully on his head with each island breeze. Thomas's mind was not on food, I could detect as he kept his hands firm on my hips. I broke his intense gaze, lingered on his beautiful smile and opened his shirt to see the tattoo, glistening from the fresh coat of salve.

"I can't believe we're here together, Phoenix." He kissed me lightly. "I love you so much." I began kissing his chest, delicately placing pecks around the fiery bird. My hands felt the contours of his firm chest.

"You know, you're crazy for getting this bird on your chest." I joked, again trying to delay what was inevitably going to happen tonight. Bradley only wanted me this bad after he broke my heart, I thought. I was nervous and uncomfortable. I didn't have the bedroom experience Thomas apparently had. I only had misadventures with Bradley. How would I stack up to all the women Thomas had been with?

"Am I?" Thomas sounded like I just grabbed his leg to keep him from floating off into space. He knew what I was doing and he took a half step back to look at me.

"Well, it's pretty extreme. It's permanent. It's so," Why was I trying to downplay his gesture of love? Oh, yeah, I was an idiot.

"Phoenix. Do you see any other tattoos on me?" There was an undercurrent of anger and impatience in his voice. "I hate needles. I got this because I love you for one thing. And, you've inspired me to write again. It is permanent, but what I feel for you is permanent. It's not just a ring you can take off when the relationship is done." Okay, I pushed him too far. I felt like I was just jabbed in the stomach. I deserved that. Thomas released me and stalked into the bedroom. Feeling like a jerk, I sunk into the lone plush chair in the living room. His absence sucked all the oxygen out of the room. He returned bearing two gifts. One small box wrapped in green foil and a white bow and one large box wrapped in red with a yellow bow.

"Phoenix. Please open these and let me know when you finally *get it*. I'll be taking another power nap. Open the smaller gift first. Please." He sounded exhausted, probably more from my wavering than jet lag. He kissed the top of my head and went to the bedroom. He shut the door and I sat there for a few minutes trying to realize the depths of my stupidity. The pressure of his kiss fading too soon.

Chapter 19

My Tongue is in a Celtic Knot

Thomas's gentle snoring told me it was safe to move again. I peeked into the bedroom. I yearned to lie next to him, be near his beauty and the exhaustion of the day threatened my own consciousness.

The two sparkling packages from Thomas drew my attention. I knelt by the coffee table. I opened the smaller package as instructed by Thomas. A book. *Grimm Brothers: The Frog Prince.* I didn't know how this could be of any connection to me, or Thomas or what we felt for each other. I knew the general storyline of the fable. I read the children's book and tried to uncover the reason Thomas would give it to me. It was evident by the end.

I was the reluctant princess who went back on her promise to the frog, Thomas. He knew our situation well.

The king forced his daughter to uphold her promise to the frog, who had retrieved her golden ball. According to the agreement, the princess had to let the frog eat off her plate and sleep in her bed. The frog's true state would be revealed. He was a prince. To say this was yet another light bulb moment in my dim comprehension of my feelings for Thomas would be an understatement. I simmered in my thoughts for awhile, then tiptoed to the bedroom to see Thomas in a deep sleep, his eyebrows still furrowed. I hope he wasn't having a nightmare about me, the reluctant lover.

I opened the second package. It was Thomas's screenplay. It looked to be about a hundred pages. I ceremoniously turned the first crisp page. It was entitled, "Firestorm." At first glance, I thought that it might have been about firefighters. Thomas never shared the storyline, and I wondered if he was hurt that I never asked. But as I read the first scene and dialogue it was apparent it was about Thomas and *me*, well more like Toby and Phoebe. I didn't realize I was the subject of Thomas's screenplay. A feeling of honor mingled with fear in me and it left a sour taste in my mouth. I buckled down to read.

I found myself at the edge of my chair. I finished reading the established scenes and dialogue. It ended at page 86. *Toby stands in front of Phoebe bared with a fiery red phoenix emblazoned on his chest.* It didn't read like a romantic comedy, but a tragic love story. I was the clueless princess in the storyline— flawed because of my hesitation to open my heart.

The incomplete screenplay was confirmed as the last page read, "TO BE CONTINUED."

It was almost nine in the evening. I knew what I needed to do, what I *had to do* and I called Pharaoh. I needed to get something accomplished tonight. I needed to stop being the stupid girl in the screenplay about to lose the best man in the world. I had to create the proper ending.

"Hello?" Pharaoh's gravelly voice was draped in sleep.

"Hey, Pharaoh. I need a favor tonight." I heard him groan.

"Tonight?" He whined.

"I want a tattoo. Call your godbrother, Christian. I don't care what he's doing. I have to get this tonight." The shock of my announcement woke Pharaoh up quick and within the hour, I met him in *Hagåtña*. I was suddenly on my back, staring at pictures of gorgeous tattooed pin up girls taped to the ceiling. Christian prepped the skin on my hip.

I left Thomas asleep and unaware. I knew his jet lag and the stress of my emotional rollercoaster ride taxed him enough that he would be out until sunrise.

The scar on my hip was a three inch s-shape, not as raised and angry as before. I asked Christian to pull up a Celtic knot on-line to match the one I had memorized from Tamara's movie cover. Christian printed up a black inked copy. He sized it to five by five inches and was able to match the curves of the knot to my scar.

"Phoenix, are you sure about this?" Pharaoh asked, concerned. "What is up with the Celtic knot? We're not Scottish."

"It's Irish. Crack open a history book sometime." I joked.

"Whatever. Why did you have to get this tonight?"

"Sorry I disturbed your sleep, brother. But did you know Thomas got a tat a few days ago? A phoenix. For me." I let that sink in. Pharaoh was intrigued. He wanted the scoop about Thomas and me. I spared no detail, starting from my humble beginnings as a field agent secret shopper to the karaoke missions and Thomas's Guam admiration. It was nice to share all this with my wide eyed brother. I never spoke to him about Bradley with such honesty. After I filled him in on our beginnings to the present, Pharaoh impressed with Thomas, finally understood the meaning of this one tattoo I was allowing myself.

"Pretty deep, sis. I love the guy already. Of course, in a future-brother-in-law kind of way." Pharaoh clarified. It was nice to have him on my side with this. He vowed not to tell mom about my tattoo. The process was not as painful as I expected, but then again, I was stabbed in the hip. Christian was a true professional, gingerly handling the area around my battle wound. An hour later, I received my first tattoo. I gazed at my hip with confidence and certainty. It was my ultimate declaration of love for Thomas.

Christian had another customer waiting and he allowed me to use his computer to type something up. I wanted to create an ending scenario for Thomas's screenplay. It took me an hour to gather my thoughts. I didn't know typical screenplay formatting, but I was sure Thomas wouldn't hold it against me. I created a scenario that would do the story justice.

I drove back to the cemetery. The gates were locked, but I prayed in Thomas's rental. I spoke to my father. "Daddy, I'm in love. I miss you. I'm sorry I got a tattoo, but I'm sure you understand. Please guide me. I think of you always."

I drove with urgency, the roads now open and free of traffic. *Tumon's* roads were still in party mode with tourists. I rushed to the room. As I expected, Thomas was still asleep, still real. I placed the ten pages I composed at the end of the screenplay and rewrapped it as best I could. I placed a hand-written note on the repackaged love story and placed it on the desk in the room next to Thomas's laptop.

Thomas was in the exact same position as when I left. His face finally relaxed and as glorious as ever. The room was frigid, so I turned down the thermostat. I undressed quietly, remaining in my lavender bra and panty, and lay on my left side on top of the sheets next to this golden god. Thomas's linen shirt splayed, I gazed at the fiery phoenix intricately designed on his chest. The steady rise and fall of the bird made it come to life.

I wanted to stay in the moment forever; but it was almost one in the morning. Thomas had been asleep for four hours and I wondered if it was selfish of me to wake him now. As I gently ran my fingers in his amber locks, the exhaustion I accumulated from the day caught up with me. I touched the bandage over my new tattoo and let my hand rest on my hips. I had gotten used to sleeping without hurting my wound. My right hand stayed near my fresh tattoo like a guard. This new day, my own crazy actions should seal the deal with Thomas. I would no longer be that stupid reluctant princess.

Chapter 20
We Have Lift Off!

I had one of those moments when you think you're doing something in real life, but you're still asleep and dreaming. Like in the mornings, when you've hit the snooze button on the alarm clock and doze off, believing that you're taking a shower, dressing, eating breakfast only to find that you actually shut off your alarm. In reality, you finally wake up and you discover that you're still in bed and almost late for work or school or whatever. I hate when that happens. I call it the dreaming to live phenomenon. I wondered if I exhausted the snooze button on my relationship with Thomas.

My dream was of me seducing Thomas like a pro, which I am not. We finally consummated our relationship. The fact that we were tattooless should have told me it was just a delicious dream.

At sunrise, the smell of coffee wafted through the room and stirred me from sleep. The windows were open, but the curtain was still drawn, keeping the room dim. Something considerate Thomas was responsible for, I thought. A thin sheet covered my nearly naked self. My hand was covering my bandage protectively. Did he see it?

The warm Guam morning crept through the room and the humidity was comforting. I wondered how long he had been awake. His internal clock most likely still on California time. I smoothed my hair back, rubbed the sleep out of my eyes and realizing more fully where I was, did a breath check. Thomas was nowhere in sight, so I made a quiet break for the bathroom. The soreness on my hip reminded me that what I did last night was real.

The gift near Thomas's laptop was left untouched. I needed him to read my words before this day could proceed. I crept back to bed and drifted back into unconsciousness.

After what felt like seconds, I was pulled out of the throngs of sleep by the sensation of cool fingers on my hip. I immediately reached to the bandage to feel Thomas's hands there instead. I met his gaze and he looked at me so tenderly.

"Good Morning." He said in a deep voice. "Actually, *neni*, it's Good Afternoon." Thomas calling me *baby* in Chamorro rocked me to the core. He looked refreshed and happy despite our rocky evening. I was certain, as probably he was too, that this morning should have played out differently. We would have been in each other's arms, completely spent from all the love making that would have happened. But, expectations don't turn into reality often enough.

"Good afternoon, Thomas." My voice came out huskier than I expected and I giggled, then cleared my throat. "Let me try that again. Good Afternoon Thomas." I exaggerated a high-pitched girly voice. Thomas smiled in response, but his eyes became fixated on my bandage. I glanced at the desk and saw the red foil wrapper in a scrunched ball. The pages of his screenplay flipped to the last section that I wrote. So, Thomas knew I got a tattoo and he probably wanted to know what was inked on my hip, since I didn't reveal it in my writing.

"May I?" He traced the white square bandage on my hip. His touch shot energy through my veins. A smile sizzled on his lovely mouth.

I responded by sitting up, pulling his face to mine and kissing him. I then fell back onto the plush pillows, taking a moment to be conscious of the movement of my hips—my inner belly dancer emerging. I raised my arms over my head seductively and smiled as I pulled my hair up and let my locks fall over my chest. If my life was a movie, this would be the slow motion sequence. I didn't want to fudge it up.

Thomas noticed and his eyes wandered up and down my body in appreciation. My blood raged throughout my body in anticipation. Thomas shook himself out of his state of hypnosis and began to slowly, considerately peel away the clear medical tape.

My tattoo lacked the color of Thomas's phoenix, but it was bold and definite and never-ending like the Celtic knot of his heritage. I watched his face intently, the sunshine peeking through the fluttering curtains, bouncing off his flawless face. As he removed the gauze, the realization that there was a tattoo over my scar, the scar Thomas witnessed coming to being, was evident on his face. His gray eyes watched me. I couldn't read his face now. Did he approve? Was this an immature move on my part? God, what if we broke up? I didn't want to think of those things. I wanted to be rooted in today. With him. Thomas's mouth gaped open slightly and he reached for his golden pendant. He pulled the pendant to his muted, beautiful mouth and I desperately wanted to know his thoughts. Thomas answered me with a flow of tears. Thomas bent down to my body and began to kiss me. He was cautious and gentle around the tattoo. I squirmed at each soft kiss. My back arched in response. Thomas viewed my puffy tattoo up close again and after realizing that I had truly done this, he created a path of kisses up my body. Each kiss Thomas planted on me brought him closer to my lips. He became more insistent and certain.

"I love you, Phoenix." Thomas's voice was so bold.

I placed my hands in Thomas's thick hair and brought his face to mine. Eye to eye I spoke from my heart.

"Thomas Patrick Roberts, I love you too." I kissed him tenderly. "Forever."

Our passionate evening that should have been turned into the passionate afternoon that was.

Chapter 21

The Princess and the Hot Frog

"Thomas and Phoenix, sitting in a tree, K-I-S-S-I-N-G." Thomas sang into my ear as the plane took off that cool paradise morning on Guam. I rested my head on his shoulder and couldn't get over the triumph I felt in my heart. After three glorious weeks with Thomas on Guam, I bid farewell once again to my family, my beloved father and my Rachel. It was like we were just coming home from a honeymoon.

Thomas completed his screenplay while on Guam, in between our many love making sessions and sight seeing for new photographs and tying up loose ends with my dad's affairs. I even started my business plan for a customer evaluation company of my own. Angelica and Ty were still going strong and excited that we were finally coming home. Angelica signed on as my business partner, glad for the opportunity to be working in Oceanside closer to the Camp Pendleton Marine base, therefore nearer to Ty.

Throughout the flights we needed to finally get back to San Diego, Thomas was constantly holding my hand. Was he afraid that I was going to bolt again?

"Are you worried about anything?" I asked matter-of-factly, as we sipped coffee on our wait in Los Angeles.

"No. I was just wondering since we're together forever, coordinating tats and all, if maybe we were going to take this to the next level." Thomas stated tentatively. I wasn't sure what other level there could be. We branded each other after all. We made love enough times in these last few weeks to make up for the angst of the last six months.

"Pray tell, kind frog. What would the next level be?" He couldn't be talking marriage. In my eyes, we were committed. We were soul mates. Marrying in church wasn't a guarantee, Bradley and me as evidence.

"Let's make it official on all levels."

"What? Like wear each other's blood in vials around our necks?" I joked. His face was stone serious. I conceded. "Tell me, Thomas. What can we do?"

"Marriage." He stated it so confidently. He took my hands in his. Thomas knelt in front of me for all present to see. I closed my eyes. God, was this really happening? On a grand scale? It wasn't the first time I was engaged, but it was the first time it was done with such emotion, where the spotlight was on me and not on the groom to be. Thomas removed his sweatshirt and revealed a cheesy tuxedo t-shirt. He winked at me and I welcomed his kitschy sense of humor.

Thomas was on bended knee smiling deliriously and I transformed into a shivering heap of sweaty awkwardness. Thomas looked at his watch then over his shoulder. On cue, my mom, Pharaoh and Rachel appeared from out of nowhere. I gasped and almost expected my dad to make an appearance. God, how I wish he was here to see this. How did they board the plane without me knowing it? Who paid for all those tickets?

"Thomas, what? Are you really doing what I think you're doing?"

"No."

I deflated. Thomas looked at his watch again. My mom kissed me. Pharaoh patted my head. Rachel squeezed me tight. Then I heard from the crowd, "We're here! We're here! Tom-Tom, we're here!" Tamara and her husband, James with baby Cassidy asleep in her stroller emerged.

"Hi everyone," I laughed through tears. "Thomas, okay. Now, really are you going to propose?"

"No." He smiled.

God, I was confused. Was a minister going to emerge next to have us marry right here in the middle of LAX? That was so rock star, but not me. My mom's tears as Pharaoh held her told me this was it. A proposal. Thomas looked at his watch again and gave a thumbs up to someone in the now growing crowd of on-lookers. Then, I saw them. Angelica and Ty, hand in hand, racing towards us. My Uncle Tony trotted behind them. His smile so large he looked like my father for a second. I buried my face in my hands. I heard Tamara on the loudspeaker.

"Hello LAX, I would like to take this opportunity to give my baby brother the floor." Tamara's voice cracked from emotion. "Phoenix and Thomas are sharing a special moment with you all.

Tom-Tom, I'm so proud of you. Phoenix, your dad and our dad are shining down on this moment. Please, proceed."

Our Jason Mraz song played from Tamara's Ipod as she placed it near the PA mic. I looked at Thomas, or tried to through my never ending tears. God, I was going to look so puffy and disheveled, but hell, I didn't care. Thomas kissed my hand, then placed his hand on his chest. Touching the unseen Phoenix there, I knew. His tears flowed too, but his voice was steady.

"Phoenix Rose Lee Lizama. Would you do me the honor of being my best friend for life. My soulmate. My wife. The mother of my children?"

James walked baby Cassidy to us. Her vibrant gray eyes matched her Uncle Thomas's. She carried a little Hello Kitty gift bag and handed it to him. She hugged Thomas. The flock of supporters made a collective, "Awww." Thomas pulled out a red velvet box. He ceremoniously opened the box and everyone went still.

I stopped breathing. The ring within was blazingly beautiful. It was a masterpiece, a twinkling platinum band embedded with a Celtic knot. Sparkling diamonds nestled in each knot. It was unreal, like it was forged by hobbits in a volcano. For a moment, my eyes flashed to Tamara who probably had a say in its radiant design. The knot matched her mother's pendant. I smiled warmly at my new sister. Her body shook with emotion and when I gave her a thumbs up she laughed.

"Thomas Patrick Roberts, descendant of the Roberts Clan of Ireland..." I joked, even now, I joked—and the people around us giggled, but wanted my answer. I made a dramatic pause, then brought my hands to my chest. "Yes. Yes!" I said loudly for the benefit of my family and complete strangers. "Yes, I would be honored to be your wife and all that other wonderful stuff." Needless to say we made an obscene display of affection.

In a flash, we stepped into the L.A. morning. Tamara and James had two vans waiting to take this newly formed wedding party down to Oceanside. The women and Thomas piled into one van and the men and the luggage were in the other.

"Thomas, you are amazing." I pinched his arm. "Are you for real?" He beamed and raised my newly engaged hand into the light streaming through the window. He kissed my hand and hummed a beautiful melody in my ear as Rachel, Tamara, Angelica and mom debated wedding details.

I wasn't sweating the particulars because I already had my prince. I leaned into my fiancé. "So what did you and my dad 'talk' about?" Thomas smiled my favorite smile.

"First, I introduced myself. Secondly, I told him that I loved you with all my heart. Thirdly, I asked for your hand in marriage. And finally, I explained to your dad that if I could get you to eat off my plate and sleep in my bed at least once, that you would become the princess I always knew you could be. *My princess*."

I kissed my handsome prince and my fairy godmothers cheered. From that moment on, Princess Phoenix and Prince Thomas set out to rule the world together.

Made in the USA
Middletown, DE
10 September 2017